One Man's
Treasure

One Man's Treasure

CHARLENE E. GREEN

URBAN BOOKS

http://www.urbanbooks.net

This is a work of fiction. Any references or similarities to actual events, real people, living or dead, or to real locales are intended to give the novel a sense of reality. Any similarity in other names, characters, places, and incidents is entirely coincidental.

URBAN SOUL is published by

Urban Books
1199 Straight Path
West Babylon, NY 11704

ISBN-13: 978-1-59983-087-2
ISBN-10: 1-59983-087-6

First Printing: April 2009

10 9 8 7 6 5 4 3 2

Printed in the United States of America

For my mother, Juliet Lorraine Simpson—
you are my heart.

For my cousin, Kevin Cornell Allen—
I still can't believe you're gone.
I wish you were here to witness this.

Acknowledgments

First and foremost, I need to thank my mother, Juliet Lorraine Simpson, for handing down to me this wonderful skill and talent called writing. Mommy, there are no words to express how much I love you. You are *the* most fabulous woman I know. Thank you for rearing my hardheaded ass all by yourself. I know sometimes I was more than a *few* handfuls, but look at me now (okay, I'm still *one* handful). Thank you for always letting me be me, even when that was difficult, and for giving me the mental space to find my path in life on my own. Hugs and kisses, Mommy. This one's for you. Can you believe it? Yo' baby wrote a BOOK! What! Grandma and Grandpa would flip! (RIP Lincoln and Cleo Simpson . . . I miss you guys so much!)

My family—Linette, Karen, Danasia, Kenneth, Gabe (and baby Gabe), Lillian, Jacqueline, Michael V. and Michael S., Pauline, Lydia, Rebecca (RIP), Al, Lenora (and family), Kevin (RIP), Kirk, June (and family), Doreen, Eric, Shea, Linda (and family), I love you all! Therezinha, I'm pickin' up where Kevin left off. I can hear him clear as day saying, "Ay, cuz . . . ay, Char . . . you did it!"

My lifelong soul sisters, Tamika Byrd, Leslie Harris, LaMonica Gardner, Joan Ferrin-Pann, Tamara Brown—ladies, we been doin' this since the beginning of time, and all I can say is, there are no better friends on this earth than you. In my next life, I want you all right by my side again. I LOVE YOU GUYS SO MUCH!

My mentor and friend, Dr. Rosie Milligan—thank

you for taking me under your wing. I am eternally grateful for all you've taught me and allowed me to do with and for you. Your training and nurturing have been invaluable, and I'm truly honored to have you in my life. Thank you for helping me release *One Man's Treasure* to the world the first time around. And thank you for believing in me every second of the way. I love you forever, Ro Ro.

Dr. Maxine Thompson, thank you for orchestrating the "rebirth" of *One Man's Treasure* so that now, *millions* of people across the country can partake in Katrice's journey. Thank you also for giving me the opportunity to work under you, and for having faith in my abilities. I'm looking forward to doing more with you in the future.

Alfreda Moore, thank you for your friendship, and for connecting me with Dr. Rosie Milligan. Had I not met you, I may not know her.

Tracy Watson, wherever you are, unbeknownst to you, you were instrumental in this book's conception. When you brought Renee Swindle's novel *Please, Please, Please* to my attention, the minute I finished reading it, I said, "I wanna write a book, too." And so it began. Thank you for being my friend.

My godsister, Dr. Elizabeth Talley, you are *so* inspirational! Keep doin' the damn thang, girl!

Maya Redfield, my *true boo!* Missing and loving you from here to Japan, baby!

The Starks family—Darren, Karren, Mary, Donovan, Tevin, Bryan, Samuel, and Betty—a million thanks for your friendship, for always opening your home to me, and for feeding me on all those holidays when a sista couldn't get up North. You're truly my L.A. family!

Bridgette Gooden, thanks for being the *very first person* to read *One Man's Treasure*, typos and all, and for giving me the good feedback.

Thanks to everyone else who read the manuscript (or parts of it) while it was still in its raw stages. Your opinions and comments were appreciated.

All of my SGI-USA friends, thank you for being there for me over the past 23 years.

A special thanks to Eric Jerome Dickey. I used your novels as learning material when I got to a point in my book where I felt the story needed "more." Thanks for writing such great stuff! Have your people call my people so we can set up a book tour! ☺

Anyone who feels they should have been acknowledged, and were not, I'm so sorry! I *swear* I didn't mean to leave you out! All I can think is, *God, I hope I'm not forgetting anybody. They'll be so mad (or hurt).* Well, I tried. If I missed anyone, I'll getcha in the next book's acknowledgments!

Okay, this is it! Round two, people. The way I always dreamed! I can hardly believe it! I've waited *years and years* for this moment. I hope you all enjoy this story. I've worked hard to try to bring you something you can laugh at, cry at, contemplate on, learn from, and talk about for a long time.

I'm out, y'all! Thanks for all your support! There's more where this came from, so don't go too far—the sequel, *And They'll Come Home,* is on the way!

Charlene Elizabeth Green
January 31, 2008
5:38 P.M.

1

I knew he was feeling me when he peered at me over his sunglasses. He came sauntering in like he thought he was everything I should want and then some. He was really tall: at least six-three, I thought. Skin the color of brown sugar, a well-groomed five o'clock shadow, and a thin, trim mustache. He smiled big, showing off his perfect teeth. You could tell he followed the rules: He saw his dentist every six months and brushed and flossed at least twice a day.

Okay, so I thought he was cute. All right, I'm lying; I thought he was scrumptious, but that's not the point. The point is I wasn't interested.

I had seen him around town plenty of times when I was out with my girls. Chantelle said her cousin Lisa used to date him about six or seven years prior. Said he was nothing but a player. He ended up breaking her heart like only a player can. Chantelle said the girl wasn't right for damn near a year after he dumped her. Didn't date anyone else until Ramon came along and showed her how a real man is supposed to treat a woman. After that, she never looked back.

Apparently, neither did he, because every time I saw him, he was with a different woman. I would shake my head and roll my eyes in disgust and think to myself how pitiful players are. So damn insecure, lonely, and weak; always putting on that "Girl-you-know-you-want-me-don't-even-front" facade. I swear. Sometimes, you just wanna slap 'em.

At any rate, Mr. Playa Playa waltzed his gorgeous self over to me and took off his shades to reveal those luscious eyes that were so light, they were borderline hazel. Or something. I had never really seen anything like it before as far as eyes go. Mixed in with the brown, I could see little splashes of green. He had lashes so long that even supermodels would be jealous. A girl could easily get lost in his eyes in the middle of a conversation and forget what the topic of discussion was.

I didn't wanna stare, so as he folded his shades and carefully placed them in their container, then inserted it into the inside pocket of his three-hundred-dollar leather jacket, I pretended to be concentrating on getting the part just right on my client's head, even though it was already straight.

I felt him pause and stare at me for a moment. Not an impatient stare, just a "look at me" stare.

As nonchalantly as I could, I looked at him and let out an airy, "What can I do for you today?"

He said, "How long is the wait? I need a fade right quick. You think you can hook me up?" Then he started caressing the back of his neck and tried to give me his best come-hither look.

Fine as he was, I paid him no mind. Instead, I

motioned toward my partner, Tiki, and said, "Tiki's wait is shorter than mine. She can take you in about ten minutes."

"Yeah, well, ten minutes is cool, but I'd rather wait for you, Miss Lady. You look like you runnin' thangs around here."

I tried not to look him directly in the eyes so as to seem as distant as possible.

"Suit yourself." I shrugged. "But you'll have about a thirty-minute wait. I've still got two people ahead of you."

"That's cool with me." He sat down and grabbed an *Essence* magazine off the table.

I hoped "cool" wasn't the only word he knew to express how he felt.

2

After he sat and thumbed through all the magazines on the table for about forty minutes, I finally called for Mr. Fine. When he stepped up to the empty chair, he told me confidently, "My name's Weston Porter," and stuck his hand out for me to shake.

Instead of shaking his hand, I looked into his heavenly eyes. "I know who you are. Have a seat." I patted the top of the chair.

He chuckled to himself as he sat down. "Okay . . . you say you uh . . . know who I am, then?"

"Uh-huh."

"So," he cleared his throat, "'scuse me for a second, but, where do you know me from, Miss Lady? I don't think we've met. I would remember meetin' *you* somewhere."

I tossed the bib around his front, fastened it up at the neck and answered, "We haven't." Then I asked him, "Now, did you say you needed a fade?" as if I had forgotten.

"Yeah, a fade," he said, as if his haircut were no

longer important. Then he pressed, "But about you knowin' me . . ."

"You know, I'm on a time schedule here, so we should probably get things moving."

He chuckled again. "Oh, okay, so you don't wanna tell me. That's cool. I'll find out later." He looked at me through the large mirror in front of him. "What's your name?"

I smiled. "Do you always let people whose names you don't know cut your hair?" I pulled out the clippers.

He gave me a sexy look. "Only today."

"Yeah, okay." I stuck a guard on the clippers and plugged them in.

He leaned back in the chair and gave me a relaxed look through the mirror, but didn't say anything.

I was having fun with this despite myself.

I grabbed a small comb from the counter and started combing his kitchen area. It was thick, curly, and soft. I had this uncontrollable urge to run my fingers through it. So I did. I put the comb down and slowly pushed my fingers through his locks, almost massaging his neck. When I peeked at him in the mirror, he closed his eyes and sort of leaned his head back into my hand and let out a low moan.

His curls hugged my fingers. "You have nice hair."

He opened his eyes and searched around for a second, then smiled and said, "Thank you, Katrice Nicole Vincent."

I looked through the mirror again and caught him eyeing my license on the wall. I gave him a flirtatious look. "I guess you know my name now."

I whipped his locks up nice and tidy as he sat quietly. I could feel him looking at me, so I made a conscious effort *not* to look at him.

When I finished, I took the bib off, shook it out off to the side of him, and gave him a mirror to look at the back of his head. I turned the chair around so he could see. He checked it out, smiled and nodded to himself, then gave me the mirror and said, "Nice job, Katrice. I might hafta become a regular around here."

I smiled and glanced at him out of the corner of my eye. "You said that like I'm not supposed to know what I'm doin'. Haven't you ever had a woman cut your hair before?"

"Just my older sister, when I was a kid."

"And did *she* do a good job?"

"Sort of, I guess. But she only touched me up every now and then. She never gave me a full cut like this." He admired my work some more. "This looks really good."

"Well, thank you. I try to make sure all my customers leave satisfied."

"Mission accomplished. So, how much I owe you today?" He started reaching into his pants pocket.

"Thirteen."

He pulled out a twenty and handed it to me.

"Lemme get your change." I turned to walk to the register.

"You keep that."

"Are you sure?"

"Yep."

"Okay then, thanks. Far be it from me to argue about a tip." I shoved the twenty into my apron pocket.

He got up out of the chair, adjusted his jacket, and looked at me like he had something else to say but then changed his mind. I pulled out the broom and started sweeping up his curly locks. I could feel him dawdling, looking for a way to start a conversation, so I purposely ignored him and kept sweeping. I wanted to laugh, because I was enjoying messing with him, but I kept a straight face.

Finally, he gave in to the silence. "So, whose shop is this?"

"Mine." I didn't even look up. I just kept sweeping.

"I never even knew there was a shop over here till a few days ago."

I finally looked at him and smiled politely. "Well, now you do."

He looked at me like he was amused and searched my face with his eyes to see where I was coming from.

Then he got bold with me. "So, are you, uh . . . involved with anybody?"

I snickered and decided to have some more fun. "Yeah. I'm involved with a lot of people."

His face dropped. "Excuse me?"

"Well, you asked me if I was involved with anybody, and I am. I'm involved with myself, my parents, my girlfriends, my coworker, my customers . . ."

"Oh boy, I see I'm dealin' wit' a comedienne, here, huh?" He showed me his beautiful, full smile.

"I'm just answering your question."

"Okay then, lemme rephrase it. Do you have a man?"

For some reason, I was embarrassed that the answer was no. I'm not sure why. I looked away, reached for the dust pan and said a quick, "Nope."

He hesitated for a moment. "Okay . . . well, do you think I could maybe call you sometime? Maybe we could go out?"

I studied his face for a minute. He seemed like an okay guy, but my thoughts drifted back to Chantelle telling me about him dropping her cousin Lisa like a hot potato, and that didn't sit well with me. I really wasn't in the mood to waste my time dealing with some dude I might only see a few times.

"I don't think so. No."

He got this shocked look on his face like someone had just snuck up on him and popped him in the back of the head. Guess he had never been turned down before.

"Can I ask why?"

And I had never been asked why before. Most guys usually slink away with their tails between their legs. This one was persistent, and I liked it, to be honest. To me, it said he had confidence. Like he felt he deserved to be told yes, and deserved to be told why he was being turned down. I wanted to change my mind right then and there, but since I had already said no, I stayed with that. Plus, there was still the issue of Lisa and all the other women.

"I'm just not interested, that's all."

He shrugged and pulled out his car keys. "Okay then, but I'll be back. Thanks for the cut."

As he walked out the door, I watched him as he stepped onto the sidewalk and slid his shades onto his face. Then he walked his fine ass away.

As soon as I got home from work, I raced to the phone and called Chantelle. I couldn't wait to tell her what had happened. I called her house, but got no answer, so I hung up and called her cell. She answered on the first ring.

"Girl, where you at?" I asked with urgency.

"'Bout to pull up in fronta the gym. I ate like a pig

today. I can feel the calories dancin' on my damn thighs and ass."

I rolled my eyes back in my head. "Girl, please! You weigh all of ninety-nine pounds, and I got more ass than you'll *ever* see! You're a damn addict."

She brushed me off the way she always does when I rag on her about being a gym junkie. "*Anyway*— wassup?"

"Girl, guess who was at the shop today spittin' game at me?"

"I dunno. That dude you met at the club a coupla weeks ago?"

"Uh-uh . . . *Weston Porter*. Can you believe that?"

"Oh, come *on*. Are you *serious?* Lisa's hit-it-and-quit-it man?"

"In the flesh, okay?"

"Lord. So, what was he talkin' 'bout?"

"He came to get a haircut, and I told him Tiki could take him sooner, but he said he wanted to wait for me."

She blew disgusted air through her lips. "Figures. Couldn't just come get a damn cut and then step. Had to get his mack on. Hound."

"Anyway, so after damn near forty-five minutes, I called him to the chair."

For some reason, I hesitated after that. I almost didn't wanna tell her he asked me out. I guess she could hear it in my voice that I hedged a bit.

"And? What happened? I know you. You didn't finish what you were gon' say just now."

"After I finished cutting his hair, he asked me out."

"Surprise, surprise. I knew that was comin'."

I didn't say anything.

Chantelle said, "Uh . . . hello?"

"What?"

"You're not gonna go out with him, are you? I mean, you *did* turn him down, right?"

I said a half-assed, "Yeah. Of course."

She paused, and I could just see her eyes squinting up as she felt my vibe through the phone. "Katrice."

"No, for real. I did. And you know what he had the nerve to say when I said no?"

"What?"

"He said, 'Can I ask why?'"

"Uh-huh . . . but knowin' you, that turned you on. You like them bold, persistent ones. You probably wanted to change your mind and say yes after he said that."

I hate it when she reads me like that.

"Girl, please. I told him I wasn't interested. He just said he'd be back."

"I'll just bet." She paused. "You gon' go out with him. Tell the truth."

"No, I'm not."

"I know when a man has your attention, 'Trice."

"How you figure he has my attention?"

"I can hear it in your tone. You sound weak."

"What? What'choo mean by that?"

"Quit actin' like you don't know what I'm talkin' about. You need to be nominated for a damn Oscar."

"I can't *stand* you!" I broke out laughing.

She laughed. "I'll bet'choo right now, if you go out with him, you'll be sprung after the first date. Bet."

"*Hardly.* He's fine, but he ain't all that. Not enough to get me twisted."

She just said, "Bet."

"You for real, huh?"

"Bet. Go out with him and see what happens."

"Okay, fine. I'ma go *just* to prove you wrong."

"No, you gon' go 'cause you *want* to. But anyway, what we bettin' for?"

"Okay—if I lose, I'll do your next four touch-ups for free, and I'll even throw in that nasty-ass blonde color you been talkin' about."

"Well, you only charge me half price anyway, but I'll take it. It's a bet."

"Wait a minute—what about if you lose? What's in it for me?"

"Nothin', 'cause I'm not gon' lose, so it ain't even no point in talkin' about it."

"You just think you know it *all*, huh?"

She laughed. "Oh, sweetie, I don't *think* I know it all, I *know* I know it all, at least about you. Now lemme go in here and kill off these pounds right quick. Call me later."

"Bye, addict."

"Shut up. Bye."

Later that evening, I hooked up with Chantelle and my other two girls, Sabrina and Genine, at my apartment. The four of us had met at a Keith Sweat concert back in the late eighties. I can't even remember what we talked about for the entire intermission, but all I know is when we left, each of us had the other one's phone number, and the rest is history.

Since Chantelle already had the scoop on my luscious customer, I filled the others in.

Genine asked me, "You think he's gonna come back?"

"I don't know . . . I kinda hope so."

"I told you . . . I knew you were feelin' him," Chantelle said.

I pointed at her. "You be quiet. I'm not feelin' him . . . yet . . ."

Sabrina said, "Well, when you finally give him some, I want all the details."

"Damn, Bree, you just jumpin' all ahead of the game. I might not even like him enough to give him some. I might not even go out with him. He thinks he's cute."

"Whatever," Chantelle said, then she looked at Sabrina and Genine. "She likes him *and* she's gonna give him some. You guys know she does this all the time. We'll have a story before month's end. Mark my words."

I gave her the finger and she flashed both her middles at me.

"Well, look," Sabrina started, "whenever it jumps off, I'm expectin' a full report."

"You're such a freak."

She smiled and gave me a sly look. "That's what they tell me, sista, . . . every time . . ."

We all laughed. Quiet as it was kept, I hoped I had a story to tell, too.

3

More than a week went by, and Weston hadn't shown his face in the shop. I have to admit, I was anticipating his return. I don't know what it was about him, but even in spite of his reputation, there was something drawing me to him. I constantly thought about that day in the shop, and even had a couple of daydreams about him. Chantelle called me every day and asked me if we had a date planned yet. I told her to quit harping on me. He might not even come back. She just laughed and told me to remember our bet.

It was about 6:30 on a Friday evening. Tiki had gone home early, and I had just let my last customer for the day out the door. While I was cleaning up in the back room, I thought I heard the door jingle. I wasn't expecting anyone, and I had no intentions of taking any last-minute Lucys or Larrys.

Without waiting to see who had come in, I called out, "We're closed!" I didn't get a response, so I put down the can of cleanser I was holding and stepped out from the back.

I thought my eyes were deceiving me, but it turned out, they weren't. Standing in black slacks, black leather dress shoes, a gray silk shirt, and a long, leather trench coat, was Weston. His one earring was sparkling like new, and he was holding a single white rose with red trim. He didn't speak, just smiled at me.

I could feel my eyes about to pop out of my head. I started taking off my cleaning gloves, cleared my throat and said, "Um . . . hi . . . ?" I moved a few steps closer to him.

"Well, hello. Is this a bad time?" He asked the question, but the confidence in his eyes said that even if I said it was, it wouldn't be for long.

I got caught in his gaze and stammered, "I, um . . . no. I was . . . I thought you were a customer. . . . We're actually closed."

He leaned himself against the counter by the door. "If I was, would you take me?"

I actually felt myself blush—and I never blush. The man made me nervous, which is rare for me.

"Well, it would, um . . . depend on what you wanted."

"Whatever you feel you can offer me."

"Why do I all of a sudden feel like we're not talking about a hair appointment?"

He rose up off the counter and stepped to me. When he got right in front of me, I could smell his cologne, Eternity for Men, which is my favorite. It drives me crazy. He extended the rose to me. "'Cause we're not."

I smiled and took the rose out of his hand. I sniffed it, then stood for a moment, just looking at him. Finally I said, "Thank you. So, what *are* we talking about?"

"Talkin' about you turnin' me down for a date, and me not takin' no for an answer. Talkin' about the fact that if you *keep* turnin' me down, I'ma keep comin' back every week till you say yes. That's what we talkin' about."

At that point, the game of Flirt began.

"So, basically, you're planning on harassing me?"

"If you plan on continuin' to say no, then I guess I am."

"Well, um, harassment would be, at best, unacceptable. I wouldn't wanna have to involve the authorities."

"Then say yes right now, and things won't hafta get ugly."

"Yes to what? I haven't heard a question yet."

He laughed, moved in closer and said softly, "I would appreciate it . . . if you would accept my invitation . . . for a date tomorrow night. Think you might be able to do that?"

I was feeling a little out of control. My stomach was turning flips, and I could feel myself falling into a trap. To keep my head above water, I said, "No."

He looked surprised. "No?"

I felt I had to gain some control of the situation. "No . . . I won't go out with you tomorrow night. But I will go out with you tomorrow afternoon— if you're free."

"Tomorrow afternoon."

"Yeah, afternoon. Is that a problem?"

"Not at all. What time can I pick you up?"

"You can't." I smiled.

"Pardon me?"

"You can't pick me up. I'll meet you somewhere . . . for brunch. Say around noon?"

I had to let him know that even though he was charming and fine, I had my own way of doing things; and if he wanted me, he'd have to play by a few of *my* rules.

He went along with me. "Fine. Where you wanna meet?"

I put the ball back in his court. "You tell me."

"Okay, uh . . ." He thought about it for a minute. "Meet me at Café Soul in El Sobrante at twelve. You know where that is?"

"El Sobrante yes; the place, no. But I'll find it."

He smiled, looking accomplished. "All right, but uh . . . you think I could have your phone number before I go?"

"I'll give it to you tomorrow. *If* things go well."

"Well, can I give you mine?"

"Tomorrow. If things go well."

He glanced at me with a mischievous look in his eyes. "Okay then. You have a nice evening, Miss Lady. I'll see you tomorrow."

"Okay. You, too."

When he got to the door, he stopped, turned to me and said, "Don't be late. I don't wanna miss out on one second of time with you." Then he headed out.

I bit my bottom lip lightly, smiled at him and closed and locked the door behind him. I smelled my rose as I watched him walk up the street. I stood for a minute and thought about what Chantelle said. She was right. Forget the bet; I was definitely going out with him because I wanted to. After he got out of my view, I smiled to myself, set my rose down on the counter, and went back into the back room to finish cleaning up. I could already tell it was gonna be a long, anxious night.

That night, Chantelle, Genine, Sabrina and I all met up at Nate's Joint in San Pablo. As we scarfed burgers, fries, and shakes, I filled them all in on what went down at the shop. Genine and Sabrina were both excited for me and wished me luck.

Chantelle just said, "Get my perm kits and hair color ready."

I threw a French fry at her, and it bounced off her forehead, and we all burst out laughing.

We spent the next hour reminiscing about past loves, good and bad. In between stories, I couldn't help thinking about Weston, and how I hoped I had a good story to share after our date.

4

I've had a few ups and downs with guys in my life, but nothing to really complain about. I've always had boyfriends, and I never really had a problem getting and keeping a guy's attention.

In high school, I fell in love for the first time with Troy Parker. We met freshman year and became fast friends. We had four classes together, and somehow we always ended up sitting next to each other. We had an English teacher, Mr. King, who had a cockeye and a speech impediment. We used to pass notes back and forth to each other and joke about him. All through freshman year we were close, but I had a feeling that soon it would turn into something much more.

One day, at the beginning of sophomore year, after a football game, a bunch of us kids were hanging out. Since Troy only lived eight blocks from me, we walked home together. When we got to my door, he kissed me, and it was pretty much on after that. He treated me like royalty, and for the first time, I knew what real love felt like.

Several months later, in the back of his brother's old, rusty van one night, I let Troy take my virginity. I know the location may not sound very romantic, but actually, it really was. We were two fifteen-year-olds who wanted to be alone together but had nowhere to go. Troy had begged his brother to let him have the keys to his van, just for one night. After twenty minutes of pleading and promising to do his brother's chores for a week, Jeff finally gave up the keys.

It was a Friday night, and I snuck out through the garage around ten o'clock. The door was stuck at half-mast, so I was able to ease under it. I was a little scared, but I boldly walked, at a fast pace I might add, over to Troy's house. I met him around the corner where Jeff had the van parked. When I got there, he was already waiting for me. He had come equipped with a big down comforter, two pillows, two wine coolers, an oversized flashlight, a compilation of some of Prince's slow jams that Jeff had made, and three rubbers. We hopped in and Troy set up our "bedroom" while I put the tape in. While Prince crooned, we propped ourselves up against the door in the back of the van with the pillows behind our backs, and we talked and drank our wine coolers. The flashlight gave us just the right candlelight ambiance, and we had turned the heat on to warm the van up, so the temperature was perfect.

After about a half-hour, we started making out. When "Do Me Baby" came on, it was as if Prince were giving us the go-ahead to do our thing. Troy laid me down nice and slow, kissed me deep, and unbuttoned my blouse. By the time the song was halfway over, we were in our birthday suits, the rubber was on, and we proceeded to bring Prince's words to life.

Troy took good care of me that night, and honestly, I don't think I could've asked for a better first time. Around one in the morning, after we lay in each other's arms for a while, Troy walked me the eight blocks back to my house. I snuck right back in through the garage, then I sent him on his way in the darkness. After that night, we became closer than ever.

Troy and I stayed together all through high school. I truly believe we'd probably still be together to this day if he hadn't moved to Washington, D.C., right after graduation. He had gotten accepted to Howard University, which was his top choice. His father was a math professor at San Francisco State University, and he loved numbers and wanted to teach math too. It had always been his dream, so when we found out that Howard wanted him, we knew what that meant. Inevitably, we would be separated. I had my own plans to attend beauty school to get my license to do hair, which was my dream. So, in mid-July, Troy packed up and prepared to leave. As hard as it was to let him go, I knew I had to.

Since our love was so strong, Troy had said he wanted to try a long-distance relationship, but I told him I didn't think it would work. I needed to be able to reach out and touch, and we both knew that wasn't going to happen. He was hurt, but in the end, he knew I was right. Having made that decision, we spent one last night together, and two days later, we said good-bye. As I saw him off at the airport, I told him not to call or write because it would be too painful. He agreed, and as he boarded the plane, he turned and blew me a kiss. I pretended to catch it, as I watched him fade out of sight, waving and mouthing "I love you."

I cried over him for months, and his being gone

felt like one of my limbs were missing. I just felt so incomplete, and for a long time, it was hard for me to function.

Troy ended up staying in D.C. after graduating from Howard. About three years ago, I heard through a mutual friend that he was teaching calculus at a local high school, and he was married and had a son. I was happy for him. We'd had our time, and I had my memories. No one, not even his wife, could take that away.

Even though Troy and I were solid in high school, and I undoubtedly loved him with my entire being, before I could even think about having anything more than a friendship with him, I had to get past a major roadblock in my heart. His name was Royce Phillip Jordan III. He was a junior when I was a freshman. He was deep chocolate and tall, had muscles like a body builder, and had the most perfect, chiseled face I had ever seen. To top it off, he was smart as hell. He was captain of the football team and maintained a consistent 3.8 GPA. He was the most popular guy in high school, and all the girls loved him, including me.

When I stepped on the scene at Oakland Tech that first day, I was with my best friend at the time, Joan-Renee. We walked into the cafeteria, and when I saw Royce, I nearly fell out. I was mesmerized by him, and I made a secret vow right then and there that one day, I would be his girl. But apparently, so had every other girl in school. Royce's name fell off the tongues of giddy girls more frequently than the words "yes" and "no." In bathroom stalls all over school, slews of girls had written that they loved him, wanted him,

dreamed about him—and some had even said they'd
been with him.

I looked forward to every break and lunch so I
could post myself outside the cafeteria and watch
him walk by with his crowd of friends. I also had two
classes with him, which made it all the better for me.
That's when I really got to scope him out. I found out
how sharp and intelligent he was. He was always the
first to raise his hand to answer a question, and even
when he was called on unexpectedly, he was always
prepared. That made me drool over him even harder.
There's nothing like a gorgeous *and* smart man.

While all the other girls had no problem gushing
over him right in front of his face, I kept my feelings
a secret from him. Sure, I ran my mouth with the rest
of the girls in school about how in awe of him I was,
and I even told them all that one day I would be his
woman. But my brother, Powell, who's six years
older than me, always told me never to chase a guy.
He also told me to never let a guy know you like him
until you know he likes you. He used to say, "Play it
cool; make him wonder about you. Guys don't like
girls who act desperate." So, with that advice under
my belt, I was determined to be the one girl that
Royce wanted out of all the others.

It was hard keeping my feelings to myself all the
time, especially since I was grouped with him for
class projects three times. Working so closely with him
was exhilarating, yet nerve-racking. I wanted so badly
to get next to him, tell him my true feelings. And it
didn't help that he was so nice to me all the time.
When he would see me in the hallways, he would
smile and say, "How you doin', sweetheart?" Just
having him talk to me used to make me nearly wet my

pants. But I made sure I played it cool, and when he would speak to me, I would say to him in my most mature voice, "I'm fine, Royce. How are you today?" He would give me a sexy smile and say, "Can't complain, cutie," then he would wink and keep on walking. We also knew a lot of the same people, so on many occasions, we would end up hanging in the same circles, engaging in conversation.

This went on for months, and with each passing day, my fascination with him grew. The more time I spent with him, the more he got under my skin. I was constantly itching to let him know that I was the one for him. Our rapport was great, and at one point, I really thought I had a chance at snagging him. That is, until the day my whole world fell apart.

I remember it like it was yesterday. One morning in early May, I woke up feeling bold. I had to let Royce know I wanted him. I didn't wanna walk right up to him and spill the beans, so instead, I made Joan-Renee stop at the store with me on our way to school, and help me pick out a small card for him. The front had a heart on it, with a little girl holding her hands out as if she were trying to hug the heart. The inside was blank. In it, I wrote, *You plus me equals perfection. Be mine. You won't regret it. Love . . .* At first, I was gonna sign my name, but then I thought about it and got scared. Joan-Renee said I should just go for it, but I wasn't so sure. I thought to myself that maybe it wasn't the right time to reveal my identity. Maybe I should let him guess for a while, then, when the suspense was too much for him to bear, I would let him know it was me. I decided to keep the truth to myself.

I had planned to stick the card in a slot in Royce's locker. I waited until the halls were quiet, and right before lunch, I excused myself from science class to go to the bathroom. I made my way to his locker, and when I got there, I stopped to make sure no one was looking before I stuck the card inside. There was nobody in my view, although I did hear a couple of students nearby, about to round the corner. I wanted to hurry up before I got caught, so I took a deep breath and shoved the card in the largest slot in his locker and ran off. I didn't even look back to see if anyone had seen me. My heart was racing, and I felt a surge of excitement rolling through me.

Just as I got back to class, the bell rang. I hurried in, snatched my books and ran back out into the hallway. I saw a few of my girlfriends and they flagged me down. I calmed myself and headed their way. They asked me where I was going for lunch. I told them I wasn't sure and I wanted to wait for Joan-Renee to see what she was doing. We all decided to meet out in front of the building in ten minutes and go from there.

I finally found Joan-Renee and I told her what I had done. We squealed and laughed, and she asked me what I was going to do next. I told her I would just wait. Let him guess awhile, then maybe in a couple of weeks, put another note in his locker and give him some clues. I wanted this to be a fun game. We put our books in our lockers and headed out front to meet the other girls for lunch.

As I was heading to my English class after lunch, I passed by the gym. Royce was coming out. He was wearing blue sweatpants and a white tank top, showing all his beautiful muscles. I felt my stomach do a flip as I looked at him and wondered if he had gotten my card. I smiled and tried to keep walking, but he stopped me.

"Ay, wait a minute."

I froze. Something in his tone told me he had something serious to say.

I turned to him, smiled and said, "Hey," as I tried to keep my composure.

He looked at me with intensity. "I got your card."

That stunned me. "My . . . what?"

"The card you put in my locker earlier. I know it was you. Somebody told me they saw you put it in there and run."

I could've died right then. Actually, I wanted to cry, but I held the tears back. I was so embarrassed. My plan had backfired, and now Royce knew how I felt. I couldn't think of anything to say, and I wasn't about to try to deny it, so I just mumbled, "Oh," and looked down at my feet.

Just when I thought the situation couldn't get any worse, he hit me with, "Look, uh . . . you know, I'm flattered and all, but . . . you're just . . . not my type. You don't really have what I'm lookin' for. But, hey, thanks for the card. It was cute."

My heart stopped, and I could feel my tear ducts about to explode. I was already humiliated and ready to slit my wrists, but I couldn't go out like a sucker, so for the second time, I held back my tears, stood proud and tall, looked him dead in his face and said, "Okay, well . . . it's your loss."

He looked at me in amazement for a moment, then, he threw his gym bag over his shoulder, sort of smiled and said, "Yeah. Maybe so." After he looked at me strangely for about five seconds, he said, "Hey, I'll see you later," and he walked off.

By that time, students were swarming everywhere, rushing to get to class. I stood there like a zombie and watched Royce fade into the growing crowd. He never even looked back at me. Three of his boys walked up to him and he gave each of them a pound, then they all began walking away together.

Since I was standing in people's way, I kept getting bumped into. Nobody said *excuse me, sorry, oops*— nothing. Then again, even if they had, I probably wouldn't have heard them. I had sunk into a comatose daze, and for a moment, it seemed as if everything around me got totally silent, and I was the only one on campus.

I'm not even sure how long I stood there getting bumped, shoved, and damn near trampled, but when Joan-Renee stopped in front of me and said, "Hey. Katrice. What're you doing?" that's when I snapped back to life.

I knew I was too damn young to be having a heart attack, but when my chest got tight and it started feeling like someone was squeezing my heart with a pair of pliers, I got scared. I dropped my bookbag, clutched at my chest, turned away from Joan-Renee and doubled over.

She screamed, "KATRICE! OH MY GOD! WHAT'S WRONG?!"

I heard some kids gasping and mumbling as I felt her trying to grab me before I hit the ground. But then, in a split second, a whole new feeling came over me. Severe and intense nausea. My lunch started making its way upward, and little beads of sweat started popping out of my forehead. Joan-Renee had me by the arm, screaming for me to answer her, but I couldn't. I broke away from her grip and ran for the nearest bush. On my way, my foot got caught in a little pothole. I tripped and fell, badly twisting my ankle, and when I hit the ground, a sharp object made contact with my forearm, ripping the skin open all the way down to my elbow, as I landed in the dirt next to a pile of dead leaves and twigs.

Before I could blink, my lunch was on its way out of my mouth. Chunks of cafeteria meatloaf, mixed vegetables, mashed potatoes, and chocolate cake blended together with orange soda flew everywhere. As I watched the liquid food hit the ground and splatter all over nature, I finally started to cry. With each painful jerk of my body came more tears. Between my aching chest, my flying lunch, my now-bloody, dirt-encrusted arm, and the fact that Royce had just rejected me without even so much as a thought, I didn't know what was making me more miserable.

By that time, Joan-Renee and a bunch of other students, as well as a few teachers, were all at my side, struggling to get me off the ground as I lay in a puddle of blood, tears, and vomit. As a few people tried to help me up, I heard at least a dozen or so overlapping remarks from the crowd.

"Wait a minute, wait! Don't move her yet!"

"Stop yelling! I'm trying to help! She's hurt!"

"Oh my God . . . look at her arm!"

"Stop arguing and get her up! She needs to go to the nurse's office!"

"What happened?"

"I don't know; she just fell out."

"You gon' be okay, sweetie . . . ?"

"I'm not touching her. She barfed all over the place."

"Shut up, stupid!"

"Don't we have algebra with her?"

"Man, she's *all* messed up."

"Is she unconscious?"

"Are you okay?"

Then, I heard Joan-Renee scream, "EVERYBODY MOVE! NOW!"

Silence fell over the crowd as she shoved her way through to get to me. The people who were trying to help me up let me go, and everybody stared at my girl while backing away from me. Even the teachers obeyed. The booming voices quickly turned to whispers as Joan-Renee knelt down and slowly began to pull me up from my stupor.

I continued to sob as she straightened out my skirt to keep my ass from showing, wiped my forehead with her palm and said, "Come on, girl. You okay? Here . . . grab my arm . . . come on . . . move slow . . . I've got you."

I started to try to speak, but nothing but garble would come out. I was slobbering; snot was making its way down my top lip, almost dripping into the opening of my mouth; my rib cage was throbbing from all the vomiting; and my eyes were burning like crazy.

"Shhh . . ." Joan-Renee said, "just . . . let's get you outta here. We're goin' to the nurse's office. Come on. We can talk later, after we know you're okay."

As the crowd opened up and made room for us, I held tightly onto Joan-Renee as she led me limping, crying, and jabbering up to the nurse's office. When we arrived, I was in so much pain, I couldn't see straight. There was a lot of commotion in the office, as the nurse and a few others got me positioned on the bed and began tending to my arm and ankle.

I was still crying, and in between trying to answer fifty different questions about what hurt and what happened, my mind drifted back to Royce. I kept hearing him tell me that I wasn't his type and that I didn't have what he was looking for over and over until it felt like my brain was about to pop.

My arm was too screwed up for the nurse's office to really take care of, so I ended up having to go to the local emergency room. The nurse called Mama at home, and it seemed like before I could even say my name twice, she was there. Joan-Renee said she would get my assignments from my teachers and bring them to the house later.

On the way to the hospital, which really was only a five-minute drive from school, Mama asked me what happened. Fortunately, I've never really had any shame in my game when it comes to talking to either of my parents, so I filled her in on every last detail of my horrid day up until that point. Mama felt bad for me when I told her what Royce had said, but she told me not to worry. If he couldn't realize what a gem I was, then forget him. I pretended to feel better when she said that, but to be honest, I still felt terrible. The fact of the matter was, Royce *didn't* realize my worth, and that hurt me more than I could ever put into words.

My arm was really messed up. It took more than thirty stitches to close up the wound, and I screamed the whole time I was in the room. Aside from my arm, the doctor told me I had a severe sprain in my ankle, and ordered me to stay off it for at least a week, maybe more. That meant I would be housebound, which was fine with me. Quiet as it was kept, I was glad he told me to stay off it, because after the day I had, I was in no shape to go back to school and face Royce, not to mention all the kids who saw me crash and burn in the middle of campus. So, after about an hour and some change, I took my stitched-and-gauzed arm, my Ace-bandaged ankle, and my new pair of crutches and headed home with Mama.

When we got home, I was starving, so Mama made me some chicken-noodle soup from scratch and a huge tuna sandwich, since I'd thrown up my lunch from earlier. I got in bed and tried to curl up to watch some television, but because of my leg and arm, I wasn't very comfortable. Mama came in and elevated both my leg and arm over pillows to ease my discomfort. Since it was my right arm that was injured, and I'm right-handed, trying to eat was a joke and a half. I had to use my left hand to eat, which messed up my flow, because I kept spilling soup all over my bed tray, and tuna kept falling out of the bottom of my sandwich since I couldn't use both hands to hold it. In the end, it took me thirty-five minutes to eat, but I felt much better afterward.

By the time Daddy and Powell got home, I had fallen asleep. When I woke up, I could hear Mama telling the two of them what happened to me. I didn't care. I would've told them myself, eventually. Mama doing it for me saved me the pain of having to relive the whole experience again. As I listened to Mama tell them what Royce said, I started to cry again. A few minutes after Mama finished the story, both Daddy and Powell came into my room to see about me.

Daddy said, "Hey, there, clumsy. How you feelin'?" He sat on the edge of my bed and wiped the tears from my face. "Heard you had a pretty rough day."

I nodded. Daddy's affection made me cry even harder, for some reason.

Powell stood at the foot of my bed, tweaked my pinky toe on my left foot and said, "Don't cry, Kit-Kat.

Bump that stupid dude. He don't know what he's missin'. Watch, one day, he's gon' try to get wit'choo. Trust me . . . you just wait. But I hate the fact that you all scratched and scarred up 'cause of him. I should knock his punk ass out."

I smiled at my big brother. He always was my hero. He would do anything for me, and I knew it.

He kissed his index and middle finger on his right hand, flashed the peace sign at me and said, "Ah'ight, love you, baby sis. I gotta go. Later y'all."

After Powell left the room, Daddy said, "He's right, you know. Years from now, this, what's his name? Royce?"

I nodded.

"One day, he'll probably look up and wonder what in the world he was thinkin', passin' you up. Don't'-choo worry, Chickadee. You'll get over this. I promise."

"Thanks, Daddy."

"All right, baby. You go on and get'choo some rest, now. I'll be back to check on you later."

He got up, ruffled my hair, and then walked out of the room. I was tired, so within ten minutes, I was asleep again.

Around six, Joan-Renee came over. She brought my homework assignments, and I filled her in on everything that happened with Royce, my visit to the emergency room, and what the doctor said.

"I'm sorry, girl. I really thought he was into you. That was hella rude, what he said, though." Then, she said, "God . . . the doctor said a week, maybe more? Are you gonna be able to keep up in your classes?"

"Yeah, I'll be okay. There's still a few weeks before finals, so I should be able to do what I need to do."

"By the way . . . I got some news for you. Your

friend Troy asked me about you today. He said he heard you had an accident and he wanted to know how you were. Told me to tell you he said hi and get well soon. He's a cutie, don't'choo think?"

I smiled. "Yeah. He's cool. I like him."

She looked at me mischievously. "You mean, *like* him like him, or just friend like him?" She started twirling her long, brunette-blonde ponytail.

"See, here you go. I knew you were up to somethin'. I like him as a *friend* . . . that's all. I mean, yeah, he's cute, but you know . . ."

"Yeah . . . I know . . . Royce." Then she mumbled viciously under her breath, "Stupid ass."

I sulked, "Yeah. Royce." I felt tears welling up, but I held them back.

Joan-Renee sighed, then said, "You know, you're gonna be okay. Pretty soon, you'll be like, 'Royce who?'"

"I don't know about all that, girl."

"You will." Then she paused and looked at me for a minute.

"What?"

"Well, back to what I was sayin' a minute ago . . . about Troy . . ."

I cut her off. "No, see, leave that alone. He's just a friend. How come you keep bringin' him up, anyway?"

"Well . . . he sort of asked me to ask you if he could call you."

"He did? For what?"

"What do you mean, 'For what,' lame duck? 'Cause he likes you, that's for what."

"No, he doesn't. Not like that."

"Yes, he does. And besides, he made a good point. Since you guys have four classes together, and you and I only have one, he volunteered to bring you the homework assignments . . . if you'll let him. Royce is in two of the classes you have with Troy, and I didn't hear him offering any help. Matter of fact, everybody heard what happened to you today, and the only person, besides me, that offered to be there for you was Troy. Now, you tell me he don't like you."

I already knew Troy liked me, but I was always too preoccupied with Royce to give him much thought. I didn't wanna tell Joan-Renee that I knew, because I didn't want her trying to push the two of us together any more than she already was. I was still traumatized behind the whole Royce fiasco, and I just wanted to deal with that for the moment.

"Whatever. And how do you know everybody heard what happened to me?"

"Girl, come on. You know news travels fast. I mean, they don't know what happened was because of what Royce said to you, but they know you fell and ended up at the hospital. And I know for sure Royce knows, because I heard some dude telling him about it after school when they were hanging out in front."

"Did you hear him say anything?"

"He just said, 'Aw, man, that's too bad.' If I had known then what I know now, I woulda socked him in the jaw."

I chuckled. "Yeah, right."

She laughed, too. "Okay, not really, but you know what I mean."

There was a short pause, then I blurted out, "You can go ahead and give Troy my number."

Joan-Renee smiled real big, clapped her hands one time and shouted, "YES!"

"Okay, hold it. Don't get excited and start plannin'

my wedding. I'm just tryina get my homework from him. *That's all.*"

She got up, gathered her things to get ready to leave and started singing, "Troy loves Katrice, Troy loves Katrice. . . ."

I laughed and threw a balled-up paper towel at her with my left hand. "Shut up and get outta here! I'll talk to you tomorrow."

She laughed. "Bye, girl. Hurry up and get back to school. I'm lonely already."

"You'll be fine. See ya."

Troy did end up calling me the next day after he got home from school. After we talked for a while, he told me he had some handouts from a couple of classes to give me, and asked if he could come by and drop them off. I told him yes.

When he arrived, he sat in a chair on the side of my bed and we talked for a long time. I was still feeling crappy about the Royce thing, but it was nice to have a little diversion for a while. Troy was a good guy, and I really did enjoy his company.

I ended up missing nine days of school. In between watching television, sleeping, and doing my homework, I cried at least once a day about what happened with Royce. Since Mama was a housewife, she was there to tend to my every need, which was great.

Troy came over every day after school and brought me my assignments, then sat and talked with me for a while. Each day that he was by my bedside, I grew to like him more and more. Not only did we have great conversation, but he also made me laugh, and I realized we had a lot in common. Not to mention the fact that he was definitely cute.

The day finally came for me to return to school,

and I was nervous as hell. Although my arm and ankle were much better, emotionally, I was still a wreck. I hadn't seen Royce since the day I fell, and I was scared about having to face him again.

I was off the crutches, but I still walked with a slight limp, and my arm, though the stitches were out, still had a bandage on it. When Joan-Renee and I arrived at school, I felt like a movie star. Students I didn't even know hovered around me to find out how I was doing and what happened that day. I told them I was fine, and that I just tripped and fell. A couple of people asked me about the vomit episode, and I told them the lunch I ate didn't agree with me, and I was already feeling sick before I fell.

As I was walking to my first-period class from my locker, I saw Royce and a couple of his boys talking. There was no other way for me to go, so I had no choice but to walk past them. As I slowly approached them, I felt all of their eyes on me. I braced myself, and tried hard not to even look at Royce, but he made that impossible.

"Hey, you. How you feelin'?" Royce inquired.

When I looked into his eyes, I felt all the emotions from the past two weeks come rushing back to me. I could tell a cry was pending, so I knew I needed to make our interaction brief. I quickly said, "Good, thanks," and kept walking. I didn't even smile. Fortunately, I didn't have a class with him until second period, so I had time to cry and get myself together so I wouldn't be a basket case right under his nose.

"All right, then . . . good to see you, sweetheart," he called after me.

I didn't respond. I couldn't tell if he was sincere or trying to be funny, but whatever the case, I just wanted to get as far away from him as possible. For the first time that year, I wasn't looking forward to being in class with him.

That first day was rough, having to sit through two classes with Royce, but I made it. I was determined to make it. Truthfully, a big part of the reason I did so well was Troy. Since the three of us had two classes together, and Troy sat next to me, I felt more at ease. Plus, our bond was growing, and I realized that even though I was still hung up on Royce, I was starting to feel a small spark for Troy.

Over the next two weeks, Troy and I spent more time together. He started walking me home from school and we began hanging out more. Soon, I finally began to feel the heaviness I felt about the Royce situation lifting. I did cry at some point every day for the first week that I was back at school, simply because it was so hard being near Royce and having constant flashbacks of that day, but after I realized that I had been crying every day for almost three weeks, I had had enough. I decided that no man was worth that many tears, especially if he didn't give a damn about me. So, I made a vow that no matter what, I wouldn't cry over Royce anymore. What happened happened, and I couldn't change it. It was time for me to move on. The more time I spent with Troy, the more secure I felt in that thought. I told Joan-Renee how I was feeling about Troy, and she damn near turned a cartwheel.

Summer vacation finally rolled around, and in addition to running the streets with Joan-Renee, I spent a considerable amount of time with Troy. By the time we started our sophomore year, I knew we were headed for a relationship, and that was fine with me. I was ready to give my heart to someone who I knew would appreciate it. So, as I mentioned earlier, the day Troy finally got bold and kissed me on my doorstep after the game, I didn't fight the feeling.

Make no mistake, I never really got Royce out of my system. I tried, but I just wasn't successful. Fortunately, I had Troy in my life, and he was wonderful. It was because of him that I was finally able to put my feelings for Royce on the back burner, even though those feelings were always simmering on low. Troy was my knight in shining armor, so to speak, and because of that alone, I knew he would always have a special place in my heart.

5

When I woke up Saturday morning at around nine, the sun was shining brightly and beating down on me through my bedroom window. There's nothing I love more than waking up to the heat of the sun on my body. I rolled over, faced the window, and basked in the sunlight while I thought about my impending date with Weston.

I lay there for about ten minutes, and contemplated what to wear. I wanted to look sexy, but not too dressy. I didn't want him to think I was trying to get his attention or impress him. I was actually feeling like I was back in grade school or something. Like the boy next door had just asked me out for a soda, the way they used to do on *The Brady Bunch*.

As I looked out the window, I wished for a moment that I had given him my number the night before. I pictured him calling me prior to our date that afternoon, and the two of us having a light, flirty conversation. First, I smiled at the thought. A second later, I was feeling discouraged. I started thinking about our date turning out sour, and the two of us not hitting it off. I started having visions of us having terrible conversation and finding one another boring. Either that or both of us being turned off by each other. To be honest, I actually started getting annoyed with myself that I was even as excited as I was to be seeing him that day. I barely knew the man, and already, I was going off on a mental tangent.

To take my mind off things a little, I got up, turned on the radio, and started cleaning the kitchen. I was feeling sort of hungry, but I didn't wanna eat before meeting Weston. The night before, I asked the girls if either of them knew about Café Soul, and lo and behold, Genine said she had been there a few times. She said the food was great, and that I wouldn't have to worry about leaving the restaurant feeling unfulfilled, because they give you more than you can eat.

After I finished sweeping, mopping, and singing my heart out, it was after ten. Just as I was about to head for my closet to pick out my clothes, the phone rang. When Chantelle's name popped up on the caller-ID box, I laughed to myself when I picked up the phone. "And just what, pray tell, do you want, Miss Randall?"

"Haaaaayyy! Today's the big date . . . what'choo wearin'?"

"First of all, it's not a 'big date,' and second, I don't know what I'm wearin' yet, so leave me alone, you pest! What'choo doin' today . . . besides tryina be all up in my business?"

"My, my! Such hostilities!" She laughed. "Well, I'm gonna go get a mani and pedi, then I gotta go see a man about tryina get my pictures put up in this art gallery."

"Good for you! 'Bout time you got back on the bandwagon. You been loungin' ever since you been on disability. I was startin' to wonder if you were ever gonna get back on track with your career. You know drawing and painting is your calling. You coulda been famous by now."

"Yeah, I know. It's just that ever since the accident, I've been a bum."

"Uh, yeah, I noticed. I know you've gotten comfortable since you've been off work these past coupla months, but damn, girl, it's time to get back in the swing of things; you need to start goin' for your goals. And speakin' of the accident, how many more physical therapy sessions you got?"

"Um, I'm not sure. My back is healing pretty good, and the doctor said as long as I take it easy at the gym and keep doing my prescribed therapy exercises, I should be able to discontinue my visits pretty soon."

"Well, good. I can't believe your job actually tried to blame you for that fall. They *knew* that floor was wet. I swear, people always rushin' to get to a damn break instead of takin' the time to finish what they start. It's called a *WET FLOOR sign,* people! I'm glad he got fired."

"Girl, you and me both. But you know what? I was mad as hell in the beginning, but then I realized that the benefit of it all is, bein' on disability is makin' it possible for me to finally spend time on my art career. I mean, I liked the job, and that clothing discount was exactly what I needed, but I was startin' to get bored there. Plus, I was comin' home tired as hell, feet hurtin', and I would be wantin' to draw, but was too damn wasted in the brain to get anything done."

"Well, take advantage of your free time while you can, girl. We ain't all able, okay?"

"I feel you."

"Okay, lemme go. I gotta get dressed and get outta here so I can go get this date over with." I tried to sound like meeting Weston was no big deal, but inside, I was about to burst.

"Okay. You know the drill . . . have fun, and of course, call me with the details later, Miss Thang. And the bet is still on; don't think I forgot."

"Bye, skank!"

"Bye, skeeza!"

After I hung up with Chantelle, I went to my closet and shuffled through my stuff. I decided to wear my new navy-blue jeans; my sleeveless, eggshell-colored cashmere turtleneck sweater; and my white, open-toed, two-inch-heeled sandals. I draped my clothes across my bed, took out my favorite olive-green satin bra and thong set, dropped them on top of my shirt, then headed for the shower.

Once I had showered, shaved, and shined, I spritzed on some freesia body spray to complement the lotion I had just slathered on my body and stuck my favorite pearl earrings in my ears. Then I put on some lip gloss, grabbed my purse and jacket, and headed out the door after checking myself one last time in the mirror.

After turning into two wrong parking lots, I finally found the café. I parked my fire-engine red, 1997 Ford Mustang near the door and hopped out. I looked at my watch, and it said eleven fifty-three. When I walked into the small-but-quaint café, it was packed. I looked around to see if Weston had arrived yet, and sure enough, I spotted him over at a table in the back, reading a newspaper.

He didn't see me, so when I walked over to the table and said, "Good morning. Is this seat taken, sir?" that surprised him.

He put his paper down, smiled, and got up. He looked absolutely delicious. He was wearing a black sweatsuit with shoes to match, and I could tell he was freshly shaven. When he got up to greet me, the air brushed past him, and once again, Eternity for Men fell off his body and danced in my nose. I wanted to throw him down right there and eat *him* for breakfast.

He looked me up and down. "How you doin'? Damn . . . you look nice. Smell good, too."

"Thanks."

"Did you have any problems findin' the place?"

"I admit, I did take a couple of wrong turns, but as you can see, I made it in one piece."

"One fine piece, at that." He smiled again.

I was embarrassed for some reason. "Thank you."

We sat down and had small talk for a few minutes, then a server came with our menus.

I asked him, "So, you come here often? This is a cute place."

"Actually, this is one of my favorite places to come for breakfast on the weekends. This dude I know turned me on to it about a year ago. It's only been here a coupla years. After today, you'll be hooked, I'm tellin' you."

"Okay. Let's see what we got, here." I opened my menu.

I ended up ordering blueberry pancakes, sausage, and eggs, and Weston ordered an omelet with home fries. We both ordered orange juice, and we were set.

Our server came back with our juices, and while we waited for our food, we talked for a few minutes about the weather and sports, then Weston got down to business.

"So, lemme ask you somethin'. That day at the shop, when you told me you knew who I was . . . what exactly did you mean by that?"

"Oh, you still trippin' off that?"

"I don't know about *trippin'*, but if someone tells me they know who I am, and I know I've never met 'em, that makes me curious."

"All right, you know Lisa Derrick?"

"Yeah, why? You know her?"

"Sort of. More like, her cousin is one of my best friends."

"Okay . . . and?"

"And . . . I heard about how you guys used to date and . . . well, let's just say, I heard about how you suddenly dropped her."

"Yeah. She wasn't right for me. So?"

"Wow . . . okay . . ."

"No, I mean, I'm just sayin' that's what I do when I'm not feelin' a woman the way I need to. Don't get me wrong; I'm not mad at *you*."

Even though he wasn't mad at me, I started feeling uncomfortable and I wanted to get off the subject. "I just . . . heard the story, that's all."

He leaned back in his chair, smiled, then looked at me like he was about to start grilling me.

"So, you heard a story secondhand, and you just automatically believed it, not having heard the other side?"

"Well, yeah, I guess."

He looked somewhere between highly amused and intrigued. "Do you always believe secondhand stories?"

I felt like I was the subject of a damn Barbara Walters interview. "Not necessarily, but I mean, it's not like the sources were unreliable. Why would they lie?"

"It's not really about folks lyin', it's more about stories gettin' twisted."

"Meaning?"

"I mean, I get the feeling you assume, based on the story you heard, that I dogged her out."

"Sort of."

He leaned forward with his elbows on the table and looked at me curiously while sporting a smile that said he was getting the biggest kick out of making me squirm. "Okay, then, Miss Lady, why don't you tell me what happened, then."

I wasn't sure where he was going with this. "I'm sorry?"

"I want you to tell me, since you seem to know the details, what happened in my relationship with Lisa."

I was embarrassed and thrown off. I hadn't expected him to be that sharp.

"Um . . . maybe we should just drop the subject. It's obvious it's a sore spot for you."

"Oh, no, it ain't no sore spot for *me, I know* what happened. But since you think you do, too, I wanna hear what you heard just to see if we're on the same page. Trust me, if what you heard is right, I'll tell you. But if it's not, I'll stand *you* corrected. So, let's hear it." He folded his arms and continued to smile at me.

My discomfort level was off the charts, and I was wishing the waitress would hurry up with our food so I could put something else in my mouth besides my foot. But she was nowhere in sight, and Weston was waiting for my answer.

"Um . . . well . . . Chantelle said that Lisa told her that you guys had gone out maybe six or seven times, and that things seemed to be going pretty good between you two, then . . . um . . ." I paused and looked at him.

"Go on."

"Um . . . okay, then she said one night you guys slept together, and after that, you stopped calling her, and you wouldn't return any of her calls, either."

He was unfazed. "And that's it? That's all you heard?"

"Yeah, pretty much."

He paused for a moment, then he broke out laughing. "That's amazin'."

"What is?"

"You know, it's crazy how two people can be in the exact same situation together and come out of it with two different stories."

"What do you mean?"

"Well, first of all, the story you heard is almost right, but there's a couple of important details missing."

"Like?"

"Like the fact that after we slept together, Lisa started jockin' me twenty-four-seven. I admit, we weren't an official couple before we made that move, but I didn't force her into that situation. It was somethin' we both wanted to do. But after that night, she started actin' like we were married or something. Started callin' me like six times a day and questionin' my whereabouts and expectin' us to spend every wakin' moment together. Now first of all, before we spent that night together, she was cool. Gave me my space, was fun and mellow, but after that night, she turned into a whole different person. I couldn't move my big toe without her tryina hover over me. I don't like that. That's not the sign of a strong woman to me. Women who act like that are insecure, and a little unstable in my opinion."

Our food finally came, and he continued with his story while we both doctored our meals with condiments.

"Anyway, so one day she called me, and I told her she needed to ease up. Give a brotha a chance to breathe. Maybe even miss her a little. She didn't like that, so she started callin' me an insensitive dog. Told me I was just like all the other men she dated. Then she slammed the phone down in my ear."

"Well," I said, while chomping on my huge blueberry pancake, "she was upset because you slept with her and then she felt slighted."

He took in a mouthful of his omelet, chewed for a few seconds and then said, "I don't know why. One night of sex does *not* a commitment make. We were two adults who did somethin' we both wanted to do. I never professed my undying love to her or said anything about long-term plans. If she hadn't started tweakin' on me, we mighta had a chance at somethin' more; but she didn't play her cards right, so I let her go."

"But, she said you didn't return any of her phone calls."

"Right. I didn't . . . *after* I told her it wasn't gon' work out and I needed to move on."

"Damn. You were kinda cold, don't you think?"

He drew his neck back and made a funny face. "Why? 'Cause I got sense enough not to waste my time, and some woman's time for that matter, when I know she's not right for me?"

"I guess you have a point."

"I'm *sure* I have a point. I never led her on, and when I was ready to go, I told her. When someone tells you it's over, if you choose to keep callin' them, that's on you. I don't feel I owed her anything after I told her where I was comin' from. Wasn't nothin' else to say after that. She chose to keep callin' and I chose not to respond. Period."

We ate for a moment before I commented, "Okay, fine. I guess you're right. I stand corrected. Maybe she didn't tell the whole story."

"Of course not. Most bitter women have a habit of half-tellin' stories when they don't get their way with a man. She told just enough to make me look like a bad person, insteada just ownin' up to the fact that she didn't go about things the right way with me. The fact is, when I want a commitment with a woman, I let her know. She won't hafta wonder and she won't hafta chase me down to get it."

The food was fabulous, and we were both grubbing pretty hard. There was a lot of fork-to-plate clanging, lip smacking and mouth wiping.

"Okay, point taken. But what I didn't mention was that after the whole Lisa thing, I saw you on several occasions around town with other women. You sayin' none of them were right for you and you had to let them go, too?"

"Yup. And no, I didn't sleep with all of 'em, either. I'm on a mission. I don't have time to be dilly-dallyin' with women I'm not feelin'."

"What kind of mission?"

He paused for a second, then took a sip of his juice before he spoke. "I'm lookin' for a woman . . . like my mother."

I was a little turned off by that. I started wondering if I was dealing with some warped mama's boy. "Come again? Your mother?"

First, the look on his face was serious. Then, a second later, he started looking at me the way you look at someone when you're trying to figure out if you can trust them with a secret. After a moment, he said, "When I was in high school, my father ran out on my mother and me and my five brothers and sisters."

"Damn. I'm sorry to hear that."

"I already knew she was a strong woman before he left, but after he was gone, my mother had to raise and care for us all by herself. I watched her keep our family together. She never complained, never cried, and she always made sure we had everything we needed. Money was funny a lot of times in the beginning, but somehow, we never went without. And she was always there for us when we needed help or encouragement or advice. She always knew exactly what to do and say. I don't know how she did it. She just had this strength and resilience and independence that just moved me. I saw sides of her I didn't even know a woman could have. After watchin' her, I made a vow to never make a commitment to a woman who didn't have the same qualities as my mother. I just . . . I treasure her. I need to be able to feel that way about my woman. So, in turn, unfortunately, a lotta the women I date get dumped early on. I just refuse to settle for less."

I was floored. I had never heard anything so beautiful come out of a man's mouth, and to be honest, I was impressed and turned on as hell. More and more, I was starting to see that Weston had a sort of confidence that I was drawn to. It was like he was solid in who he was and what he wanted, and didn't care in the least if people didn't agree or understand.

"That's . . . really beautiful. Damn. I don't even know what else to say. But where'd your father go?"

Then his vibe changed to bitterness. "Don't know, don't care. A real man just don't run out on his family like that."

I went back to feeling uncomfortable.

"Um . . . well, have you seen or spoken to him?"

"Once. 'Bout six years ago. I went home when my mother had hip surgery and he came to the hospital one day. I was mad as hell, too."

"Home . . . where's that?"

"I'm from Chicago."

"Oh, okay. So, um, and you guys didn't talk then?"

He got real short with me. "Nah, we don't talk."

Something in the way he said it told me I needed to change the subject. To lighten the conversation up, I asked, "So, how'd you end up here?" That seemed to do the trick.

"Aw, I moved out here wit' my boy Eric when I was eighteen. When we were juniors in high school, we used to talk about movin' out here together. We were tired of the same old scenery—plus, the weather is harsh in the winter and we got tired of always freezin' our asses off. We heard California was the place to be, so one day, we had a serious talk about it and decided we would move out here after high school. We both got part-time jobs at McDonald's and started savin' our paychecks. We wanted to make sure we had enough money to be able to afford more than some roach motel, so after graduation, we started workin' full time to really build up our savings. We made some calls, did some research, found us a crib, packed our bags and jumped on a plane to Oakland. Been here ever since."

"That's cool. You guys still room together?"

"Nah. We did for like four years, but then Eric got his girl pregnant, so they decided it was time for the two of them to get they own place, settle down. I still see him all the time, though. We like brothers. That's gon' always be my dawg."

"So, what'd you do after he moved out?"

"Aw, it was cool, 'cause by then, I had my job at Goldman's Gym and I was makin' enough money to go on and do my own thang."

"What do you do at Goldman's?"

"I'm a personal trainer, but I don't work there no more. I work at the gym over on Webster now. Still a trainer."

With that body of his, I really should have guessed he would have a job like that.

The more we talked, the more I was feeling him. I thought about the little bet Chantelle and I had made, and I started planning to hook her hair up for free, 'cause I was losing. I liked him, and already, I wanted to see him again.

"So, you like it out here?"

"Yeah, it works for me. It's a far cry from Chi-Town, but I get home about once a year, so I get a dose of my roots. Can't stay away from my family too long."

"You said there's six of you?"

"Yeah. It goes my sister Leslie, me, my twin brothers Kevin and Cornell, my sister LaMonica, and the baby, Tamika. Well, I guess she ain't a baby no more; she's almost sixteen."

"Sounds like you guys are close."

"Oh, yeah. My family, man, they mean everything

to me. But, what about you? We been talkin' about me since we sat down. I wanna know all about you, Miss Vincent. What'choo got goin' on?"

"Well, I'm from California, lived in Oakland all my life, my parents are William and Eleanor and they're still married, and I have an older brother, Powell Jerrard . . . P.J. for short. And my family means everything to me, too." I smiled.

"Okay, short and sweet; I guess that works. Got any other friends besides Lisa's cousin?" he joked sarcastically.

I laughed. "Yes, as a matter of fact, I do. There's Genine Young, Sabrina Thomas, and my shop partner, Tiki Jones."

"Tiki . . . is that her real name?"

"No, Tiki is a combination of her first and middle names, Tina Kiara. But nobody calls her Tina. She's been Tiki since she was, like, seven."

"So, you got a shop all your own, huh? How'd that come about? What are you, like twenty-six or seven?"

"Close. I'm twenty-eight. What about you?"

"Just turned twenty-nine five days ago."

"Oh, well happy belated."

"Thanks."

"I'll be twenty-nine next month on the twenty-fourth."

"I'll hafta remember that."

"Oh, you plan on being around that long?" I joked.

He smiled. "Just get back to you and your shop, smarty pants."

The waitress came with our bill, and Weston pulled it towards himself. I told him, "Lemme get it. It'll be my birthday gift to you."

"You can do something for me next March. How

'bout that?" Then he smiled, picked up the bill, looked at it, and reached in his pocket for his wallet.

"Anyway," I cheesed, "about my shop."

He laughed. "Yeah, can we git back to that, please?"

"Okay, well, my mother's best friend, Miss Marie Louise Lawson, used to do my hair back in the day. I think I mighta been, what, eight or nine when I started goin' to her for my wash, press, and curl. My mother was doing it originally, but my hair was so thick and long, and it just got to be too much for her to deal with, so she sent me to Marie Louise." I took a long chug of my orange juice.

"Anyway, so I went to her once every two weeks, and every time I was there, I was just so intrigued and interested in every little thing she did. I must've had a hundred questions per visit," I chuckled.

Weston said, "I know you were in there drivin' that woman crazy, huh?"

I smiled. "You know what? Actually, she really didn't mind. I think she kinda got a kick out of it, myself. But, anyway, after a while, I think she realized even before I did, that I had a growing interest in the whole art of doing hair thing, so one day after she did my hair, I think I was ten or eleven by then, she asked me if I wanted to help her out around the shop on weekends for a coupla hours. Said she'd pay me five dollars a day, and I jumped at the chance."

He was amused. "What kinda help were you gon' give at that age?"

"Well, I mean, little simple stuff. Things she knew I could do without screwin' up. Like washing out hair utensils, organizing her shelves and counters with all the products she used, sweeping up hair, keeping clean towels and bibs out and ready, cleaning out the sinks—

stuff like that. She even let me answer the phones and set up appointments for her regulars when she was busy doing someone's hair."

"And you liked doin' all that stuff?"

"Yeah. I mean that was the thing . . . I loved the whole scene. *Everything* was fascinating to me, not just the idea of doing someone's hair. So, I was more than happy to do the little grunt work."

"So, I know you never got to do anything to anybody's hair, right?"

"Well, no, but if I had a few free minutes between prepping and cleaning, I would be reading the ingredients on the backs of all the bottles and jars, and I would ask questions about what certain stuff was and what it does for your hair, so I was always learning about hair, even though I wasn't actually doing it."

"Damn, you were a little fiend, huh?"

"I'm tellin' you, I had my hands in everything."

"Sounds like you found your passion early on."

"Yeah. Marie Louise taught me everything she knew. We used to have these long talks when I would get my hair done, and we got really close. She really was like a second mother to me. Anyway, I worked for her for a few years, till I started high school, then, I got off into other things. I had twice the amount of schoolwork, and I was hanging out with friends more, so my time wasn't as free. But she still did my hair, though, and one day, while she was curling me, she asked me if I thought I might wanna actually do hair for real . . . like as a career, and I was like, 'Hell, yeah!'"

He laughed. "You didn't say 'hell yeah.'"

"Actually, I did. But it was just a little slip of the tongue, and she knew it, so she laughed at it. So, I told her yeah, and she said that if I was really serious and if I went to beauty school after high school and got my license, she would set up a space for me there and I could come work in her shop with her."

"For real?"

"Uh-huh. I told her it was as good as done. So right after I graduated from high school, I enrolled in Alameed Beauty College and about a year later, I had my license and I started working at the shop."

"You can learn all that in a year?"

"Oh, yeah, but you're there full time. It's just like a job; it's not a coupla hours a week. I mean, you're immersed in it, so you gotta be committed."

"So, whose hair were you doin' when you first started out?"

"Hell, all my friends, their friends and family, and I even did my parents' hair. Pretty soon, I had people I didn't even know callin' me for appointments. Word of mouth should never be underestimated."

"So, when did you get the shop?"

"Oh. Well, when I was about twenty-three, Marie Louise got really sick. So sick that I even had to take over her clientele for a while. One day, her husband Freddie called and said they found out she had colon cancer. We couldn't believe it. She passed away about a year later, and I went into this deep depression. She was my mentor, plus she was my mother's best friend, and really she was a good friend of mine, too."

"I'm sorry to hear that. Musta been hard."

"You don't even know. We were all a wreck. I found out from Freddie that she had left the shop to me in her will. They didn't have any kids, and Freddie said I was just like a daughter to her and she wanted me to have the shop."

"Damn . . . she did? That's cool."

"Yeah. At first, I didn't wanna take it, just because I thought the shop would carry too many memories and I would always be sad, but after I talked to my mother and Freddie about it, they convinced me to take it and do her proud. So, here I am, doin' my thang."

Talking about Marie Louise made me a little emotional, and my eyes started to tear up. Weston noticed and asked me, "You okay?" and handed me a napkin for my face.

I thanked him and dabbed my eyes. "Yeah, I'm fine."

"You sure? I didn't mean to bring up no heavy memories for you."

"No, no . . . it's not your fault. I just get sad about it sometimes, that's all. I'm fine."

"Okay . . . we supposed to be havin' fun on our first date, not cryin'." He smiled warmly at me.

"I am. I'm enjoying our date."

"Well, good. I am, too. So, where'd your shopmate come from? I wanna hear the rest of the story."

"Oh—Tiki and I met in beauty school. She's from Oakland, too, but we lived in different areas and went to different schools growing up. We got to be real tight during the time we were in college together, and afterwards, we kept in touch and hung out a lot. After Louise died, I called her up and asked her if she wanted to come work in my shop—be my partner—and she said yeah. There was some beef goin' on between her and another girl at the shop she was workin' at, so leaving there was right up her alley. We been at CUT! for about three and a half years now. It works out well for us."

"That's good. You got a nice setup over there."

"Yeah. She's getting married next May to a friend

of mine from high school, Charles Hamilton. I used to cut his hair when I first started out. But when Tiki came to work in the shop with me, one day he came in for a cut, and when he saw her, suddenly I wasn't good enough to do his hair anymore, and I got kicked to the curb." I laughed at myself. "Naw, I'm just playin'. But, yeah, they hooked up, and she started doin' his hair, and they been together ever since. I'm not sure how much longer she's gonna be workin' with me, 'cause she may open her own shop sometime after the wedding. We'll see what happens."

Weston just sat there and smiled at me after I finished talking.

"What . . . why you lookin' at me like that?"

"Nothin' . . . I'm just . . . enjoyin' listenin' to you talk. I like your company."

"Well, thanks, that's good to know."

"So, you 'bout ready to head out?"

"Yep. I'm stuffed. This was good, thank you. And you're right, I *will* be back."

He started getting up. "I told you, girl. Best place in town."

Weston paid the bill, and when we stepped outside, he asked, "What'choo drivin'?"

I pointed to my car. "This is me, right here."

"Nice . . ." he eyed my personalized license plate in the front. "FASTKAT, huh?"

I smiled. "Yeah, but not the fast you're probably thinkin' of. I got a heavy foot; all my friends tell me I'm a speed demon. When I got this car last year, I thought that would be cute to put on the plates. Where are you?"

He pointed to the middle of the lot. "Over there . . . black Dodge Durango."

"Oh, I love those. Love my 'Stang more, but that's a hot car, too. You like it?"

"Oh, yeah, I love it." He looked out into the distance and said, "Aw . . . speak of the devil . . . there go Eric right there. . . ."

I turned to see who he was looking at and saw a milk-chocolate-colored man—about five-foot nine with extremely long, neat dreadlocks and a thick mustache and beard—approaching us. He was walking hand-in-hand with a little boy that looked about five or six years old. Eric saw Weston and waved at him.

Weston said, "Come on . . . meet my boy." We met Eric and the little boy halfway.

"Ay, man! Wassup?" Eric asked.

"Aw, you know—just tryina do my thang." He looked down at the little boy and said, "Wassup, li'l man? Gimme some," then he stuck his fist out and the little boy tapped his on top of it, pound style.

Weston asked, "So, where y'all headed?"

"Right over here to Marty's so I can get this one's hair cut," he ran his hand on top of the little boy's head. "He lookin' kinda wild."

"All right, then . . . ay, this is my friend Katrice. Katrice, this is my dawg, Eric Townsend."

Eric stuck his hand out in the traditional way and said, "How you doin'? Nice to meet you. This is my son, Eric Junior. We call him E.J."

I shook his hand. "Nice to meet you, too. Hi, there, E.J." Eric Jr. blushed and smiled at me, but didn't speak.

Eric said to his son, "Say hi, boy. You know how to speak."

He mumbled, "Hi . . ." then looked away and smiled.

Eric asked us, "Y'all comin' from the café?"

I nodded, and Weston answered, "Yeah, had to get us a little somethin' to eat."

"Ah'ight, then, we gon' head on in here. Ay, hit me up later on, man."

"Ah'ight, dawg. Say hi to Tamara for me."

"Fuh sho'. Ay, you take it easy, Katrice," Eric said.

"You too," I answered.

After they walked away, Weston turned to me and asked, "So, what's on your agenda today?"

"I dunno. Why?"

"You not workin'?"

"Nope. Closed on Saturdays."

"Really . . . that's unusual. Most shops are open on Saturdays."

"Yeah, but I decided to do something a little different with mine since I have that freedom, so what I do is open up on Sundays for three or four hours to take care of my church clientele. I found that a lot of them want their hair fresh for their Sunday services, so it works out well."

"Hmm . . . I like that. It's different. So, since you're free, spend the day with me."

"Uhhh . . . doing what?"

"Well, nothin' in particular. I'm'a wash my ride, hit the mall right quick, then, I don't know. But whatever I do, I want you to come along. Just . . . roll wit' me . . . talk to me . . . keep me company. I like you. I wanna spend time with you. Plus, I'm just not ready to let'choo go yet."

"*Dang,* like *that?*"

"Yeah. So, is that gon' work for you?"

"Well . . . I guess so . . . but what about my car?"

"Leave it here. We not gon' be gone long. Few hours maybe."

"You sure it'll be okay out here? They won't tow it?"

"Nah. It'll be fine."

"Okay, well at least let me move it from in front of the door to where it's not so on display."

"Okay, I'll meet you over at my car."

"All right."

After I moved my car, I went and hopped in Weston's fresh-smelling Dodge. I had a good feeling about him, and I was glad he asked me to extend our date.

As I was fastening my seat belt, Weston said, "Thank you."

"For what?"

"Not turning me down again. That first time drove me crazy."

I laughed. "You're welcome. And the only reason I turned you down was because of that whole Lisa-and-various-women issue."

"But we straight on that now, right?"

"Yeah, we straight. And you know what? I apologize for assuming things about you. That wasn't cool."

"Hey, you didn't know. I'm just glad I got a chance to explain myself, or you mighta kept envisionin' my picture in the dictionary next to the word *dog*."

I cracked up.

Our first stop was one of those little coin-operated, self-service car washes. Together, Weston and I washed, dried, and vacuumed his car as we bounced our heads to the music on the radio.

After we left the car wash, we rode to the mall in Richmond. We talked and laughed all the way there. It was amazing how comfortable we were with each other. Weston was fun, witty, and a true gentleman, and I was definitely on my way to being smitten.

At the mall, we stopped in Macy's so Weston could find an outfit for a function he was going to with some people from his job. He wanted something casual, yet classy. Being the fashion freak that I am, and not to mention that I love to shop for men, I had no problem running through the store helping him pick out clothes. I must have found at least six different 'fits, all of them he liked. Every time I would show him one, he would say he wanted it, until I showed him the next one, and then he would change his mind. For nearly a half-hour, I saddled him with clothes to try on. He told me how much he usually hates clothes shopping, but with me there, he was actually having fun.

Finally, he decided to go with the tan silk pants and the tan, black, and blue silk long-sleeved sweater, which actually was my top choice, too. After that, we went over to the shoe section and found him some sharp Kenneth Cole loafers that were sinfully butter soft, and the fact that they were forty percent off made it all the better.

Weston was happy with his purchases, and he couldn't thank me enough for being there to help him out. He told me he needed to make sure to have me with him when he went clothes shopping in the future, and that I saved him a lot of time and a huge headache.

Since we were there, I told him I wanted to go to the Fashion Fair counter to get another tube of lipstick. On our way, we had to walk past the Clarins counter, and I stopped to sniff my favorite perfume, Elysium. I commented, "I love this stuff."

Weston asked me, "Is that what you're wearin' today?"

"No, I have on freesia today. This is my favorite, but I haven't bought any in a while."

He didn't comment, and we walked over to the Fashion Fair counter.

After I got my lipstick, we milled around the store for about another fifteen minutes. It was after three when Weston asked me, "Wanna go to the movies?"

"Um . . . yeah, that sounds good. What movie you got in mind?"

"I wanna go see that new one, *U.S. Marshals,* with Tommy Lee Jones and Wesley Snipes. I think it's playin' at the theater in Pinole."

"I heard that was good. My brother and his girl-friend went to see it a couple of weeks ago."

"Cool. Come on. I think there's a four-something show."

"Okay. Let's hit it."

As we pulled out of the parking lot, Weston popped in a CD by a new group called Destiny's Child. I asked, "Hey, is this that 'No, No, No' song?"

He nodded while bobbing his head. "Yeah. These girls can sing! That lead singer, Beyoncé, is fine, too."

"That's what everybody keeps saying. I guess she looks all right, but I don't know about fine."

"Well, you're a woman, so I don't really expect you to get excited over her, 'less you happen to swing 'that way,'" he joked, then looked at me out of the corner of his eye and smiled.

"Uh, nope, don't think so, sweetie." I pointed south. "This is a man's world."

Weston fell out laughing. "I heard *that!*"

We let Beyoncé and her crew take us to Pinole, as we bounced, sang, talked, and laughed.

We just barely made it to the four o'clock show. When I reached in my purse and pulled out the money to pay for my own movie, Weston looked at me like I was crazy and asked, "What'choo doin'?"

"Payin' for my movie."

"No you not. Put that away. We still on a date, girl."

"Well, I didn't just wanna assume . . ."

"Woman, put'cho money back in yo' purse and come on, here. I got this."

"Well, alrighty, then."

We both loved the movie, and agreed that the plane crash scene was the best we had seen in a while as far as crash scenes go. Weston said he'd pay to see the movie again, just to sit and watch that one scene alone. I told him I didn't blame him, and when it came out on video, I was buying it.

For some reason, neither one of us bothered to look at our watches after we left the theater. The sun was just about gone, and it was getting dark, but it was a gorgeous evening. It was comfortably warm, and I had my jacket draped across my arm. We stood outside for a minute, talking about the movie with two other couples that were in our row inside.

After they walked off, Weston said, "I want me somethin' sweet. Hey . . . wanna go get some ice cream across the way at 31 Flavors?"

"Yeah!" I sounded like a damn twelve-year-old.

We jumped in the car and rolled over to the other side of the shopping center to 31 Flavors. Weston ordered a double scoop of something with vanilla and caramel in a cup, and I ordered a small hot-fudge sundae with chocolate and pralines and cream. Of course, Weston insisted he pay for me again, but I didn't argue with him. We sat at a small table in the front and ate our ice cream like two kids at a birthday party.

I noticed I had gotten fudge on my right arm, and when I lifted it up to wipe it off, Weston said, "That's a helluva scar you got on your arm. What's the history behind it?"

"Oh . . . I fell in high school. Took thirty-something stitches to close it, and it never quite healed right. It started to keloid and I couldn't stop it."

"You fell, huh? Ain't that what all abuse victims say?" He smiled.

I laughed. "Seriously, fool! I did!"

"Okay, so tell me about it."

I filled him in on the entire Royce saga from beginning to end. I didn't leave out a single detail. It had been so long since I told the story that I actually found myself laughing at it as I was talking. Weston found it amusing, too. When I told him about how I fell and what all happened, he looked at me like he couldn't believe all the drama that had gone down in that small amount of time. To be honest, telling the story did take me back a little, and it brought those old feelings I had for Royce to the surface again.

Weston said, "And after all that, you still never hooked up wit' ol' boy?"

That stung a little, but I didn't let on. "Nah. I had to move on. Better things came along for me."

"Oh, well. Like you said, that was his loss. Where is he now?"

"I'm not sure . . . living somewhere back East, I heard. I haven't seen him in about ten years. Last time I saw him was at a party that a mutual friend of ours threw when I was about eighteen or so. He didn't stay long, so we really didn't even talk. Just a quick hello and that was it."

All of a sudden, I didn't wanna talk about Royce anymore. That surprised me, because I hadn't really tripped off him in a long time. I admit, I thought about him on many occasions after that last time I saw him, and I knew I still carried a small torch for him, but this particular conversation was starting to make me feel sad, and I was having much too good a time with my new friend to have it ruined by bitter thoughts of Royce, so I changed the subject.

"So, what about you? You got any scars from old crushes, physical or mental?"

Weston told me about one girl named Janet who broke his heart when he was thirteen. We laughed at his memories, then he started telling me a little bit about what it was like growing up in the Windy City.

He kept me entertained with stories for what seemed like an hour, but I really don't know how long we sat there, since I don't know what time it was when we showed up.

When I looked down at my watch, I let out a small gasp. "Damn. When did it get to be seven-thirty?"

"It's not that late, is it?"

"Yeah. I mean, it's not really late, but the time just got away from me today. I forgot all about my car, too."

He smiled. "I guess that means you fully enjoyed your day, then, right?"

"Definitely."

"Good. Me, too."

"I really should get back. I need to make sure my baby is still in the parking lot and in one piece."

"I feel you. Come on, let's make that move."

When we got back to the parking lot, my car was the only one there, and sure enough, it was just fine. Weston parked next to my car and got out to say good-bye to me at my door.

I stuck my key in the door, then turned to face him. "Well, Mister Man, thank you for today. I've never been on a first date quite like this one. It was fun. I sorta felt like a teenager again."

"It was my pleasure. So . . . you remember what you said at the shop about us exchangin' numbers?"

I knew what he was talking about, but I said, "Refresh my memory."

"You said it would be all good if things went well, remember?"

"Oh, yeah . . ." I said in an exaggerated tone, "I did say that, huh?"

"Yeah, you did. So, wassup?"

"Hmmm . . . well . . . I dunno . . . I don't really think things went very well, do you?" I said through my large smile.

"Tease . . . you know things went better than well today. And they'd be even better if I could kiss you right now."

I wanted to slob him down but I decided to keep him in suspense a little.

"Oh, a kiss, huh?"

"Uh-huh."

"Well, I guess a small one wouldn't hurt."

He leaned in a little, and I threw him off by saying, "Right . . . here . . ." and pointed to my right cheek, while smiling at him.

"Oh, all I get is the cheek?"

"Well, yeah. I gotta make you wait a little to get the good stuff."

"Fine. I'll take the cheek . . . for now. But I'll be back for some of that 'good stuff' real soon."

"'Kay."

He stepped to me and planted those warm, soft, juicy lips on my cheek with as much passion as if he were kissing me on my mouth. I closed my eyes, and I felt my nipples start to get hard as he lingered on my cheekbone for a good three or four seconds. When he stepped back and looked at me, those damn eyes were glowing in the darkness, and I almost shoved my tongue down his throat.

"So," he started, "I'm not leavin' without the digits, so you might as well break me off right now, beautiful."

With that, I reached in my purse and pulled out one of my business cards with all my phone numbers on it and handed it to him. If I had a number to reach me in the bathroom, I woulda given him that one, too.

Weston did the same, and pulled out one of his business cards and handed it to me. "Now, you know I'ma call you tomorrow, right?"

"You do that."

"All right. You be safe drivin' home, FASTKAT."

"I will. You, too."

"No doubt. I'll talk to you tomorrow."

"Okay."

He walked away and I got in my baby and sat for a second. As he was pulling off, he honked his horn at me and waved. I waved back and smiled.

Chantelle was right. I was sprung after the first date, and I couldn't wait to admit it to her.

6

Home is not *hardly* where I went after I left the parking lot. I made a *serious* mad dash to the Hilltop Bayview complex, where Chantelle and Sabrina shared a two-bedroom apartment. I was flying high from my awesome date, and there was no way in hell I was gonna go home and twiddle my thumbs. I called the house as I was pulling out of the lot and Sabrina answered.

"Hello?"

"Bree—what'choo doin'? Chantelle home, too?"

"Girl, where you been? We been callin' you since four o'damn clock! How come your phone wasn't on?"

"Oh—we were at the movies and I turned it off when we got there."

I heard Chantelle shout in the background, "Tell her slow butt she better be on her way over here to kick down some details! Hell . . . keepin' us waitin' all day!"

Sabrina said, "I know you heard that."

"Yeah, yeah; tell her I said I'll be there in fifteen minutes. I gotta get some gas."

"Okay—but ay—how'd it go? Thumbs up or down?"

"Just wait till I get there, damn!"

"I hate you. Hurry up."

"Bye."

I hung up and called Genine's cell since I knew she wasn't home. It was Saturday night and she was babysitting her three-year-old cousin. I didn't wanna call the house phone, just in case little Danielle was sleeping. Genine answered on the fourth ring.

"'Bout damn time you called. What's the dealio? Been waitin' all day."

"Girl, you need to call Bree and 'Telle's house in like fifteen minutes and have them put you on speakerphone so you can hear this story."

"It must be good, or else you wouldn't be soundin' so damn chipper."

"I'm sayin'—call over there. I'm on my way now. Fifteen minutes."

"Okay, bye."

"Bye."

I zoomed to the gas station and filled up. I was in such a rush that I accidentally pulled the pump out from my tank too soon, and spilled gas all over the ground and on the side of my car. I cussed at myself, snatched some paper towels and quickly wiped my fireball down.

After I paid for my gas inside, I ran to the car, jumped in it like somebody was chasing me, and skidded off. I didn't even bother to turn on my music. I kept thinking about Weston bobbing his head to Destiny's Child, and that made me smile.

When I got in the door, before I could even say hi, Sabrina said, "Come on . . . talk. What's the verdict?"

Chantelle snapped, "You ain't right . . . cuttin' off phones and keepin' folks in suspense. The damn date started at twelve and you showin' up here at eight o'clock. What the hell you been doin' all day?"

"You need to be quiet, *Disability Queen*." I chuckled, took my jacket off and plopped down on the couch.

"Ay, don't hate, baby. I told you at the end of last year that when 1998 hit, I was gon' make some moves and get my art career goin.' Who knew I'd hafta damn near break my back at work in order to do it?"

Sabrina got impatient and interjected, "Enough of all that . . . are you and dude gon' be soilin' up some sheets soon, or what? That's what *I'm* tryina find out right about now."

Chantelle said, "Oh, yeah, fuh real. When's my next *free* appointment?"

I gave Chantelle the finger, then told them, "First of all, I'm not sayin' anything till Genine calls. You need to put her on speaker. She should be . . ."

The phone rang and I said, "That's her."

Sabrina raced to the phone, snatched the receiver up and said, "Hey, girl . . . hang on. . . ." and clicked on the speaker. "You there?"

Genine said, "Yep."

"Ah'right, go . . . spill it," Sabrina demanded of me.

I got up, moved closer to the phone, and started telling them all about my date. I could barely finish two sentences at a time without one of them interrupting me with a question or comment, and me having to yell at them to shut up.

After I told them the part about Weston and Lisa

and why he dumped her, Chantelle paused for a moment, kind of chuckled to herself and said, "You know what? I mean, really, if it wasn't for the fact that I actually *have* seen her act like that over a coupla different guys, I probably wouldn't believe that story. But that was so long ago . . . I thought she'd advanced since then, but I guess not."

I was surprised. "For real? She's done that before?"

"Yeah, back in the day, but I guess she ain't changed. You see she's not with Ramon anymore, either. Prob'ly ran him off, too. That's my damn cousin for you."

The three of us chitchatted about the Lisa issue for a couple of minutes, then I got back to my story. When I told them the part about Weston looking for a woman like his mother, everyone was shocked.

Genine said, "*Damn*. He said that?"

Sabrina told me, "Girl, he's *deep*. You know they say men who love their mamas are the bomb . . . treat they women like queens."

Genine cosigned over the speaker. "Yuuuup, I heard that, too."

And Chantelle said, "She hit the jackpot. I can tell already."

I said to her, "And you called him a hound."

"Well, how was I supposed to know? Lisa had me thinkin' that. I'm'a clown her too, next time I see her."

"Don't say nothin' about it to her," Sabrina said, "just leave it alone. That's old news. She probably moved on and forgot all about him anyway."

Genine chimed in. "Okay? It took her long enough to get over him, and if you tell her what she missed out on, she gon' be feelin' stupid."

Then I jumped on the bandwagon and added,

"Plus the fact that you not even supposed to know she played herself like that."

"Whatever," Chantelle grunted while frowning.

I asked her, "Why're *you* so annoyed?"

"I don't know. . . . I think because I shoulda known she wasn't tellin' the whole story. I mean, like I said, I've seen her do that type of mess before, and I think I feel kinda like a buster 'cause she had me thinkin' bad stuff about a decent dude."

"Oh, well," Sabrina said, "at least now we know."

"Yeah, don't trip," Genine told Chantelle.

She ignored them both, then looked at me. "Okay, so finish the story."

As I spent the next twenty minutes dishing every detail of the rest of the juicy story, Chantelle and Sabrina were all up in my mouth like the goddamn dentist, and Genine was so quiet that a few times, I had to ask if she was still there. She just kept saying, "Hell yeah!"

After I was finished, Genine asked me, "How come you ain't give him no tongue, fool?"

"That's what *I'm* sayin'!" Chantelle and Sabrina shouted at the exact same time, in the exact same tone.

I told them all, "I asked myself that same question when he drove off . . ."

Genine said, "And you came up with . . . ?"

"God . . . I don't know. I think I was nervous or in-timidated or somethin'."

"WHY?" That was all three of them together.

"'Cause . . . I don't know . . . he just threw me all off track. I wasn't expectin' him to be so together and re-spectful. And we clicked like I've *never* clicked with a guy before . . . so early on, I mean. We talked and laughed and bantered back and forth all day long."

"But," Sabrina started, "what does that hafta do with you failin' to put one on him? I don't get it. If y'all hit it off, then what was the problem?"

"Okay? 'Cause Miss Cutsey Katrice *never* gets intimidated by a man," Chantelle said sarcastically.

"Shut up. I know I don't *normally,* but this is different . . . *he's* different. I ain't never met nobody like him before."

"Okay, Miss Harlequin Romance," Genine jabbed.

Chantelle and Sabrina laughed.

"*Anyway,*" I continued, "he's just not like a lot of the other guys I've been out with, and I was scared to kiss him. Like I was afraid I'd lose control of myself or somethin'. I didn't want him to see me like that just yet. It's too soon."

"Well, I say you shoulda capped off the night with some spit-and-tartar exchange," Sabrina said.

I gave her a slightly disgusted look. "You're *so* subtle."

"And that's why you love me," she gave me a fake, cheesy smile.

"But I don't," I joked.

"Anyway," Chantelle began, "what now? When y'all gon' hook up again?"

"I dunno. He said he's gonna call me tomorrow. We'll see."

"No you *didn't* just say 'We'll see.' Like you really got doubts about him callin'. Shut the hell up!" Genine called out over the phone.

Chantelle jumped in. "I know! Don't she make you wanna slap her? She know he gon' call."

Then Sabrina added her two cents. "You know?

Tryina act like she ain't sure." She turned to me and said, "Y'all both sprung."

"And speakin' of bein' sprung . . ." Chantelle started.

I knew what was about to come outta her mouth, so I didn't even let her finish. "Shut up! I know— I owe you!"

"Oh, now," she tweaked my left cheek, "don't be mad 'cause I know ya better than ya know ya'self, Boo-Boo!" She cackled.

"Git off me!" I laughed, and knocked her hand away from my face.

Genine said, "Ay—I gotta go y'all . . . Danielle just woke up. I'll talk to you tomorrow."

We all said, "Ah'ight."

"Bye—and congrats, 'Trice. Hope it works out for ya. I'm out."

"Thanks, girl," I called out, and she hung up.

Sabrina went and clicked off the speaker phone, then she asked me, "So, you think you might be on to somethin' wit' this dude?"

"I hope so, girl. I need some good lovin'."

"Not just you," Chantelle said. "But I'm glad for you, girl. He sounds like he might be a keeper. We gittin' older now. It's time for us to be serious about dealin' wit' quality men."

"Okay? You ain't neva lied," Sabrina said. "We all knockin' on thirty's door, and none of us are in a healthy, valuable relationship with someone who's worth our damn time. I *would* like to get married and maybe have me a kid or two."

I said, "Girl, I know what'choo mean. I saw a woman and her man in the store the other day, and they had a son and it was the cutest sight. The three of them were holdin' hands, and they just looked so peaceful together. I found myself feelin' a little envious of the woman, you know? Like, how did she pull that into her life? And she looked younger than me."

Chantelle cautioned, "Yeah, but don't be too quick to envy a situation you ain't seen up close. You never know what's goin' on behind closed doors. Homeboy might be whoopin' her ass, and the child's, too. I mean, I ain't tryina be morbid or nothin', but . . ."

"No, I know, but it was just . . . lookin' at them together . . . just the whole scene gave me a pang. I was like, *I want that,* you know?"

"Yeah . . ." Chantelle and Sabrina both said, with a twinge of heaviness in their voices.

We sat for a few seconds in silence, each of us in our own private world, then, I asked Chantelle, "Hey—how'd it go today?"

"How'd what go?"

"Didn't you go talk to some man about your artwork?"

"Ohhh . . . yeah. You know what? He called me to reschedule our meeting, but we did talk for a few minutes, and I don't know. . . . I'm discouraged."

"Why?"

"Well, he started tellin' me about all these procedures and obstacles and pros and cons about getting my work into a gallery, and I just didn't realize it was such a big deal. I was hopin' I could just take my work in and they'd beg me to let them put my pictures up in their place, but it don't work like that. There's applications, fees, policies, and then a lotta places only deal with well-known, reputable artists. This one guy I talked to a coupla weeks ago told me he only deals with dead artists' work."

Sabrina laughed. "Oh, that's *real* encouraging!"

"Okay? That's what I'm sayin'." She sighed, then said, "I'm havin' second thoughts about this already. Maybe I should just go back to my little retail job and forget about this art thing."

I tried to lift her spirits. "Come on, 'Telle. First of all, that man don't even know you—or nothin' about your work, for that matter. He was just givin' you the facts. I don't think he was tryina discourage you. You need to know what you're up against, but that don't mean you gotta concede to it. You gotta go for yours, girl. Nobody said it was gon' be easy. You just need to decide exactly what you want, and figure out a game plan for how you gon' go about gittin' it."

Sabrina added, "Yeah, and then you just gotta be prepared to bust ass until you accomplish whatever goals you set. You know your work is the bomb. You just gotta catch the right people's eye."

"I wanna sell my work so bad, I can taste it. I can just see myself, drawin' picture after picture and sellin' them bitches like hotcakes; gittin' rich and loungin' in my five-bedroom house in the Oakland hills, havin' hella classy parties and get-togethers— just livin' large and righteous, y'all. A fine, about-somethin' brotha by my side, supportin' the hell outta me, and an art career that never stops. Makes my head spin just thinkin' about it."

"Well," I started, "if you feel like that, it'll happen, long as you stay focused and don't let nobody dis-courage you, bring you down or get in yo' way."

"Yeah, I gotta be more determined. You know how I am. One little thing even *looks* like it's gon' throw my plan off track, and I start to crumble."

"And you gotta work on that if you gon' make it, girl," Sabrina informed her.

"Yeah, I know."

I was starting to get hungry, so I asked them, "What'choo got to eat up in here? Feed me. My brunch done wore off, and sista needs some sustenance."

Sabrina said, "It's some leftover spaghetti in there that I made the other night."

"Good." I jumped up from the couch. "I'm 'bout to tear it up, too."

"Help ya'self," Chantelle told me. "And bring me a soda out the fridge when you come back."

I chowed down like a hog on a big-ass plate of some of Sabrina's screamin' spaghetti, while the three of us sat and talked some more. Chantelle and Sabrina were both laid out, Chantelle on the couch and Sabrina on the loveseat. I was slouched in my favorite recliner in the corner.

Around eleven-thirty, I was full and tired, and I told them, "I need to jet, y'all. I gotta open up at eight-thirty tomorrow morning; my churchgoin' folks need their hair tight." I got up to get my purse and jacket.

They both said a sleepy, "Ah'ight, girl."

Then Sabrina said, "Keep us posted on yo' new friend."

"You know it."

Chantelle just had to say, "And git my color ready. I'll be in next week for my appointment."

"I'm sicka you." I smiled, then put my jacket on and my purse on my shoulder.

"Uh-huh," she said, barely hanging on to consciousness, "and it's only gon' get worse." She let out a weak chuckle.

"You better be glad I love you. Bye, y'all." And I headed out the door.

"Bye," they said together.

I knew I needed to also talk to Tiki about my day, but I didn't bother to call her, since I knew she and Charles were out for the evening. He was taking her to dinner in San Francisco, and then to a jazz club after that. I decided I would just fill her in when I saw her at the shop the next day.

When I got home, the light on my answering machine was blinking twice. I prayed to God one of the messages was from Weston. No such luck. Instead, I had to listen to my brother harass me about not returning his leather jacket that I loved, which, according to him, I had "borrowed" three weeks prior. I ignored him and erased both messages, since I had no intention of returning the jacket. He said I could have it, but swore I misunderstood him. I decided to deal with him much later.

I wanted to talk to Weston, but since it was late, I decided to just have some patience and wait for him to call me the next day. I couldn't help but fantasize about my phone ringing and having Weston be on the other end, telling me what a great time he had with me that day, and that he couldn't wait to see me again. I wanted to look into those sexy eyes of his again so bad I was about to explode.

In attempt to take my mind off him a little, I went and turned on the radio, but left the volume down low, so I wouldn't disturb my neighbors. Wouldn't you know it, "No, No, No," by Destiny's Child, had just come on. I laughed at the irony of the song being on at that moment, then, sang right along with the group, all the while picturing Weston bouncing his head to the same beat earlier that afternoon.

I tucked myself in at around twelve-thirty, but

couldn't sleep a wink. Thoughts of Weston were rolling through my head like an Amtrak train, and I was going out of my mind. Finally, after about an hour, I felt myself drifting off to sleep, and I remember hoping I would dream about Weston all night long.

I went to sleep smiling, looking forward to picking up where we left off in the parking lot; and when we did, I vowed to do more than just put one on him. I was determined to steal his heart.

7

Fortunately, Tiki and I had some time alone in the shop that next morning before our clients began to arrive. I was able to break down every detail of my date with Weston, just as I had done the night before with the girls. Talking about him gave me such a rush, I wanted to start doing backflips and turning cartwheels.

Tiki was excited for me and couldn't stop squealing with joy, even after I was finished talking. She said, "Hey, now! Look like we gon' finally get to go on us some double dates around here! I can't *wait*, girl!"

"I sure hope so. But I'm trying not to put too much on this. I already feel weird 'cause I'm feeling things for him that I think it's too early for me to even be thinking about. I mean, damn, we just met."

"So what? When Charles asked me for my number that day, somethin' in the way he looked at me told me he was the one, and we hadn't even been out yet. So I don't know what'choo talkin' 'bout, 'cause sometimes, your heart tells you things before you have a chance to get your head together. That's how love is. Ain't no rule book on when you supposta feel stuff. You just gotta roll with the feelings when they come."

I rolled my eyes back in my head. "*Gawd,* you have *truly* been bitten by the bug. You sound like a damn Hallmark card."

"Uh-huh . . . you clownin' now, but just wait. In another coupla weeks, you gon' be singin' a whole nother song. *'Specially* after y'all do the do."

I laughed. "You're probably right."

"Oh, I *know* I'm right. I saw his fine ass . . . the way he was all into you. And he's so tall and solid, too. I'ma tell you what: That brotha got a serious surprise for you when he come out them boxers, you hear me? That thang gon' fall out his draws and roll across the floor like the red carpet. Watch!"

I rolled. "Girl, *shut up!*"

"I'm serious!" she laughed. "You know I done *had* many a Mandingo man in my day. You ain't had the pleasure yet, and I'm tellin' you, it ain't no joke, so get ready. You might be paralyzed the next day! I'ma know when he pops the coochie, 'cause you gon' roll up in this bitch in a wheelchair wit' a bandage between yo' legs! Matter of fact, he ain't gon' pop it, he gon' bust it wide open!"

I was laughing so hard that tears were coming to my eyes and I couldn't stand up straight. Tiki was trying hard to keep a straight face, but it wasn't working. She burst into laughter right along with me.

After we cackled for another minute or so, we pulled ourselves together, wiped our eyes and Tiki said, "But seriously, girl, don't fight it. If you feel somethin' for him and he seems to be feelin' the same way, then I say, take it as far as you can. Maybe soon, I'll be makin' plans to come to *your* weddin'."

"Yeah . . . wouldn't that be something? And you know what? I can see that happenin', too. I can't explain why. . . . I just . . . can."

"Hell, you ain't got to explain it. I know all about it. I'm livin' that dream right now. I mean, I know the wedding is still fourteen months away, but I feel so solid and confident about me and Charles. And I know he feels it, too. That's why we didn't rush to get married as soon as he proposed. We knew we didn't need to, 'cause it was like, what for? We know we're soul mates, and we gon' be together whether we got that piece of paper between us or not, so why rush into it? We gon' take our time, enjoy bein' engaged, I'm'a have fun wavin' this rock on my finger in people's faces, and we gon' do this right. One time. That's it."

"I feel you, girl."

"And I've never been this confident or secure about *any* relationship in my life, and I've had some pretty damn good ones, too. But this one . . . this is definitely the one."

"Yeah, you do have a top-notch man. You know I know. That's my boy. Always has been. I was glad to see y'all hook up, 'cause Charles is such a sweetie and these *so-called women* he was messin' with were takin' advantage of him and steppin' on his good heart. He was really startin' to turn sour. Even started talkin' about doggin' women like he was gettin' dogged, since he couldn't find a good one. We had some long talks, and I told him to come from that place, 'cause it wasn't gon' help, and it wasn't gon' make him feel any better."

"See, that's what I mean about how close we are. He told me that, you know? Told me how you tried to help him keep hope alive, and I'm sure glad you did, 'cause my baby is the bomb."

"Well, you just make sure you hold on to him, girl. He's one of a kind."

"You ain't said nothin' but a word." She pointed her index finger at me. "Let a bitch come try to dip her hands in my cookie jar. I'll beat a ho down so fast and so hard, she'll wish she went and bought her ass some Mrs. Fields instead, okay?"

I laughed and shook my head. "Girl, you *kill* me wit' that mess! You are *truly* ghetto! But I feel you."

"Hmm, I know you do. And once you and Long Fat Dong get *really* involved, you gon' be just as protective of yours as I am."

"Yeah, I'm sure I will—but you know what? I'm sure his dick is *not* that big, so you need to quit, you damn freak!"

"Okaaaay," she sang, "I know what I know. That's all I got to say about it."

"Well, hopefully, I'll get the chance to find out real soon."

"Oh, honey, you will. I feel it."

It was a long and stressful day. Weston didn't call or come by the shop, and by five o'clock, I started getting scared. I wanted to call him, but I simply refused. I thought to myself, *If he wants me and he's sincere, he'll hafta come get me. Period.*

By eight-fifteen, I was at home, in my pajamas, curled up on the couch, letting the television watch me, and feeling lousy. My home phone hadn't rung all day; I could tell because my caller ID was empty. The only people that called the shop and my cell phone were clients, Genine, and my mother. Weston hadn't dialed any of my numbers the whole day, and I was damn pissed. Really, I was more or less mad at myself for getting caught up so soon. One nice date and a few flattering compliments, and I was already attached, and that made me insane. But part of me was also mad at him. I hate when guys just throw out the words, "I'll call you," like it's nothing, and then you never hear from 'em. I can't *stand* a liar. I started thinking that maybe Lisa was right, that Weston really *was* the dog she said he was. Then I thought about Chantelle calling him a hound, and decided she probably was on target with that observation.

After nearly twenty minutes of poisonous thoughts, I got up, stomped into the kitchen, flung open the freezer door so hard it banged against the wall, snatched out my pint of chocolate-chocolate-chip ice cream, pouted my way back to the living room, tossed myself onto the couch again, and commenced to polish off the almost-full carton of ice cream.

Around eight-forty-five, as I was crunching furiously on the last of the delicious, calorie-ridden semisweet chips and desperately scraping the bottom of the carton with my spoon for remnants, my home phone rang and scared me. For some reason, it sounded three times as loud as it normally did. I was so into eating my sorrows away that, actually, I had forgotten about Weston for a minute, which I found ironic, since he was the reason I had started the binge in the first place. I didn't bother to fall over myself to get to the phone, because it never even crossed my mind that it could be him, since I had already given up on him calling by my tenth bite of ice cream.

As the phone continued to ring, I let out an angry

sigh, cursed whoever had the nerve to be interrupting my depression, and finally headed across the room to answer it. When I picked up the receiver and spit out an annoyed, "Hello?" my heart smiled when Weston said a tired, deep-voiced, "How you doin', beautiful?"

I held back my joy at hearing his voice. "Oh, hey . . . I'm fine. How're you?"

"Tired. I had the longest day. Had two meetings this morning, had to go to a class this afternoon, and then I met with five clients. I'm beat down. How was your day? You whip the hell up out some hair?"

I smiled to myself, relieved that he actually had a good reason for not calling until then. And what I loved was that I didn't even have to ask what took him so long. I took the "liar" label off him, and put the good guy label back on.

"Yeah, I hooked up about seven heads today. I'm tired, too."

"I wanna see you . . . tonight. I know it's gettin' kinda late, but I been thinkin' about you all day. I wanted to call you earlier, but I was so busy, and then I wasn't sure if I should call you at the shop, 'cause I didn't know if I would be disturbin' you, so I just decided to wait till I got off work."

"Oh—you coulda called the shop. You don't hafta worry about disturbing me there." I decided to open up a little. "And to be honest, I wanna see you, too."

"So, what we gon' do about this?"

"Well, I usually try to walk Lake Merritt every day, and I haven't done it today. You wanna walk it with me now? It's still warm out, and it'll give us a chance to talk some more."

"I'm down for that. Where you wanna meet?"

Since I lived on Lee, and Weston lived on the other side of the lake on Boden, I asked him, "Um . . . can you meet me down in front of the Quick Stop on Grand? We can go from there."

"Cool. Be there in ten minutes."

"'Kay. I'll see you out there. Bye."

"Ah'ight."

I was out of my pajamas and into my lake-walking attire in less than two minutes. I was so excited, I tripped over the phone cord and damn near broke my neck trying to get out the door. I didn't bother to drive, since it would only take me a few minutes to jog down to the store.

It was really warm out that night. Weston and I ended up strolling leisurely around the lake twice, which took us about three hours, and it was awesome. We talked about everything under the sun. Likes, dislikes, each other's home life growing up, pains, joys, insecurities, our friends, families, goals and dreams, fears, and the list goes on. As we talked, laughed, and joked, we were so connected that we barely noticed all the other people out getting their evening jog, stroll, or power-walk on. It's funny, before we headed out that night, we were both grumbling about how tired we were, but it seemed like the more we walked and talked, the more energized we both became. We were like two old friends who hadn't seen each other in a decade. The conversation just went on incessantly, and we had so much in common, it was almost scary.

By the time we reached our starting point the second time, it was a little after midnight. Both of us had to get up early and knew that we should head home, but neither of us was ready to end the evening.

We stopped in the store for some water, and when we came out, Weston said, "So, I know you got an early day tomorrow. So do I . . . damn. I'm not ready to say goodnight yet."

"I know . . . me either."

We chugged our waters and stood in front of the store for a minute, just looking at one another, almost as if we both knew something big was about to happen for us. I think in that moment, it was pretty clear to both of us that we were about to embark on a life-altering relationship. The initial nervousness I felt around him in the beginning had faded away. Now, all I felt was a calm, comfortable, and secure feeling when I was with him, and I could tell the feeling was mutual.

Finally, after guzzling down most of my pint of water, I said, "I guess I *should* put myself to bed, but, will you walk me home?"

"I don't even know why you askin' me that. You didn't think I was gon' let'choo walk home by yo'self, did you?"

"Well, I only live, like, a six-minute walk away—it's no big deal. I was only asking 'cause I wanted to spend a few more minutes with you, not because I'm afraid of the dark."

"Well, whether or not you scared of the dark, I was still gon' make sure you got home safe. It's after midnight. You don't have no business bein' out here alone at this hour."

"What if I told you I do this all the time?"

"Then I'd say after tonight, all that madness is gon' stop. I'm not gon' have you runnin' around out here in the streets for one of these crackheads or rapists to snatch you up. I'm tryina keep you around for a long, long time."

"Is that right?"

He looked right through my eyes and straight into my soul and said a resounding, "That's *damn* right. Now, let's get'choo home. I don't want'choo dozin' off while you pressin' hair tomorrow. You might mess around and burn a hole in some po' woman's neck."

I laughed and tossed my empty bottle into the trash. "Come on here, you. Let's go."

When we got to my door, I stuck my key in the lock, turned to him and asked, "You uh . . . wanna come in for a minute?"

"If I do, I might not leave."

I smiled. "Yes you will. I promise."

As much as I wanted to tuck him into bed with me and show him my true feelings, I also knew I didn't wanna do too much too fast. I wanted this—whatever it was gonna be—to be right, and sex at that moment, though I could tell would have been earth-shattering, might have put a damper on our growing bond. I wanted to wait for a special moment, and even though I didn't know what moment that would be, I was sure that night wasn't it.

He said, "You gon' put me out, huh?"

I gave him a coy look, opened the door and stepped inside. "Only temporarily."

He looked at me like he was ready to devour me, licked his lips, and stepped in behind me.

He looked around for a few minutes, admiring my apartment, while I went to the bathroom. When I came out, he was standing at my entertainment center, which had about nine framed pictures of me, my family, and my girls sitting on top of it.

He said, "Damn, you look dead on yo' pops. I mean, I see yo' mother in you, too, but yo' pops straight took over."

I walked up beside him to see which picture he was looking at. It was the one of my mother, father, Powell, and me the day I graduated from beauty school.

"I know; and Powell looks like Mama. That's a trip how that happens."

"Yup. You got a real nice-lookin' family."

"Thanks."

He scanned a few more pictures and I schooled him on who was who. Finally, he turned to me. "Well, since I'm bound to git put out, I guess I should make my way down the road."

"Don't worry, this is all to be continued. But, did you want a ride home? 'Cause that wouldn't be a problem."

He laughed at me. "Naw, girl. I can git *my*self home alone in the dark. You go on and go to bed." He paused before he said, "I need to cool off anyway."

He gazed at me, lust spilling from his golden eyes. My look matched his.

Before I could even respond, he stepped so close in front of me that I could see the dampness resting on his paper-thin mustache. My heart started pounding quadruple-time. I knew what was next, and this time, I had no intention of redirecting him to my cheek.

He stood there for a couple of seconds, staring me down, then, he gently cradled my face in his soft, warm, massive hands, leaned down, and introduced me to the most succulent, passionate kiss ever. His lips were full, and they felt like pillows as they pressed against mine. First his mouth lingered on top of mine, then he teased me with a succession of short, soft kisses, and I felt myself melting into the floor. Several seconds later, he took it to the next level, and slid his tongue between my lips. I closed my eyes, and let my mouth fall open. Our tongues met, and his mouth was still sweet from the Juicy Fruit gum he had chewed earlier. I savored every bit of the flavor, and for the next thirty seconds, we told each other with grunts, moans, and plenty of heavy breathing about the feelings we had brewing inside of us.

He leaned my head back slightly, and his lips began to travel slowly from my mouth to my chin, and then to the left side of my neck. I wrapped my arms around his muscular back, and reached under his shirt so I could feel his moist, bare skin. He tilted my head to the right while I squeezed his flesh, then he began skillfully sucking on the sensitive spot on my neck, right under my jawbone. I let out a long, low moan that let him know I was close to losing consciousness, and then I felt one of his hands resting in my cleavage area. I knew if he even so much as scraped up against a breast, my panties would come flying off, and even though my body was ready and willing to go that extra mile, my heart wasn't quite there yet.

I caught my breath, pulled back a little and whispered an urgent, "Oh my God . . . wait."

He stopped in his tracks, eyes glazed over, breathing sporadic and asked, "What's wrong?"

I swallowed hard, gathered some air. "I want . . . this . . . I do . . . I *really* do . . . just not right now. It's too soon. I want it to be right."

He pressed his lips tightly together and nodded his head with a quick pace. "I understand. I'm sorry . . . I just . . . got a little carried away."

"No, no . . . you didn't do anything wrong. I got caught up, too. It's just that . . ." I licked my lips, and I could still taste him. "I don't know where this is headed, or—where *we're* headed, but I like you— a lot—and I don't wanna potentially ruin whatever this is by jumping in the sack in the first few days, you know?"

He collected himself and said a calm, "Yeah. And you know what? I respect that. I really do." He let out a heavy sigh. "So, on that note, I'm'a go, 'cause now I *really* need to cool off."

He had on a pair of loose-fitting sweatpants, and when I glanced down, I could see the bulge that had formed inside of them.

I got worried. "You're not mad, are you?"

He scrunched up his face. "*Please*. Gimme *some* credit, here. I mean, it's not like we been seein' each other for a year and you still holdin' out. We just met. And even though we already clickin' like crazy, you probably right . . . we should wait a minute. So, that's what we gon' do. When you ready, I'm sure you'll let me know. But in the meantime, I ain't goin' nowhere, if that's what'choo thinkin'."

"It's happened before."

"Yeah, but that was then, wit' somebody who ain't me, so don't even let that cross yo' mind again, okay?"

I smiled. "Okay."

He kissed me again on the lips, then rested his palm on the left side of my face. "Now go to bed. It's damn near one o'clock. I'll call you tomorrow—well, later today, ah'ight?" and he headed out the door.

I mocked him. "Ah'ight."

I stood in the doorway and watched him trot down the stairs and jog across the street. Finally, I let out a small sigh and went back in the house to get ready for bed.

I tossed my soaking-wet thong underwear in the hamper and tried my hardest to shake the vision of Weston tonguing me down from my brain. I could still smell him all over my clothes, and I wanted to stay close to him that night, so instead of changing back into my pajamas, I slept only in the T-shirt I'd worn that night. At first, I was a little cold, since I'm not used to being completely bare at the bottom when I sleep, but repeated thoughts of Weston sucking my neck quickly warmed my bones, and took care of all the cold chills I felt that night.

After that night, Weston and I were pretty much joined at the hip. We talked on the phone and saw each other every day, even if it was just for a few minutes, and our connection just got stronger and stronger. My girls teased me because I couldn't stop talking about him, but I didn't give a hell. I was falling in love, and I wasn't ashamed to admit it. Not in the least.

Although things continued to be hot and heavy with us physically, somehow, we managed to hold off on the sex. Day after day, we exercised self-control. This was challenging as hell, considering the fact that several times while we were curled up on either his or my couch kissing, his hands made their way inside my bra, where he caressed and fondled me, paying special attention to my nipples, and when he played with them, I spiraled into a panting frenzy.

One night, while we were cuddled up on his chaise lounge, supposed to be watching *NYPD Blue,* but once again got caught up slobbering on each other, my pants "magically" came undone, and his fingers went on a little fishing trip between my legs, and met up with Girlfriend. She was sopping wet, and those Ball Park Frank–sized fingers of his slip-sliding around inside of her had me hitting high notes that even Mariah Carey couldn't reach.

By then, I knew the time was near.

About four days before my birthday, Weston and I were walking the lake, which had become a regular thing for us, and he asked me, "So, what'choo got planned for yo' birthday? We ain't even talked about that yet."

"Oh my God . . . you're right." Then I paused. "I can't even believe you remembered."

"I remember everything that's come outta yo' mouth since the day we met."

I just looked at him. The time was most definitely near.

"What?" he asked.

"Nothing . . . I just . . . can't believe you. You blow my mind."

"Why, 'cause I remembered your birthday? Woman, please. Don't let *that* blow ya mind. I got all *kindsa* tricks and treats in *my* bag o' love. Buh'lieve that."

"Oh, I don't doubt it."

"So, wassup? You got plans?"

"Well, sort of. My family's got kinda this weird thing—all of our birthdays are in April."

"All of who?"

"Me, my mother, my father, and P.J."

"Are you serious?"

"Yeah."

"I didn't hear you mention nothin' about nobody's birthday this month."

"I know. That's because my parents weren't even in town for theirs, and P.J.'s isn't till after mine. I didn't even think about it."

"So, what's the order?"

"My mother's was the second, dad's was the twelfth, me on the twenty-fourth, and P.J. on the twenty-eighth."

"Damn. How the hell did that happen?"

"I know; it's freaky. Anyway, my parents left for Hawaii on the first and they just got back on the fifteenth. We're having a family dinner on my birthday to celebrate all four of ours together, since my parents weren't here, and P.J. and his girlfriend are going to Vegas for his. You wanna come? You could meet everybody—I mean—if you're ready for all that."

"What'choo mean, if I'm ready? Hell yeah, I'm ready. I don't have no problem wit' meetin' yo' family. It's about that time anyway. Time for me to let them know I got'choo on lockdown."

"Oh, really?"

"Yeah. I ain't lettin' you go. You all mine now."

"Oh? Since when?" I kidded.

He draped his arm around my shoulder as we walked, kissed my cheek and said, "Since right now. I thought'choo knew. *I'm* fillin' this position. *Permanently*."

I laughed and nudged him in the ribs. "Well, congratulations—and welcome aboard."

We laughed and kept walking.

And so it was official. He had made it clear that we were now a couple. I was thrilled, and looking forward to a long and prosperous future with my new man.

I had dated and been in several relationships since my breakup with Troy, but not with anyone as special as Weston. He just had a different effect on me altogether. Something about him was unlike the other men in my life.

For a long time, I was convinced I had made a huge mistake in letting Troy go, and that maybe I should have tried to have a long-distance relationship with him. I was so sure that I had shut down the only guy who would ever really be right for me, but Weston's coming into my life proved me wrong; and for once, being wrong was something I was more than happy to be.

8

I ended up working on my birthday, which really wasn't a big deal, since Weston had to work, and so did Genine and Sabrina. Chantelle had some business to take care of during the day, so she was all booked up, too. Besides, since I love my job, it didn't pain me in the least to have to be there even on my special day.

Weston called me early that morning around seven-thirty to wish me a happy birthday. He said he was sorry we couldn't spend the day together, but that he was looking forward to dinner with my family that night. We had planned to ride to my parents' house together, so he said he'd pick me up at six.

I had a great morning. Tiki surprised me with a hundred-dollar gift certificate to Jamba Juice since she knows what a fiend I am for that place, and one of my customers, Mrs. Wallace, got me a new day planner. She said she noticed that the one I kept at the desk up front was tattered and falling apart, which was true. I was just too lazy to go get another one. I kept saying I was going to, but never got around to it.

Chantelle called the shop around noon and said that she and the girls had something for me, and that they would stop by my house when I got off work. I told her that was fine, but that they needed to be there by five-thirty, because I needed to be ready to leave by six.

My mother called right after Chantelle to say happy birthday and to confirm that my "new beau" and I were still coming to dinner. I told her yes, and then asked her what was on the menu. She told me to mind my business and just be on time. Dinner was at six-thirty.

At about two-thirty, I was just about finished rinsing the perm out of my customer's hair when I heard a guy say, "Excuse me . . . are you Miss Vincent?"

I hadn't even heard him come in the door. When I looked up, I saw a short white guy in a black T-shirt and black shorts, standing and looking confused.

"Oh, hi . . . uh, yeah, I'm Miss Vincent. May I help you?"

"Yeah, uh . . . we just need to know where you want us to put all these flowers."

"All what flowers?"

"We got, like, three dozen flowers out on the truck for you, but we didn't wanna bring 'em in until someone told us where to put 'em."

I turned off the water, wrung Mrs. Carson's hair out, then tapped her to let her know it was time for her to sit up.

"I'm sorry . . . you said you have three dozen flowers for *me?*"

Shorty got impatient with me and half-snapped, "Yeah. If you're Miss Vincent, we got flowers for you. Where do you want 'em?"

I wrapped a towel around Mrs. Carson's head and

told him, "You can just put them over there," and I pointed to an empty corner about ten feet away from where I was standing. Shorty turned and walked out.

Tiki was just coming back from getting some lunch. Right after she walked in, the same guy plus one other came back with a dozen roses—half of them red, the other half yellow—and two dozen beautiful carnations of mixed colors.

When I saw the carnations, my heart skipped a beat. It dawned on me that on my first date with Weston, I had told him that my favorite flower in the world is the carnation. We were talking about the day he brought me the single rose to the shop when he asked me out for the second time, and he asked me if I liked roses. I told him yes, but even though they come in beautiful colors, they're such sometimey flowers—they don't always open, and they die fast. Carnations live a lot longer and, to me, are just prettier.

The guys put the flowers down, I thanked them, and they left. I excused myself from Mrs. Carson and looked over at Tiki, who was wearing the widest all-knowing grin I had ever seen. I smiled too, because by then I knew who the flowers were from.

I saw a card sticking out from the roses, so I rushed over, snatched it out, and tore open the envelope. The card read: *Beautiful flowers for the beautiful woman in my life. Happy Birthday. Love, Weston.*

It said, *Love, Weston.*

Even though neither one of us had said the L-word yet, I knew it was coming soon. I had been ready to say it for at least a week or two, but I didn't wanna scare him off by saying it too soon. We had only been seeing each other for five weeks.

I was so outdone; I just stood there for a minute,

staring at all the gorgeous flowers. No one had ever sent me flowers before. Sure, men had given them to me, but never had I had them sent special delivery, and I most *definitely* had never received three dozen all at once. The whole scene almost brought tears to my eyes. And I don't know how he managed to do it, but somehow, Weston sent me roses that were already in bloom. All the flowers were stunning, and they smelled heavenly.

Tiki called from across the room, "Um, excuse me? Can a sista get the 411, please? You know it's not nice to keep secrets!"

Mrs. Carson said, "Honey, she over there lookin' like she in a trance. Must be from a new boyfriend. My husband use'tuh send me flowers like that when we was first startin' out. Hmph, I ain't got so much as a twig from him in the last thirteen years. Enjoy it while you can, baby."

The three of us laughed. I shared the card with them, then, I filled Mrs. Carson in on the new love of my life, while I blow-dried her long, thick mane. Tiki stuffed her face with a huge burger while she sat and listened, even though she had already heard the story.

Mrs. Carson got up to go to the bathroom before I flatironed her hair, and while she was gone, Tiki said, "Hey I got three words for you. Long . . . Fat . . . Dong."

"Shut up!"

"Girl, I know you said you wanted to wait, but seriously—*please* tell me it's goin' down tonight."

And it was. I had already planned to make my move that night. I couldn't take the heat any longer. We were already officially a couple, I was in love, and frankly, I needed a good tappin'. It had been almost a year since my last romp, and Girlfriend can only take so much neglect. So, whether he was Long Fat Dong or Average Joe, I was gettin' me some that night. And what better occasion than my birthday?

I told her, "*Hell yeah!* I've waited long enough. Girlfriend's been cryin' in her sleep at night!"

"Woo—ha ha! I *know* that's right! Been there, suffered *through that,* girl! *Plenty* of times! I sang praises to heaven when Charles waxed my ass that first time!"

"I know you did. Girl, when—"

Mrs. Carson opened the bathroom door, and before she came out of the back room, I waved Tiki off and mouthed, "Later," to her. She smiled, nodded, and started getting her products ready for her three o'clock customer.

In between yapping with Mrs. Carson, Tiki, and her customer, I kept peeking over at my flowers and smiling to myself. Six o'clock couldn't come fast enough.

Chantelle, Genine, and Sabrina got to my house at about five. I hadn't even been home fifteen minutes, and I was already rushing. They knew my time was short, so after all the happy birthdays and quick small talk, they presented me with my gift. I ripped the package open while they all watched me with big smiles on their faces. They had all pitched in and gotten me two supersexy, not to mention skimpy, lingerie sets from Frederick's of Hollywood, plus, a collection of love oils, edible massage lotions, and flavored condoms. I had already told them that I had planned on consummating our relationship that night, so their gift was right on time.

I thanked, hugged, and kissed them, then quickly

told them about my plethora of flowers sitting at the shop. They all agreed that the buck should stop with Weston, and quite frankly, I was ready to second that.

After a few more minutes of girl talk, I put my dear soul sisters out. I barely had time to get ready by the time they left. I had wanted to take another shower so I would be extra fresh, considering what was on the agenda with Weston later, but that was out, since I'm slow as molasses when it comes to getting ready, so I opted to just brush, floss, wash my face, and change clothes.

At six-eleven, Weston arrived. One thing I noticed about him was that he had a slight late problem. Almost every time we made plans to do something, he was anywhere between five and ten minutes late. If there's one thing that makes me wanna scream, it's standing around waiting for someone with my jacket on and my purse on my shoulder. The only time he'd been early was the day of our first date. I chalked that up to anticipation and excitement . . . and wanting to make a good impression. Several times, I wanted to mention his lateness to him, but since it was so early on in our relationship, I didn't say anything for fear of sounding like a nag. But one thing I determined was that if it kept up once we were more deeply involved, I was going to have to have a talk with him.

When I opened the door, Weston smiled big and said, "Happy birthday, baby. Damn, I missed you today," and stepped inside.

I didn't wanna be rude and rush him, but he was already more than ten minutes late, and Mama had already made it clear that she wanted us there on time. Plus, I was hungry as hell. I hadn't eaten all day, simply because I knew dinner was gonna be on hit, and I wanted to save all my appetite for that night. Fortunately, my parents only lived fifteen minutes away, so I tried to relax a little.

Although we were pressed for time, I hadn't forgotten about my flower delivery, and I made sure to let him know how I felt about it. After he had gotten in the door, I flung my arms around him, pulled him down to my level and planted a serious tongue-kiss on him. When I finally pulled my lips off his, he smiled and said, "*Damn,* baby! What was that for?"

"That," I began, "was for my three dozen flowers today. They were gorgeous, and I can't believe you did that for me. Thank you, baby. That made my day."

"Aw, hell . . . that wasn't no thang. That was just a little somethin' to let'choo know I was thinkin' of you. But I'm glad you liked 'em."

"I did. No one's ever sent me flowers before. And you remembered that I love carnations. That was major. I almost fell out behind that one."

"Serious? That was your first time havin' flowers sent to you?"

"Yeah. I mean, I've gotten flowers before, but nobody's ever sent 'em."

"That's a damn shame. I'm glad I did that, then, 'cause I started not to, just on the strength that I figured you had that kinda stuff done for you all the time. But then I decided that even if you did, I still wanted to do it anyway."

"Well, I'm glad you did, too. That was a perfect surprise. I . . ."

I almost slipped up and told him I loved him, but I caught myself. Just barely.

He heard me stop, and asked, "You what?"

I had to think fast. "I just . . . I'm really glad you're in my life. You amaze me."

He smiled. "Come here." He pulled me in and hugged me. "I'm glad you in my life, too. But, wait now . . . I got something else for you."

I broke away from our hug. "What? You got me something else? You didn't hafta do that—the flowers were enough."

He turned around and picked a bag up off the floor. I hadn't even noticed he'd come in with it; I was so busy kissing him. He handed me a package wrapped in pretty gold paper, with a white bow on top.

"Baby . . ." I looked at him, "what . . . ?"

"Just open it, woman."

I put my purse and jacket down and started ripping open the package. When I finally got the paper off, my mouth fell open. It was a huge Elysium perfume gift set, complete with a large bottle of eau de toilette, two bottles of lotion, shower gel, soap, powder, and a one-ounce bottle of perfume. I was beside myself. I wanted to cry, actually.

"Oh my God, Weston . . . how did you know? This is my favorite perfume. . . ." I stared at him with a confused look on my face.

He laughed at me. "I know that. That's why I bought it."

"What do you mean you know?"

"You told me. Don't'choo remember? On our first date . . . at Macy's. We stopped by the counter and you sniffed it and told me you loved it, but you hadn't bought any in a while."

I thought back to that day, and after a few seconds, I did remember doing that, but it was such an insignificant event that I had to really think hard to recall it.

I sniff scents at counters and make comments all the damn time, so my doing that wasn't anything special.

"And . . . you remembered that? I mean, that was like, over a month ago. I can't believe you. I barely even remember that."

"Didn't I tell you that I remember everything you've said to me since the day we met?"

"Yeah, but I didn't think you really meant that— I thought that was just a figure of speech."

"Naw . . . I got'choo . . . up here . . ." he tapped his index finger on the side of his forehead. "That wasn't no joke."

I was speechless. I just looked at him for a moment. He looked at me like nothing he had done that day was any big deal. But, it was to me. Very big.

"I don't know what to say to you. 'Thank you' sounds so . . . so not enough or something."

"Come on, now. Thank you is all you need to say."

I hugged him again, extra tight, and lingered in his arms for a minute, silently.

Finally, he said, "Hey. We better go. It's almost six-twenty."

I pulled back. "You're right. Come on."

I had also packed an overnight bag, which was sitting off to the side of the front door. Weston didn't know it, but I had no intention of coming home that night. More than ever, especially after all that he had done for me that day, I wanted to take our relationship to the next level. After I put my jacket on and flung my purse on my shoulder, I picked up my duffle, put my gift set inside, and got my keys ready to lock up.

"Ay, uh . . . what's wit' the bag?" he asked. "You stayin' at your parents' house tonight?"

I grinned. "Nope. I got other plans after dinner."

Then, I gave him a look that told him exactly what that meant.

I wish I had a picture of the look on his face at that moment. It was worth two million bucks. I didn't even give him a chance to respond. I just smiled and sashayed by him. "Come on, baby, let's go. We got a big night ahead of us."

After a second, he said, "I'm right behind you!" and followed me out the door.

I called Mama when we got in the car and told her we were running a few minutes behind schedule. She said that was fine, because she was still getting the food ready to put on the table.

In the past, when I had brought guys home to meet my parents, I was really nervous. Not that I took any shabby folk to the house, but, you know, it's normal to feel a little on edge when your family's about to meet a mate. But with Weston, I wasn't the least bit concerned. I already knew he would be a hit, hands down.

When we walked in, all I could smell was the scent of delectable foods that were sure to leave me at least ten pounds heavier by the end of the night. Mama ran up to greet us before we could even really get all the way in the door. I gave her a hug, kissed her on the cheek, then introduced her to Weston.

She said, as she hugged him, "It's so good to finally meet you. I feel like I know you already. Treecie has nothin' but great things to say about you."

Weston chuckled. "It's nice to meet you, too, Mrs. Vincent," then he looked at me and smiled. "*Treecie* has told me a lot about you guys, too. I'm glad I could make it tonight."

I gave him a playful, evil-eyed look. "Okay,

okay—don't start with me about my nickname. My daddy gave me that name when I was three."

Mama said, "You mean you haven't told him about your pet name?"

"No, but he knows now, Mama."

I guess she could tell I was embarrassed, because she told me, "Oh, child, you don't have nothin' to be shame about."

"Yeah, I think it's cute, Treecie—I mean, baby," Weston said, as he helped me out of my jacket and held back his laughter.

I nudged him in the arm lightly and he winked at me.

"Hey! Y'all come on in here wit' all that love!" Daddy shouted.

I laughed. "Here we come, Daddy."

Mama took our jackets and put them in the hall closet, while we headed into the living room.

Daddy, P.J., and his girlfriend, Lateshia, all got up off the couch at the same time and came toward us. I introduced Weston to everyone, then got my birthday hugs and kisses from the three of them.

P.J. and Lateshia had been together for four years, so she was like family already. The two of us got along really well, and had even hung out quite a few times. She and P.J. had met at his job. He'd just started working at Honda of Oakland and was the top salesman at that time. Lateshia had come in to trade her 1987 Ford Escort in for a new Accord one day. To let him tell it, Lateshia was "all up in his grill" from the moment she walked in, but to this day, she swears it was the other way around. Long story short, P.J. was her salesman, and after all the papers were signed and the deal was closed, he went in for the kill and asked if he could call her. She didn't hesitate to break him off her number, and it's been on ever since.

She and P.J. moved in together and were living in Daly City, so I didn't see them too often after that. I hated the city, so I hardly ever drove out to see them. Most of the time when they came to visit, I was either working or busy doing something else, so I always ended up missing them. The last time I had seen P.J. was before I met Weston, when he *gave* me the leather jacket that he started accusing me of ganking him for.

After all the introductions and first-meeting chitchat was over with, Daddy roared, "Well, come on, y'all! Dinner's on the table, and I'm ready to git it onnnnn!"

Everyone agreed and scattered here and there to wash their hands. A few minutes later, we all met back in the dining room, where Mama had our feast all laid out for us to hurt ourselves with. Mama always makes everything from scratch; none of that canned or boxed stuff jumpin' off with her. There was garlic bread fresh out of her bread maker, her special herbed au gratin potatoes that no one can make better; my favorite vegetable in the world, collard greens, which I had been begging Mama to make me a pot of for months; and individual Cornish hens, each stuffed with a little ball of dressing and smothered in a mouthwatering orange glaze sauce. And for dessert, another favorite of mine: Mama's to-die-for cherry cobbler. That was the only thing I'd known for sure we were having, because she had asked me the week before if I wanted cake or cobbler, and I told her that cake wasn't even an option if cobbler was in the running.

Dinner was delicious and fun. We all laughed and talked while we smacked on Mama's food. Weston couldn't stop ranting and raving about how good everything was. He told Mama that her cooking reminded him of his mother's, and made him miss being back home.

He held his own, engaging in conversations with everyone at the table. It was as if he had met them all before, and I could tell they loved him. Before dinner was over, he had already made plans to go fishing with Daddy and P.J. Several times, in between running his mouth with my family, he took a second to look over at me and give me that special look he always gave me. It was a soft look that let me know that I was important to him, and that he was into me, and it made me melt inside every time he did it.

Needless to say, every morsel of the food on the table was perfect, and all the cleaned plates were proof of that fact. By the time we finished dessert, we were so full that we could barely breathe. We all sat at the table for a few minutes and let out satisfied moans and sighs while rubbing our bellies, looking heavy-eyed.

Around a quarter to eight, we all moved into the living room. We sat and talked for a while, then Daddy got up and left the room for a few minutes. When he came back, he had my birthday present in his hand. Mama and Daddy had chipped in together to get me some books they knew I wanted. I'm one of those people who're always meaning to go buy something, but never gets around to it . . . like my day planner that Mrs. Wallace replaced. Anyway, I was happy they hooked me up.

Next, P.J. reached behind the couch and pulled out a large box wrapped in cute birthday paper. The little card on top said it was from him and Lateshia. I tore through everything, and when I opened the box, my eyes lit up. They had gotten me a leather jacket exactly like the one P.J. "gave" me. I had always loved that jacket, and it had taken me almost six months to convince him to let me wear it.

When I saw the jacket, I started squealing, and snatched it out of the box to try it on. Everyone laughed at me, then P.J. said, "Now gimme mine back, thank you very much."

Of course, I agreed to do so, pronto.

After I put my gifts away, the six of us sat around and shot the breeze for about another hour and a half. Around nine-thirty, I suddenly blurted out that Weston and I had to be going. To be perfectly honest, I was ready to get to the sex. I couldn't take it anymore. Weston looked at me kind of strangely when I made the announcement, but after I gave him the same look I did right before we left my apartment, it dawned on him why I was in such a rush to leave, and he fell right in line with me.

"Uh, yeah . . . we got one more stop to make before the evening's over."

I finished his sentence for him. "Yeah, so we need to hit the road before it gets too late."

I was anxious as hell to get home and top off the night's events. Quiet as it was kept, all through dinner, I kept thinking about us wrapped up in each other's arms, butt-naked in a pool of post-sex sweat. At one point, I was so hot and bothered that I was damn near ready to start wrapping our plates up to go and skipping out right then and there.

I gathered my gifts, and Mama went and got our coats from the hall closet. She had already packed both of us some leftover food to take with us. We

spent the next few minutes saying our goodbyes, and
Weston and P.J. made sure to exchange numbers so
they could hook up at a later date. Mama and Daddy
told Weston what a joy it was to have met him, and let
him know that he was welcome back any time. Daddy
reminded him about the fishing trip they had talked
about, and told him to get back to him on when he
wanted to go. On the way out, Weston hugged Mama,
and gave Daddy a firm, friendly handshake. After I
did my last-minute hugging, kissing, and thanking,
we headed on out.

It seemed like we got back to Weston's house in
two minutes, even though the ride was just under fifteen. When we got in the door, I put my bags down,
then we headed into the kitchen to put our food away.
Weston pinned me gently up against the refrigerator,
kissed me, then started running his fingers through
my hair while looking at me like he had something
really important to say.

"You know," he started, "I knew when we met you
were gon' be someone real special to me, but I ain't
never felt this deep for a woman this soon into a relationship."

Before I could even get excited about what I hoped
would come out of his mouth, he said it.

"I love you, Katrice. I mean really—I'm in love
with you. I been wantin' to say that for a coupla
weeks, but I just couldn't believe I actually felt it so
fast—but I do. And every time I see you or talk to
you, the feelings just get deeper and deeper. It's like,
I don't even wanna let you outta my sight for one
minute. I don't know what the hell you did to me, but
I'm gone offa you. Straight up."

I couldn't speak. I knew I had been on the verge of

spilling my love beans for a couple of weeks as well, but I had no idea Weston felt the same way. I had tried to imagine him saying it to me on several occasions, but of course, the imagination don't have nothin' on the real thing. I felt my whole body get warm, then I noticed that Weston started looking worried.

He said, "Can you . . . say somethin'? Please?"

I didn't waste a single second with my answer. I wrapped my arms around his waist, looked up into his eyes and told him, "Yes. I can. I'm in love with you, too. I've just been holdin' it in 'cause I didn't wanna scare you off by sayin' it too soon."

"You ain't gotta worry about scarin' me. It's just not possible. I told you already . . . I'm in this for the long haul."

"Well, I'm glad, because so am I. And now that we got our true feelings out in the open, I need you to do something for me right now."

"What's that?"

I reached up, wrapped my hand around the back of his neck and pulled his head down to my face. I licked my lips, then whispered in his ear in a soft, sexy tone, "I need you to go into the bedroom, turn back the covers on the bed, take off all your clothes, and get in it."

He pulled back and looked at me with excitement, and just as he was about to say something, I pulled his head back down to me and continued. "While I . . . strip . . . down to nothing . . . and go and take a hot shower and uh . . . put on . . . shall we say . . . something I know you'll like a lot, but I won't have on for very long."

He tried to speak again, but I cut him off by resting

my index finger on his lips. Then I said, "And when I come out of the bathroom, the only thing I wanna see is you . . . waiting for me . . . with a rock . . . hard . . . dick." I looked at him and smiled innocently.

His breathing became heavy, and since he was still leaning up against me, I could already feel him hardening, which turned me on no end.

"Now," I concluded, raising my voice only one mere notch, "I need to go and get fresh, so I'll meet you in the bedroom in twenty minutes. Yes?"

All he did was nod his head. This time he didn't try to speak. He just looked at me like a teenaged boy who was on the brink of losing his virginity. I held in my amusement as I slid out from under him and switched away, leaving him in the kitchen with whatever thoughts he had rolling around in his head.

I grabbed my bag, went into the bathroom, turned on the shower and started snatching products out left and right. I broke into my new perfume kit and pulled out the shower gel and one of the bottles of lotion. After that, I pulled out my feminine wash, my toothbrush, toothpaste, razor, shave gel, shower cap, and mesh shower sponge. The last thing to come out of the bag was the skimpiest of the lingerie sets that the girls had bought me. It was a cobalt blue, no-crotch one-piece with lace in the midsection area and in the back, and satin sides and straps. I set everything up, put on my shower cap and hopped in the steaming shower.

I applied some of my special bikini-area shave gel, grabbed my razor and gently glided it over Girlfriend. After that, I sudsed her up real good with a large squirt of feminine wash. I made extra sure to hit all the nooks and crannies, just in case Weston wanted to have a little snack.

I washed my face with the bar of plain soap that Weston had in the caddy, then I opened up my new Elysium shower gel and squeezed large amount onto my mesh sponge. The hypnotizing scent filled the bathroom, and as I rubbed the suds all over my body, I thought about how my day had gone thus far. Every moment had been perfect, and there was still more to come. I thought about us professing our love to each other in the kitchen just minutes before, and the way he looked at me right before he said those magic words. I got turned on, and Girlfriend started throbbing.

After I had sufficiently scrubbed myself down, I got out of the shower, patted myself dry, and slathered on some delicious Elysium lotion. Once that was done, I slipped into my Frederick's gear. I brushed and flossed again, even though I had already done that before we left for dinner, then I fluffed up my hair and looked at myself in the mirror. I was looking and smelling good, and I was ready for action. I packed all my stuff back in my bag and opened the bathroom door.

I set my bag in the hallway and went into the bedroom. I couldn't believe my eyes. He had changed his regular lamp light bulb and put in a low-wattage red one. There were several candles lit and placed strategically around the room. The ambiance was beautiful, but what was even more gorgeous was Weston. He was lying under the covers, but the only part of him that was covered up was his lower area. When I stepped all the way into the room and approached his side of the bed, his eyes got big as saucers as they traveled from one part of my body to the next.

He mumbled, "Oh my God . . ."

I was just about to speak, but when I looked down at his nightstand and saw the three extra-large condoms sitting there, I stood motionless for a second. I thought about what Tiki said, and all of a sudden, I was nervous. But I had waited entirely too long for this moment, so, without anymore hesitation, I walked up to the bed, leaned down, kissed him, then pulled back the covers.

All I could think when I saw what I saw was, *Lord, help me.* The man was, as I had ordered him to be, rock hard. But I'll be damned if Tiki wasn't right on the money with this one. Staring back at me were not six, seven, or even eight inches of dick. I was faced with a whopping nine and a half to ten inches. I had never seen such a sight in real life. Sure, I had watched my share of porno movies, and I had seen some big-dicked men swinging their packages around on camera, but never in my life had I been about to embark on anything this large in person. And not only was it long, it was thick, too. Long Fat Dong was definitely in the house. I almost fainted as I stared at his member, wondering how in the hell he was gonna get all of it up in me. I wondered if the extra-large rubbers were even gonna fit over it.

Weston saw the shock on my face and he grinned. "Somethin' wrong, baby?"

I lied and tried to sound sexy. "Not at all. Everything's just fine."

"Then come here. We got business to take care of."

He pulled me down on top of him and kissed me like he never had before. He ran his hands all over my body, while his dangerous-looking friend poked and jabbed me in my stomach area. Finally, he pushed me up into a sitting position, with me straddling his six-pack. He slid his fingers underneath the straps on my lingerie and gently pulled them off my shoulders. Then he took both hands and pulled the lace off my breasts, and out they popped. He caressed my swollen breasts in his large hands, then began pushing them lightly together as his fingertips slid across my nipples.

That was it. I was gone. I tilted my head back and purred like a satisfied cat. I closed my eyes and let out a huge breath of air. His hands moved, as he caressed my hips, thighs, and back. I wanted to scream. I opened my eyes and looked down at him, and he was staring me right in the face. Then, he lifted me up slightly and started sliding himself downward. My heart raced. He moved at the speed of light, because before I knew it, he had slid himself all the way under me so fast that I had to grab onto the headboard for support, and within seconds, Girlfriend had moved from straddling his six-pack to straddling his face. I almost died. He was breathing long, slow breaths, and I could feel the heat from his mouth blowing against my lips. I closed my eyes again in preparation for the journey I was about to be taken on.

And what a journey it was. First, he just lingered there while he sniffed me for a minute. Elysium was all over my body; I'd made sure of that. He turned his head from side to side, kissing my inner thighs, which made me tingle all over. But when he started kissing Girlfriend, I started feeling weak in the knees. He reached underneath me and separated my lips with his fingers. I was already hot and juicy, but when I felt his tongue touch the inside of my lips, I felt new juices release, as I held onto the headboard for dear life. His tongue made its way around and around in slow motion, as he mapped out every crease and fold of my box. Every time he breathed, the heat from his open mouth wafted into my canal. I heard him grunting and moaning as he sopped up all my love, and I could barely contain myself.

My moans became increasingly louder each time his tongue circled, flicked, and pressed against my skin; but when he finally sealed his plump lips around my magic button, that's when I really got vocal. Instinctively, my hips started to gyrate as he ate me like a pro. He sucked, teased, and slurped like he was born to do it. He used gentle, fluid motions that nearly sent me into convulsions. He knew exactly how much pressure to apply to my button and when. He also knew when to speed it up and slow it back down. I could barely breathe. His lips felt like butter. I sped up my hip motions and started calling out his name in whispers, telling him how good it felt, and that I loved him, and didn't want him to stop.

My talking made him pant and moan even harder, and I could feel him about to turn up the heat a notch. Girlfriend was throbbing, and so was my head. All the excitement was giving me a headache, but I simply ignored it. Then he did something I had never had a man do before. He slid his entire tongue all the way inside me and worked it up, down and around, like a mini dick. I hollered out loud and pounded my fist against the wall as I moved myself in accordance with him. He worked it there for a minute; then, just as I was about to come, he pulled his tongue out and ran it around my button with fury. After a few seconds, he wrapped his lips around it again and closed his mouth, while sweeping his tongue back and forth, applying light pressure every other second.

My time was up. I started screaming. Literally. I couldn't help it. My hips were swaying out of control.

He knew I was about to burst, so he wrapped his arms around my thighs to keep me still as I released the dam of juice into his mouth. He lapped it up like a dog that had just run across a bowl of water on a scorching hot day. I went into a mild cardiac arrest, gasping for air, screaming out to God, yelling Weston's name, and about to pass out. I was still clutching the headboard while Girlfriend pulsated harder than I've ever experienced before.

Before I even had a chance to catch my breath, Weston was already out from under me. He said, out of breath, "Turn over, baby. We not through yet."

I turned around and slid onto my back. Weston snatched a rubber off the nightstand, ran his palm over his mouth, then looked at me and said, "That was just an appetizer. You ready for the main course?"

I looked down at Dangerous, whose one eye was pointing straight at me. "Bring it on," I told him.

He opened the package, pulled out the king-sized sheath and rolled it on nice and tight. He reached down and slowly pulled my lingerie all the way off and tossed it on the side of the bed. He pulled me down towards him, and I went spread eagle. I was scared to death, but I was trying not to let it show.

I think he sensed my nervousness, because he leaned down, kissed my forehead and said, "I love you, girl."

I caressed his face in my hands. "I love you, too."

The closer in he moved, the harder I breathed. He grabbed hold of Dangerous and inched his way in between my legs. I was tight, since I hadn't had any in a minute, so when he gently began to push his head into my opening, I gasped.

He looked concerned. "You okay? You want me to stop?"

"No, no . . . don't stop. Just . . . go slow. Real slow. You're kinda packin', and the store's been closed for a while."

"Okay. Just . . . relax. I'll take good care of the store, I promise."

Ever so slowly, he began to push that engorged pipe of his into me. I held my breath with each centimeter of insertion. To be honest, I was scared to death he was gonna get in there and rupture something vital. I had never tangoed with that much manhood before, and I wasn't sure I would be able to handle it.

He stopped for a moment, looked in my eyes and whispered, "I need you to breathe, baby. You not breathin'."

Small bits of air escaped from me. "Sorry—I'm—sorry. . . ." I felt like a damn virgin all over again.

He moved his face close to mine. "Don't be sorry; it's okay. I'm'a open this store if it takes all night. Just try to relax, all right?"

I nodded and closed my eyes. He stopped pushing for a second, leaned down, and planted the most tender, loving kiss on my lips. I opened my mouth and let his sweet tongue fall on top of mine. I got lost in the moment, and I felt the store beginning to flood. As soon as it did, Weston gave one long, slow push, while making sure to keep our kiss going long and strong. His entrance caught me off guard, and I let out a small whimper as I dug my nails into his back. A chill ran down my spine and I felt my legs start to shake.

He broke away from our kiss. "Hang on, baby; we almost there."

He spread my legs as wide as they could go with

his knees, then with one last smooth stroke drove the rest of his nine-plus inches into me. I saw a million stars, and I moved my hips a little to loosen myself up some more. It felt like heaven once he was in, and when I looked in his face, his eyes were closed, and I could tell he was in a wonderland of his own. He let out several deep moans, and his breathing quickened. He moved his hips from side to side, and I ran my hands down the front of his solid chest.

He continued with a slow-moving groove, grazing his thick, cement-hard package up and down the sides of my walls. My tightness finally subsided and I was able to relax. After a while, his forehead started to sweat. He stopped to catch his breath, paused, and looked at me. Before he moved again, he asked, "You okay, baby? You wit' me?"

I arched my back and pressed the back of my head into the pillow; then I closed my eyes and moaned, "Yesssss."

By now, I was totally loose and no longer afraid of the big, bad Dangerous. I had my own groove going. I tossed my hips 'round and 'round and from side to side, and I squeezed, fondled, and rubbed everything I could get my hands on. I wrapped my legs around him, grabbed his ass with both hands and pushed him deeper into me. Then, I pulled his face down to me and began sucking on his left earlobe, which I had discovered a couple of weeks prior was one of his hot spots. He whimpered, gasped, and started thrusting with fervor.

I locked my legs around him as tight as I could and started contracting my walls, which sent him into a frenzy. Sweat was dropping from his face into my eyes, and into my hair. To get his attention again, I ran my hands over his face to wipe the sweat, then I whispered in his ear, "Spell my name."

Still thrusting with all the passion he had, he panted, *"K-A-T-T-T—OH, SHIT—R-I-C-C—FUCK!—E!!"*

I knew he was about to explode, so I ran my fingers through his hair and ordered gently, "Look at me." He opened his golden eyes, looked me in mine, then pounded me with every bit of energy he had left.

He shouted, "KATRICE! KATRICE! AW . . . SH . . . SH . . . SHIIIIIITT!" And then he collapsed on top of me.

For the next five minutes, we lay in silence, nothing but our heavy breathing between us. He rested his head in between my breasts and I stroked his back. He whimpered softly as he caught his breath, and I was simply in heaven. I wasn't worried about the fact that I didn't come, because I usually don't when I'm with a guy for the first time. I have to get used to the feel of him first; that's when the real fun begins for me. But no matter. I got mine when Weston went deep-sea diving, so I was totally satisfied. One thing I knew for sure was that we wouldn't be having any problems in the bedroom.

Finally, he lifted himself up and said, *"Damn,* woman. I can hardly breathe up in here! Look what'-choo did to me."

We laughed, then he rolled off of me and sprawled out on his back. I thought he was about to go to sleep, but instead, he started talking to me. He told me that even though it was hard not knowing when I would be ready, he was actually glad we waited until that night to make love. I agreed. I also told him it was the best birthday I had had in a long time. A minute later, he draped his arm around me, and we cuddled and talked for a while.

After about twenty minutes or so had passed, we got up, and after we had both emptied our bladders, we took a short shower together. We spent the rest of the night lying in bed, making plans for our future. Finally, around two or three o'clock, we conked out.

The next morning, I woke Weston up with a little oral surprise of my own. That kicked off a two-hour lovemaking session that blew the one from the night before out of the water. After we had worked each other over, we were starving. Since it was Saturday, and neither of us had to be at work, we decided to do a repeat of our first date, and went to Café Soul to get our grub on.

After we were full and satisfied, we went to Blockbuster, rented four movies, then went back to Weston's and locked ourselves in the house for the rest of the day. That was just fine with me, because there wasn't any place I wanted to be more than in the arms of my new man. We were happy, in love, and nothing else mattered.

9

From May all the way through July, I was so busy that my head was spinning. Between working and going out, I barely had time to take care of myself. I had forgotten how much your life changes when you're in an intense relationship, and how much work it really is. Just adding one special person to your life can cause all kinds of drama and chaos. I had to keep my Palm Pilot close at hand at all times, because I kept getting confused about which events were when. Movies with Weston, Tiki and Charles; bonding night with the girls; barbecue at P.J. and Lateshia's; Bodega Bay with Weston; visit with my parents; dinner in San Francisco with Weston, Tiki and Charles; lunch and shopping with the girls; concert with Weston, P.J., Lateshia, Tiki and Charles; comedy show with Weston and my parents; quiet night alone with Weston; on and on and on. I was so damn tired I couldn't see straight. A few times, when I didn't have my Palm Pilot right in front of me, I had to call people to make sure what, if any, the plans were for that particular day.

I didn't complain, because I had a lot of fun. Everyone loved my man, and because of that, someone always wanted us to be at some type of activity. I loved the fact that I never had to babysit Weston when we were with other people. I've been in situations with guys where, as soon as they got around someone other than me, suddenly, they were mute. But not my baby. As a matter of fact, several times I had to actually vie for his attention because he was so into a conversation with Charles or P.J. or my father. Even Mama and Tiki a couple of times. But in the end, I wouldn't have had it any other way.

Probably the biggest event for us as a couple was the trip to Chicago we took in mid-August. Weston had invited me to go home with him for four days to attend his family reunion. I jumped at the opportunity, since all I heard over and over were a zillion and one stories about his family. He didn't have a lot of recent pictures of everyone, so I was always trying to picture his mom, brothers, and sisters when he would talk about them. So when he told me he wanted me to go with him, I didn't even hesitate with my yes. Quicker than he could cough twice, I had made arrangements to have Tiki fit my clients into her schedule while I was gone. She was more than happy to do it, and she was just as excited as I was about the trip.

When I told the rest of the girls about it, they all had different responses. Genine said, "Uh-oh! You know what it means when a man wants you to meet his family! He's thinkin' about *marriage*! Go on, girl! Git that ring!"

Chantelle said, "Girl, that is *not* true. Not that he don't love her, but it just means he thinks she's worth bringin' around his peeps. You know—it's safe, now that he knows she ain't all ghetto fabulous and won't embarrass him."

And Sabrina said, "I think you're both wrong. When a man takes a woman to meet the fam, it's like the final test. If his family takes to her, then he knows for sure that she's a keeper. You know how families have a way of peepin' out little stuff about your mate that either you don't see, or you don't wanna *admit* you see. But, whichever the case, if the family don't like her, he gon' hear about it. Same goes for women bringin' men home. It's the 'Can my mate pass the family inspection?' test."

I ended the debate with, "Well, you know what? I'm not about to sit up here and put a label on his motive for wantin' me to meet his family. We're a couple, we're in love, he's met my friends and family, now it's time for me to meet his. Period. I'm excited as hell. I need to get away for a minute. I ain't been out the state since I went to Texas for Joan-Renee's wedding. That was almost three years ago. It'll be good to see and experience something new."

"Well," Genine started, "have fun—and *please* don't come back here without pictures. You know how you are. Have a camera danglin' right from yo' damn wrist and won't snap no shots."

"I know, I know . . . but I'ma hook it up this time."

Sabrina asked, "When you guys leavin'?"

"Three weeks. I can't wait."

10

Those three weeks dragged by slower than slow. The closer our departure date got, the more anxious I became. The night before we left, I barely slept two winks. I didn't leave the shop until late because I squeezed in four "it can't wait" heads, and by the time I got home, it was after eleven. Since I still had to finish packing, which took me well over an hour, I didn't end up getting to bed until after midnight. That would have been fine, except for the fact that we had a seven-thirty flight the next morning, and had to be at the Oakland Airport by at least six. Because I was so excited, I didn't get to sleep until one-something, and had to be right back up at four-thirty.

Weston had wanted us to spend the night together so we could leave together, but I didn't think that would be a good idea, since we had a bad habit of distracting each other so heavily. I could just see us at either his or my apartment getting caught up in each other; then, when it came down to the wire, we'd both be out of our minds trying to get ourselves together individually and get out of the house on time. After he thought about it, he realized I was probably right, and told me he'd see me in the morning.

By the time my alarm went off, I was still tired, I had a headache from being so anxious, and I was feeling cranky, which, for my Taurus ass, is not a good thing. I remember hoping when I got up that morning that Weston would have his act together just for once, and not be late. Things hadn't gotten any better since April, and I had already spoken to him several times about his problem. I tried to be nice about it, and he said he knew he had issues in that area, and would work on it. All I knew was that the morning of August fifteenth would have been the perfect time to make that change.

But apparently, I was asking for a little too much. We were supposed to be on the road by five-thirty. I had told Weston I would be waiting outside when he picked me up, so he wouldn't have to bother getting out of the car. Getting up in the morning was never a problem for him, so I knew I didn't need to make a wake-up call to his house . . . it was everything that went on *after* he was up that concerned me. I had seen him in action many times, and no matter how early he would get up to be somewhere, he was a mess trying to get ready. He never picked out his clothes the night before, so he always spent what seemed like an eternity with his head shoved in the closet, pushing stuff from side to side, trying to find something to wear. And if he had to iron? Let's not even talk about it. Once he finally did find and prepare something to wear, he was the slowest dresser I ever saw. To top it off, he always had to floss twice, rinse nine doggone times after he brushed, clean off his shoes before he put them on, shave his face even if he had no stubble, spend ten damn minutes picking out a cologne to wear, and believe it or not, the man actually pondered for un- believable amounts of time figuring out which jacket to wear . . . or if he was gonna wear one at all. Watch- ing him drove me out of my mind, and to be honest, tired me the hell out.

When I got outside, it was exactly five-thirty on the nose, and Weston was nowhere in sight. I sat my big suitcase down and posted myself on top of it. It was nippy out, and I couldn't put my jacket on be- cause it was packed away, and there was no way I was going up in all my stuff to get it out, so I just said forget it. I figured Weston would be driving up any second anyway, so it really didn't matter.

I couldn't have been more wrong. Any second turned into almost twenty-five minutes, and I was livid. Just as I was about to pull out my cell and call him, he came around the corner. I knew the doors would already be unlocked, so I stomped over, slung open the back, and tossed my stuff in. I say tossed, but my stuff was extra heavy, and since I had an adrenaline rush from being mad, it felt like I tossed it up in there.

I got in the car, slammed the door, folded my arms and looked out the passenger window, not speaking a single word. Since it was obvious that I had an at- titude, Weston copped one, too. He threw out a tart, "Well, good morning to you, too, *Miss Vincent*."

I was silent. I knew it was rude, but I didn't care.

He glared at me. "You plannin' on speakin' or what?"

I mumbled an attitudinal, "Hello," and didn't even look his way.

He sighed real hard. He knew why I was mad. "I *tried* to get here on time. I'm sorry, okay?"

"You're always sorry," I snapped.

"Look woman, I'm tired and I don't need this. It's too damn early."

"Well, I'm tired too, shit. Let's just go." I cut my eyes at him. "*We're late.*"

"Ay, you know what? You need—never mind. Shit . . . fuck this."

And he skidded off.

He drove like a bat outta hell, and all the way to the airport, neither of us spoke a syllable to each other. I sat with my lips poked out, and he drove with his brow all crinkled up while he blasted Public Enemy's "911 Is a Joke," the one song by them he knows I can't stand. He put the song on repeat and played it the entire time we were driving. Then he had the nerve to rap along with them, all loud and obnoxious. I wanted to sock him. Men act like such assholes when they get mad, I swear.

When we got to the airport, of course, we had to rush, since it was well after six. For some reason, it was crowded as all get out, and everyone there looked like they had gotten thirty minutes of sleep or less. We went through baggage, security, and to the waiting area without speaking. Fortunately for us, our flight was delayed fifteen minutes, because we barely got there on time to begin with. I was glad we had a chance to sit down for a few minutes. My head was throbbing and my feet were hurting. I had made a dumb choice and put on some new shoes I bought the day before, and I was paying for it.

We sat across from each other at a diagonal, in total silence. Weston was looking evil, and I was still pouting. At one point, I looked over at him while he was staring out the window watching the airplanes roll in and out. It occurred to me that I had acted a straight-up ass, and that I needed to check myself real quick. I had a good man. A man who invited me to go with him two thousand miles away to meet his family and paid the four hundred dollars for my plane ticket on top of that. A man who treated me like a queen and who would do anything for me. Sure, he had a late problem that didn't seem to be improving. And yes, he was stubborn, picky, quick-tempered, slightly closed-minded, and a know-it-all. But I loved the hell out of him, and instead of appreciating him in the moment, all I could think about was the fact that he was twenty-odd minutes late. Yeah, it pissed me off, but I could've let it go, just that once. I studied his face for a moment, and I saw all the stress and worry he held in his expression. I felt bad. I was so busy thinking about how I felt that I had forgotten about him.

I hate to admit when I'm wrong, but I knew if we were gonna talk at all before we got to Chicago, I was gonna have to eat humble pie. I gathered my purse and my carry-on and moved to the seat right next to him. He turned and frowned at me, then went back to staring out the window. It was clear to me that making nice with him wasn't going to be easy.

As I sat and tried to figure out what I was about to say, I watched him for a few more seconds. He looked exhausted and sad.

I ran my hand lightly along his thigh. "You want me to go get you some coffee, babe? I saw a little shop back there, and I know how you are about missing your morning mocha."

He didn't bite. Just shook his head and continued staring out the window, so I dug a little deeper and took my make-up tactics to the next level. I removed my hand from his thigh and ran the back of it down the side of his face. He didn't pull away from me, which was a good sign, but he still wouldn't speak or look at me.

"You sure there's nothing I can get you?"

No answer. At that point, I knew there was only one thing I *could* get him that would make things right: a bona fide apology. I stopped rubbing his face and went on and did what I hate to do.

"I'm sorry, baby. I know I was rude earlier. I'm just tired, that's all."

I felt his vibe shift just a little; but the problem was that on top of pissing him off, I had hurt his feelings, and it was always a struggle to get him to come around when I pushed his buttons like that. Over the short time we had been together, I came to realize that he was even more sensitive than me. Go figure.

"Weston. I really am sorry. I know you're tired and stressed out, and I know you tried to get there in time." Then, to lighten the mood some, I joked, "Don't trip off me, baby. You know I think I'm perfect and my shit don't stink," then I nudged him playfully in the arm.

He cracked half a smile and finally looked at me. "Oh, so you admit it, huh?"

I smiled, and after a second, he smiled right back. Finally, his guard was down.

He took my hand. "But I'm sorry, too. I don't know *why* I can't be on *time*. I'm'a work harder on that, baby; I promise."

I thought about all the unnecessary things he had

going on in the mornings, and almost went into a whole speech about it, but I decided to save it for another time. Instead, I just said, "We'll work on it together," and kissed him on the lips.

When we got off the plane, Weston took me by the hand and led me down the corridor into the airport. His palm was damp, which meant he was nervous. I didn't blame him—all of a sudden, I was scared, too. I wasn't really afraid his family wouldn't like me; it was just that I was about to meet so damn many of them all at once, and that thought alone was overwhelming me. It's one thing to meet your man's immediate family, but walking into a family reunion is a whole different ball game. Nevertheless, I was glad I was there. I couldn't wait to see the tribe Weston had emerged from.

No sooner than we stepped off the platform, Weston dropped my hand, spread his arms out as wide as he could, grinned like I had never seen him grin before, and sang, "Wasuuup, beautifuuuul?"

That caught me off guard, because I didn't know who the hell he was talking to. There was a huge crowd of people flocked in front of the doorway, all looking for their loved ones, and I couldn't figure out how he had managed to spot anyone familiar in the half-second we had been in the room. Before I had a chance to ask him anything, a petite woman of about five-foot-two, with long, thick hair that was tied up in a ponytail, a gorgeous figure and flawless face, and dressed in a lightweight red jogging suit flew into Weston's arms, hollering, "There's my baby booooyyy!!"

Baby boy? I thought. This was his *mother?* She

looked like she was all of twenty, and from what I could tell, she and Weston didn't really look alike. She was a lot darker and had deep brown, almond-shaped eyes and a completely different nose and mouth structure than Weston. About the only similarities between them were their eyebrows and dimples. The few pictures I did see of her were old, and they were mostly upper body shots that didn't do her any type of justice. This woman was perfect. Not an ounce of fat on any part of her body, and just as toned and firm as she wanted to be. I was almost jealous.

I just stared at them while they hugged. They were like best friends coming together after years of separation. It was a touching scene that made me break into a smile, as I watched him literally swing her from side to side with her legs dangling in the air.

After the two of them showered each other with a thousand kisses and hugs, he finally put her down and turned to me looking proud, slid his arm around my waist while he pulled me close and said, "Mama, this is Katrice Vincent. Baby, this is my mother, Lorraine."

Lorraine smiled warmly at me and we both said, "Nice to meet you," at the same time. Then she reached out to hug me. It's funny, I'm only five-foot-seven my damn self, and I found it amusing that I had to reach down to hug her. While embracing me, she said, "I've heard *so, so much* about you!"

"Same here," I told her. "It's good to finally put a face to all the stories your son tells me. You are *so beautiful*. And I hope you know you're *workin'* that outfit, okay?"

She laughed. "Oh, thank you, baby. I just recently turned fifty-two, but honey, I ain't tryina look like it!"

"Well, you sure don't."

Weston draped his hands over Lorraine's shoulders and said, "Yeah, that's why I gotta watch her. Every time I come home, I gotta damn near fight some young dude, pushin' all up on her."

Lorraine turned around and popped Weston in the rib playfully. "Boy, quit tellin' stories!"

Weston looked at me. "I'm tellin' you baby, my moms be gittin' *play.*"

"I don't doubt it."

Weston looked at his watch. "Well, come on, y'all. Let's hit up baggage claim before it gets too crowded over there."

It was too hot for words, and the humidity had all of our clothes sticking to us by the time we got to the house. It was almost five o'clock when we pulled up to the garage. We piled out of Lorraine's Rav4, and all of us grabbed some bags. Fortunately, all our luggage made it to the airport, so we didn't have any drama and were able to get out of there pretty fast. I, of course, had four suitcases to Weston's one and a half, plus my carry-on. I started off with only two, but after I thought about all the uncertainty of what kind of activities would be taking place over the course of the four-day trip, I started to panic about being too far away to just double back and grab something else. Before I knew it, I had pulled out two smaller suitcases and stuffed about ten more out-fits into them along with six more bra-and-thong sets and nylons, and I even managed to shove a few extra pairs of shoes in, too.

Weston clowned me about my alleged overpacking as he rolled the largest of my suitcases up the walk-way. Lorraine and I said at the same time, and in the same tone, "Better safe than sorry," then looked at each other and cracked up. Weston just smiled and shook his head at us.

As Lorraine opened the front door, I could hear loud music and scattered voices throughout the house. No sooner than we stepped in, I heard a voice scream, "Weston!" When I looked up, all I saw was a tall, lanky body barreling toward him. She jumped into his arms and wrapped her long legs around his waist, hugging him tight.

Weston laughed. "Wassup, Meekymu? I missed you, baby girl! Come here . . . lemme look at'choo!"

She was a beautiful female version of Weston. She had long, silky, lion's-mane-colored hair that sat at her shoulders and was parted down the middle. She had clear, brown-sugar skin, just like her brother, and had the same dimples. The biggest difference was her eyes. They were the most gorgeous sparkling green: large and innocent, with lashes even longer than Weston's, which I didn't think was possible. She was built a lot like me when I was her age: full and round in all the right places, a prime target for some little hornball to live out a fantasy or two, given the right opportunity.

Weston spun her around and looked her up and down. "Awwww, sookie! Look at my baby sista up in *here!* Do I need to move back home so I can watch over you? You didn't have all this *p-pow* last time I was here, girl! Might hafta rough up a few of these dudes around here."

Tamika was embarrassed. "Shut up, Weston," she smiled. Then, she plastered her right hand on her hip, said a sassy, "Besides, I already got a boyfriend," and stuck her tongue out at him playfully.

"Ohhh . . . like *that?* What's his name?"

"Patrick. He's seventeen," she said proudly.

"Yeah, okay, *seventeen*. Am I gon' get to meet him while I'm here?"

"Yup, he's comin' to the barbecue on Sunday."

"Yeah, well, I'm'a hafta have a talk wit' him."

"No you not!"

"Uh . . . *yeah,* I am." He ruffled her hair and she pushed his hand away playfully.

"Watch out, boy! Don't be messin' up my hair. I just got it done."

"Oh, I see you think you cute now that'choo *sweet sixteen* . . . okay, then." He pulled her over in my direction. "Come here, you . . . say hi to my girlfriend, Katrice."

She smiled at me. "Hi. Dag . . . Weston said you were gorgeous. For once he was tellin' the truth." She smirked and peeked at him.

He popped her upside her head. "I'm'a whoop yo' butt!"

I chuckled. "Well, hello . . . and thank you. So are you."

She beamed. "Thank you."

From somewhere upstairs, someone yelled, "Meeeeeeek! Phone!"

Tamika got that familiar look on her face that said her little man was waiting on the other end. She said a hurried, "Nice to meet you . . ." and rushed off to a phone in another room.

Weston bellowed, "Hey! Monica! Bring yo' tail down here, girl!"

"Weston . . . ? Ay, y'all, they're here!"

In less than ten seconds, everyone came running down the stairs. They all took turns attacking Weston, and once that was done, for the next several minutes

I had the absolute pleasure of meeting the rest of the Porter family. Suffice it to say, they were all "lookers."

Leslie was really tall with a svelte figure. She had perfect, mocha-colored skin and dreadlocks to match that cascaded down the middle of her back, and she looked a lot like Lorraine. Her smile was warm and comforting, and when her big hazel eyes twinkled at me, I could tell we were gonna hit it off real quick.

Monica was a teeny-tiny little thing—maybe an inch shorter than Lorraine—had green eyes like Tamika's except smaller and about a shade darker, and was cute as a button. Her hair was in goddess braids, and I could tell she worked out because she had on a yellow tank half-top that showed off her sculpted little arms and abs and a pair of white jean shorts that bared her tight, defined legs.

Then there were the twins, Kevin and Cornell. Good Lord, those men were heart-stopping fine. I mean that literally. When I looked at them, I actually felt my heart pause for a second. I had to catch myself before something like, "*Goddamn,*" flew from outta my mouth, instead of a proper greeting. They had left Weston in the dust in the height department by at least three or four inches. They both had clean-shaven bald heads, not a razor bump in sight; they were milk chocolate and high-cheekboned like their mother, both slender and muscular, and had smiles that would melt butter. Even though they had brown eyes like Lorraine, they were the most heavenly, hypnotizing brown bedroom eyes I had ever seen. I was staring so damn hard when Weston introduced us that I had to ask twice who was who. They were most definitely identical. After staring for a few more seconds, I finally figured out I could kind of tell them apart by their smiles. The right side of Kevin's mouth turned up slightly higher than Cornell's. Weston said that by the end of the visit, I'd be an expert at telling them apart, but I didn't see that happening.

After all the introductions were finished, Leslie, Kevin, and Cornell all left together to go to the store to get the rest of the ingredients for the fish fry they had planned for that evening. Monica went back upstairs to start getting ready for her date with her boyfriend, Earl, and Lorraine went into the kitchen to start making the potato salad. Tamika was still off in some corner of the house talking to her young suitor.

Weston and I took our things to the den, which also doubled as a guest room when there was company. There was a sofa bed, twenty-five-inch television, and a large sliding door closet, which I was glad to see since I had so much stuff. Off in the corner was a sewing area complete with a huge sewing machine, a bunch of different colored fabrics, patterns, drawings, at least four pairs of different-sized scissors, some thimbles, and spools of thread everywhere.

Weston saw me looking and said, "Sorry about that, babe. Moms'll straighten that up before we hit the sack tonight."

"Oh, I'm not trippin'. So, this is where all the magic happens, huh?"

"Yeah, this is her little haven."

Weston had told me all about how Lorraine had started her own clothing business awhile back. It's how she made her living after she quit teaching elementary school. It started when Leslie was in high school. A boy she liked had asked her to the junior prom, and at the time, money was really tight. Leslie wanted Lorraine to buy her this fancy-schmancy dress from some high-class department store that cost nearly two hundred dollars. Lorraine went through the roof at the request, and Leslie went into a tizzy when Lorraine turned her down cold. After days of pouting, Lorraine told Leslie she would make her a dress just like it. She had always liked to knit and sew, and had made a few small items such as sweaters and shirts, but she had never attempted anything more complicated than that. To be honest, she really wasn't sure she'd even be able to pull it off, but she wanted to try.

Long story short, by the time prom night rolled around, Lorraine had created a dress even more stunning than the one in the store, and Leslie bragged to all her friends that night about how her mother made it with her own two hands.

Soon, Leslie was coming home from school with requests for Lorraine to make dresses and outfits for hordes of fashion-conscious girls wanting to look cute for upcoming events, or just in general. Lorraine had just about had it with her teaching job, and had been searching for a new way to make ends meet so she could quit. When the requests started rolling in by the dozens, Lorraine decided that was her cue to make her move. She finished out the school year, and by the following June, she was raking in almost double her teaching salary in clothing sales per month and was having the time of her life doing it. She was amazed at how much people were willing to pay for her services, and had dozens of regulars as well. She had so many calls coming in that she had to add a phone line with a separate number and turn it into the business phone.

Fifteen years later, Lorraine's business was still

going strong, and had grown by leaps and bounds. She had long since graduated from just making clothes for women, and had branched out into all types of clothing, including men's, boys', even baby clothes, which were her best seller since babies grow so fast and need new clothes every doggone month. With all the money she had made over the years, she was able to remodel the house twice, travel around the world three times, spend two months in Africa and a month and a half in Paris, and pay cash for both her cars—and had saved enough money that even if she decided to take a break from the business, she would be financially stable for quite a while.

When I asked Weston why she never sold her clothes in stores, he said she liked the fact that when she made an item for someone, it would be tailored specifically for them, and they'd be the only one wearing what she called her Lorraine Porter Original. That explained the LPO I saw engraved on the collar of her jogging suit when we got off the airplane. Weston said every item she makes has that moniker engraved on it somewhere.

We put our bags down, and he took me on a tour of the house. It wasn't terribly large, and Lorraine had a classy sense of style. She had lots of artwork hanging on the walls in the living room, most by Samuel Byrd, the famous artist from Philly. She had met him back in the day through her best friend, Marguerite, who was good friends with him, and had been buying his artwork ever since.

There were tons of plants of all kinds, and out in the patio area she had started a small flower garden. I loved the fact that she had scented candles in every room, and she had the most beautiful chandelier hanging in the dining room.

Upstairs, there were three bedrooms—one for her, one for Monica, and one for Tamika. Lorraine had a bathroom in her room, and Monica and Tamika shared the one at the end of the hallway. They were the only two of the siblings still living at home. Leslie lived about forty-five minutes away with her husband, Joe; Cornell lived all of five miles away; and Kevin was only visiting. He still had one more year to go at UCLA.

By the time we finished with the tour of the house, Leslie, Kevin, and Cornell were back with the food. The five of us went outside on the patio and talked while Tamika helped Lorraine get dinner ready.

We sat for an hour and a half, and I got my bond going with the family. Leslie and Joe had been married for three years. Joe was a pharmacist, and she was working on her career as a stand-up comedienne. After spending fifteen minutes with her, I saw why. Everything she said was funny, even when she was trying to be serious. We howled so loud out there that I started getting scared we were disturbing the peace.

Kevin was at UCLA studying film and television. He was working on a screenplay for a movie about a man who goes to Brazil to find his soul mate, falls in love with a beautiful woman named Therezinha, and tells the story of their struggle to build a life together.

Cornell was attending business school so he could get his license to start a small school-bus line, appropriately named Schooler Line.

By the time I filled them in on my story, Joe had shown up and dinner was ready. We scarfed on snapper, which was fried and seasoned to perfection, and we also had mouthwatering potato salad and a huge, delicious green salad that Tamika made with three kinds of lettuce, carrots, mushrooms, onions, tomatoes, avocado, cucumbers, and a homemade Italian dressing.

By ten o'clock, we were all stuffed, and I was beat. Weston, Kevin, Cornell, and Joe all went out to a sports bar to do the "guy thing," and I stayed in with Lorraine, Leslie, and Tamika. Monica was still out with Earl, but Lorraine said she would be home soon.

We stayed up late, flapping our gums, and I was so at home, I felt like I had known them my whole life. Monica came in around midnight and joined the party.

Close to two in the morning, after I had already turned in, I felt Weston creep into bed next to me. He was wide awake and wanted to make love, but I told him I couldn't do that in his mother's house. He assured me that we wouldn't be heard, and that it was fine, but I was still leery. But when Weston got on top of me, and started kissing me, and I felt Dangerous come alive, I changed my tune real quick.

Around ten that morning, Weston and I borrowed Lorraine's car and Weston took me all over Chicago; we ran nonstop. We visited his old high school, Paul Robeson, and drove through all the neighborhoods that Weston used to hang out and get in trouble in. He even took me to the spot where an old, abandoned building used to be, where he lost his virginity at thirteen, to a sixteen-year-old named Sylvia.

Later that afternoon, he took me to lunch at a Mexican restaurant, and the food was so good I wanted to lick my plate. After that, he told me we were going for "a drive," but wouldn't tell me where.

I tried to squeeze it out of him, but he just kept telling me it was a surprise.

The surprise was the Chicago Botanic Garden out in Glencoe. When we walked in, my mouth dropped open. It was the most beautiful sight I had ever seen. We took a tour by tram, walked around, sat, and talked, and I tried to smell every flower I could shove my nose up to. I fell in love with the place quick, and when I found out that weddings were one of their specialties, my wheels started turning. After about three hours, we headed back to the house.

I was exhausted, but there was still more. Weston, Kevin, and Cornell all wanted to go out to a club called The Lounge. Weston said he had been hearing about it from some of his old buddies from the neighborhood that he kept in touch with, and wanted to go the next time he was home. I could have fallen asleep right then and there, but instead, I summoned up a second wind, got dressed to the nines, and headed out with the gang.

I was glad I went, because we had a ball. I watched Kevin and Cornell mack nearly every woman in the club; and even though I had to evil-eye a few hoochies who were trying to push up on Weston when they thought I wasn't looking, I enjoyed every minute of the night. We all danced until the sweat poured off our brows. Thank goodness there were couches to sit on, because after nearly two solid hours of shaking my ass to jams and flailing all over the place, I needed a break.

We fell into bed at almost three, and as tired as we both were, the only lovemaking that was going on was in our dreams, because we were both asleep before we could count to ten.

We all got up at about seven o'clock to get ready for the reunion, which was to be held at Lincoln Park. Weston had told me that there would be scads of relatives attending, and that they had booked enough space for at least 150 people, but he thought there might be more.

When we arrived, at around eleven, I couldn't believe the amounts of food I saw. I mean, you name it, and it was there. Just loads and loads of barbecued ribs and chicken, links, beef hamburgers, veggie burgers, potato salads, green salads, macaroni and cheese, corn on the cob, vegetable skewers; every kind of cobbler, pie, and cake imaginable; and of course, more soda, water, and beer than a grocery store could shelve. I had never been to a family reunion, so this whole situation was a new and exciting adventure for me.

Weston introduced me to I-don't-know-how-many people, none of whose names I remembered, and the kids were the cutest things on the face of the earth. Some of them were bad-assed kids, some were well-mannered, but all were cute nonetheless.

There were definitely more than a hundred and fifty people there, but somehow, everyone had a place to sit.

We started grubbing at around one-thirty, and things were going really well at first. Everyone was happy and having the time of their lives.

Then, in two seconds, everything fell apart.

Weston was talking to his cousin Luke who was sitting across the table, while sucking on an over-sauced rib, and all of a sudden he stopped talking mid-sentence.

He tossed his rib onto his plate and his expression turned to stone.

"What the hell is *he* doin' here?" He looked around at everyone at the table. No one said a word, but everyone looked like Weston had just discovered something that, up until that moment, had been on the hush tip.

From about seventy-five feet away, cautiously approaching the festivities, was a tall, solid man with salt-and-pepper head and facial hair who looked and walked exactly like Weston. It only took me a second to figure out who he was. It was like looking at Weston twenty-five years into the future.

A couple of people cleared their throats, and a few others slowly wiped their mouths while peering at the scene with shifty eyes. You could hear dust falling from the sky it was so quiet at our table. Some people were still holding food in their mouths looking like they were afraid to even swallow.

Weston noticed that no one was answering him and snapped, "AY! I said what's he doin' here?"

Everyone was still deaf-mute.

Lorraine was standing at the cooler fishing out more sodas and beers, when she heard Weston's outburst. She spun around, looked at the man approaching, then looked at her son with fear in her eyes. She dropped two of the beers back down into the cooler from under her arm and set the other four sodas down on the table.

Weston slammed his napkin down, jumped up from the table on the defensive and exploded, "Mama! You see this? You see him comin' over here?" He rushed towards her.

His mother panicked. "Weston . . . baby . . . just hold—"

He didn't let her finish. Instead, he redirected his

focus, realizing the man was just about up on them, and started walking toward him to intercept his arrival at the scene. As the two came face-to-face, Weston demanded to know, "Man, what the hell you doin' here?" He stepped to the man like he was a trespasser on his property, ready to throw down.

People started whispering to one another and squirming in their seats. I started getting scared. I had never really seen Weston in an outrage, and things weren't looking good.

The man said a simple and straight-faced, "Hello, son."

I could see Weston's nostrils flaring and his hands twitching. After a second, he balled one of them up into a fist.

"Man, I ain't tryina hear all that *son* shit. I *said* what the hell you doin' here? Don't nobody want'-choo around here. You not welcome."

A wasp landed on my potato salad and started crawling toward the edge of my plate, making its way over to my arm. I was petrified, because my fear of bees goes deeper than you'll ever know, but at that moment, my bigger fear was that Weston was about to crack his salt-and-pepper-look-alike in the jaw. Between Weston and the wasp, I was paralyzed.

"Look . . ." he started.

But then Lorraine stepped in, gently pulled Weston's arm and said, "Weston . . . stop now . . . go on and sit back down."

He faced her with a perplexed look. "What'choo talkin' 'bout, Mama? You act like you ain't even surprised."

His father interrupted. "Your mother invited me here, Weston. I *am* still family."

Two bumblebees flew down to join the party with the wasp, which was now dangling from the edge of my greasy paper plate, and I nearly peed on myself. I wanted to jump up and run, and I guess I started looking wild-eyed and started breathing heavy, because one of Weston's cousins leaned over and said in a low tone, "Just don't move and you'll be okay. They want the food, not you."

I nodded my head frantically and looked up at Weston, who practically had smoke coming out of his ears.

He glowered at his father and hissed, "You a damn liar. Ain't nobody invited you up in here. Git outta here, man! It's a little late to be tryina be somebody's family now!"

Lorraine's face got stern. She yanked Weston by the arm and reprimanded, "Weston. Stop it. I asked him to come. You causin' a scene out here." Then she turned her focus to his father and said, "Sonny, go on and fix you a plate. Lemme handle this."

Sonny looked down, nodded, stepped away from the two of them, and made his way over to the food.

Disappointment like I've never seen before fell across Weston's face. He cocked his head to the side, dropped his shoulders, looked his mother deep in the eyes and questioned, "Mama. You actually invited that man here? Why would you do that after the way he did us? You shouldn't even wanna look at him."

Lorraine pointed her index finger at Weston and chided, "Listen. That man is your father. This is a family reunion, and he's still family, whether you like it or not."

Weston protested, "But, Mama . . . he don't give a damn about us. . . ."

She shook her head quickly, waved her hands in his face to cut him off and told him, "No, no, no. Now, we not gon' argue about this today. I'm tired of this mess between you two. You all need to work past this. Now, I'm sorry if you got a problem with Sonny bein' here, but you not the only child he has. Your brothers and sisters wanna spend time with him. They all wanted him to come."

Weston looked back at the table, scowled at everyone for a second, looked back at Lorraine again and asked, "You mean to tell me everybody knew he was comin' but me?"

Lorraine didn't answer, which was answer enough, and Weston looked deceived.

By this time, Sonny had piled food on two plates and found a spot at our table. No one from the other tables further away seemed to be paying much attention to what was going on over in our direction, which was best, because something told me it wasn't over yet. Most of the attention at our table had gone back to eating and talking. Sonny had put his plates down for a moment, and was making his rounds to all the family members, hugging and shaking hands with everyone.

I continued to peek at Weston and Lorraine. I had given up on my plate of food, even though the bees finally flew away. My man was upset, and now I was worried.

He inquired, "Why didn't somebody tell me he was comin'? I'm not understandin' this."

"Because we knew if we told you, there was a chance *you* might not come."

He paused for several seconds while staring at

Lorraine. "So, what about you, Mama? *You* wanna spend time wit' him, too?"

She hesitated. "I miss your father, yes."

"So, what? Y'all gettin' back together or somethin'?"

"No. What Sonny and I had is over. But you hafta realize that your father and I had been together since grade school. We loved each other long before we got married. Just because you divorce someone doesn't mean you stop caring about them, no matter what they did."

"So, you sayin' you forgive him for cuttin' out on us? He didn't write, didn't call, didn't send no money . . . how can you forgive that? I just can't see it."

Lorraine sighed, then, studied her son's sad and confused expression for a moment. "Honey, I'll never forget what your father did. But it takes too much energy to hold lifelong grudges against people that hurt us. At some point, you gotta learn to accept folks for who they are and let the past go. Your father and I are on decent terms these days. That's the way I want it. And he does give a damn about us, whether you believe it or not. He just couldn't give us what we needed back then. I'm not excusin' it, just acceptin' it. Now git'cha attitude in check, 'cause honey, *my* kids don't show they ass in public; go back over to the table and introduce that beautiful woman of yours to your father. I won't have you ruinin' this special occasion with your bitterness."

Right then, Lorraine Porter became my hero. She had class and wisdom, and it was then that I saw where Weston acquired his solid foundation and sense of decency. And I finally understood why he searched so hard to find a woman like his mother, and why he loved her so much. I felt honored that he chose me.

Weston scooped his mother up in his buffed-out arms, hugged her tight, planted a passionate kiss on her cheek, and said, "I'm sorry, Mama. I didn't mean to upset you."

She smiled at him. "I know you didn't."

Then he added, "I'll try . . . today . . . but only for you. I still don't appreciate him bein' here, but if it's what you want, I'm'a give you yo' respect."

"Thank you, baby." She grasped his hands in hers.

Weston released his mother and made his way back to the table. I pretended to pick at my sweet-potato pie with my fork to make it look like I had been minding my own business the entire time. Normal conversation and laughter had resumed, and Sonny was stuffing his face with corn on the cob.

Weston stopped at my side and asked me, "You okay, babe? You need anything?" He looked at me tenderly.

I shook my head, then I asked him, "Are *you* okay?"

He grabbed my hand and lightly pulled me up from my seat. "Yeah. Come here. Got somebody I want you to meet."

We walked around to the far end of the table and a few people looked up at us nervously as we approached Sonny. Weston cleared his throat, slid his arm around my waist, pulled me close and said, "'Scuse me, uh, Pop . . ." I could tell it was hard for him to be polite.

His father looked up from his plate and I stared at him for a second. There, looking back at us, were the brilliant green eyes, the luscious mocha skin, and full, supple lips that had been strewn randomly throughout the Porter siblings.

Weston continued, "I, um . . . want you to meet my girlfriend. This is Katrice Vincent. Baby, this is my father, Sonny Porter."

Sonny smiled the same wide, toothy smile that I saw on Weston every day. He got up from the bench, and instead of shaking my hand, he hugged me tight. That caught me a little off guard, but it didn't bother me one bit. I hugged him right back.

He said, "So good to meet you, young lady."

"You, too."

"I hope we'll have a chance to talk later on."

I smiled. "I'd like that." Then I looked at Weston, who was looking tense. I rubbed his back, but he didn't respond.

Sonny told him, "You got a beautiful woman here, son."

Weston looked away. "I know that."

Sonny sensed that was pretty much all the politeness his son could manage for the moment, so he cleared his throat and muttered a small, "Well . . ." and sat back down.

Weston clenched his jaw and led me back to my seat. When we sat down, he looked at the food on his plate and grumbled, "I don't even want this no more. Lost my appetite. I'm'a go for a walk." He grabbed his plate, grimaced at it, jumped up and tossed it in the garbage. Then he stormed off.

Lorraine had taken her seat next to me again, and I looked over at her. I wanted to go after him, but given the fact that I had never been in this type of situation with him, I wasn't sure what to do. I guess she could read the uncertainty on my face, because she rested her hand on my arm, gave me a light pat and shook her head. I guess a mother knows her children, even if she doesn't see them that often.

Thirty minutes later, I was engrossed in a conversation with Jackie, Weston's aunt, about the pros and cons of wigs and weaves, when Weston startled me by blurting out coldly, "Lemme talk to you for a minute." I hadn't even seen him arrive at the table. When I looked up at him, he was standing over me looking like he was ready to cause yet *another* scene. I wasn't sure what to make of the way he approached me, and I was almost offended, but I caught myself from letting it show. I excused myself from the conversation and got up. Weston walked ahead of me with heat in his steps. We walked over to a large tree and he stopped and abruptly turned around.

I asked him, "What's goin' on?"

In a huff, he announced, "I'm ready to *go*."

"Okay . . . I mean, yeah . . . we can go ahead and go back to the house if you want."

He clarified himself. "Naw. I'm ready to go *home. Tonight.* We need to be out. I'm not stayin' here wit' his punk ass hangin' around like he's somebody. He don't have no business comin' around here minglin' and eatin' our food like he ain't did nothin' wrong. Fuck him. We packin' up and gittin' the hell outta here."

I can't lie, I was stunned by his hostility, and I really didn't know what to say. So I reminded him, "But, your mother invited him . . . and everybody seems to be enjoying his company . . ."

He frowned and sucked his teeth. "That's bullshit. They all just frontin'. My mama is the one who really wanted him to come. They just bein' nice outta respect for her."

"But . . . how do you know that?"

I guess I must've hit a nerve, because he just about ripped my head off. "Look, I know my family, all right? My brothers and sisters got as much hate for him as I do. They ain't tryina mess wit' him. They just caterin' to Mama 'cause they know she still love his sorry ass!"

Things weren't going too well, and my next comment didn't help, which was, "Well . . . you haven't been home in a while—maybe they all got past what he did and decided to let bygones be bygones."

Bad choice of words.

He retorted, "Bygones? Man, you don't know what the hell you talkin' about."

"Wait a minute, all I'm saying is—"

Contempt filled his voice. "Naw, I don't wanna talk to you about this no more. You gittin' on my nerves wit' this ol' bullshit you spittin'. You don't even know nobody in my family well enough to be talkin' 'bout how they feel and what they done got past. You just need to *be* quiet and come on here so we can go to the house, pack, and leave."

I felt my heart hit the grass. I was so mad, I could've spit in his face, but I was also hurt, because he had never spoken to me that way before.

I told him point-blank, "First of all, don't you *ever* disrespect me like that again. You don't order me to do *shit,* okay? If you want me to do something with you or for you, you *ask* me. Second of all, I'm not goin' *nowhere* with you. I'm not the one runnin' from my issues, here, you are. So if *you* wanna pack and leave tonight, you go right ahead. I'm not packin' a *damn* thang and jumpin' on *nobody's* plane this evening. I'm enjoyin' myself. And guess what? Your family is enjoyin' *me,* and I'm *not* ready to go. So if I hafta fly back by myself, then fine. I'll see you back in Oakland tomorrow night."

I turned and started walking away. Weston realized what he had done and who he was dealing with, and jumped right to attention. He grabbed my arm before I could take three steps and pleaded, "Baby, wait . . . please . . . don't leave. Please . . . I'm sorry . . . I'm just trippin' right now. My father got me ready to blow a fuse."

I just frowned at him.

He looked me dead in the eyes. "Katrice . . . I apologize. I didn't mean to disrespect you. I can't even believe I just said that to you. This ain't your fault. I'm just scared, that's all."

I softened up a bit. "Scared of what?"

He paused before he started speaking. "You know, I got a lotta issues to work through about him, and I'm afraid to stay here wit' all this pent-up anger in me. I'm afraid he's gon' say or do somethin' that's gon' set me off, and if that happens and me and my Pops get into it, that'll destroy my mama. You know she's my heart. I don't wanna take no chances of hurtin' her like that, and right now, I don't think I'ma be able to control my anger around him. So I just . . . I don't think I can stay here, baby. My blood is boilin'."

I knew this was the moment that I was supposed to do what every great girlfriend is supposed to do, which would be say something supportive, but again, this type of relationship was totally new to me. I was used to relationships filled with fluff. You know—I like him, he likes me, we hook up, we have fun, we have a spat or two here and there, we grow apart (translation: I get bored), we break up. Kind of like what happened with a few of my exes over the years, like Isaiah, Anton, and Greg. They were great guys, and I did care for all of them in different ways, but there was just no real depth to what we had. What I was experiencing with Weston was completely different. With the others, nobody was going through any major emotional turmoil, nobody was dealing with deep issues that appeared to warrant therapy, and nobody was threatening to do bodily harm to people they loved. All of my relationships had been, well, fluffy . . . up until that point.

I knew that before I spoke a single word to him, I had to be on top of my game, or else the next time I tried to walk away, he might not stop me. Then, in an instant, something awesome came to me, and I knew exactly what my man needed to hear. Whether he would listen or not was another story.

I let out a heavy sigh, the kind that says you're about to embark on a make-or-break situation. I took Weston's hand and coerced, "Come—sit down with me for a minute." I pulled him lightly off to the side of the tree and sat in a healthy, vibrantly green patch of grass. He didn't speak a word and sat down next to me. Then I studied his face for a second. His wheels were spinning a hundred miles an hour as he looked out into the distance.

I took a deep breath and began. "You know, my father and his brother never got along. I remember every family function we had, somehow or other, they would always end up in a verbal war, and they almost came to blows more times than I could count. I don't know what their deal was. I couldn't even begin to tell you. But my father used to talk about my uncle like a dog. Never had anything nice to say about him. Now, I don't know what my uncle was doing behind my daddy's back, but my mother used to always tell my father that if he and his brother didn't work their problems out, one of them was gonna be sorry for the rest of his life.

"I was young then, so I didn't really understand what she meant by that, but I knew whatever she said, it was for a deep reason, and I always knew she knew what she was talking about, even if in the moment, I didn't." I glanced over at Weston, who was still looking out into nothingness, but I could tell he was hearing me.

I continued. "So, anyway, this fighting and dogging each other out went on for like five more years. Then, one day, out the blue, my uncle just fell over at the dinner table and died. Turns out, he had an aneurysm. Everyone thought that when my father found out, he would almost do a cheer, he hated my uncle so much . . . or so it seemed. But what ended up happening was, when my mother told him, before she could even really finish her sentence, my father started clutching his heart and yelling *no* at the top of his lungs, then his knees buckled and he fell to the floor and started wailing like I've never seen anyone do in my life. When my mother tried to comfort him, he pushed her away and said if his brother was gone, he wanted to go, too. For like five minutes, he kept saying, 'If my brother's gone, I wanna go, too.'"

By now, Weston was looking at me with this intense stare that almost scared me. Then I saw it in his eyes, I was reaching him. I went on. "So, we were all standing there and nobody knew what to do because we weren't expecting him to react like that. Eventually, my mother told us all to just leave him alone, so we did. At his funeral, my father didn't say a single word. He just sat there expressionless, looking like he was in a trance. Then, when it was time to view the body, he waited for everyone else to go, and he told my mother that he wanted to do his last viewing alone. After we all left the room, we waited outside the door. We could hear my father crying and talking to my uncle, telling him how sorry he was for all the fighting. Then he started telling him how much he loved him and he would never get over his being gone. We kept hearing him say, 'Wake up, so you can hear me say I'm sorry. I need you to hear me say it.' It was the saddest thing I ever saw, I'm telling you. And you know what? My father hasn't been quite right since."

I was on a roll, and I was damn proud of myself, too. My man looked at me with childlike innocence and waited for me to finish my story. So, I concluded with, "So, my point is that . . . I know you think you hate your father, and I know you think you never wanna talk to him again, and I'm not even gonna try to pretend I understand where you're comin' from. *But,* I love you, and I plan on bein' around for a real long time, damn it, and I don't want *you* to be the one who ends up bein' sorry for the rest of your life. You never know . . . anything could happen.

"Now I just met your father, so I hafta say, my concern is really for you right now. I don't ever wanna see you go through what my father did. It just doesn't even need to happen. So, I really think you need to talk to your father before we go home. You don't hafta have a long, drawn-out conversation. Just take a minute to ask him why he left, and hear what he has to say. That's all. Just start there. You gotta start somewhere, so why not start at the bottom line. You don't know why he left, and he's got the answer. So, go get it. I'm willing to bet my life savings he'll tell you what you wanna know. And don't sit up here and try to tell me you don't wanna know, 'cause I think you'd be lying. Even if on the surface you *think* you don't, deep down, I believe everyone wants to know why someone they love hurt them."

Weston closed his eyes real tight and held them like that for a good ten seconds. When he opened them, he looked at me with anguish on his face and said, "If I talk to him, you gotta be there with me. I can't talk to him alone. I don't trust myself."

I wasn't sure about that. "You know, I really think you should try to talk to him one-on-one and—"

"No. For real. If you don't come with me, it ain't goin' down. I can't do it. I need you there."

At this point, even though the whole idea made me uneasy, there was no way I was gonna turn my back on my man, so I assured him, "Okay. I'll come with you. Whatever you want me to do, I'll do it."

He nodded, pursed his lips together and said, "I don't know what I'd do without you. I might lose my mind if somethin' happened to us. I love you so much, and I'm already knowin' I can't lose you to nothin' or no one." Then he pulled me into him and kissed me on my forehead with passion and put his arms around me.

I was so overwhelmed, all I could manage to say was, "I feel the same way."

After a moment, I got up, brushed myself off and asked him, "You ready to go back to the table?"

"In a little bit. I just wanna sit here and think for a while. You go ahead. I'll be over there soon."

I returned the action, and kissed him on the forehead. "'Kay." I smiled and then slowly walked away.

As I walked back to the table, I had a whole new sense of myself and who I was. I felt like for the first time, I helped someone over a hurdle that they didn't think they would jump. It made me feel good. Really good. Especially since the person I helped was someone who was rapidly turning into the love of my life. I stopped to glance back at Weston, who was deep in thought. I realized at that moment that my relationship with him was far from fluffy, and that was just fine with me.

Later that evening, after all the festivities were over, a bunch of Weston's family members wanted to go out to the club, but Weston declined. He said he had something he needed to take care of first. After he said that, he looked at me as if silently reminding me of what I promised him.

When we got back to Weston's mother's house, as fate would have it, the only people there were Lorraine and Sonny. Weston's brothers and sisters were all over at his cousin's house, so nobody would be expected back anytime soon. Sonny was helping his ex-wife clean up and put things away. When we walked into the living room, we could hear the two of them in the kitchen, yapping like old friends.

Weston stepped into the doorway of the kitchen and cleared his throat, to announce that we were there. Lorraine and Sonny both turned around at the same time and looked at us. Weston said an apprehensive, "Hey, y'all," then he looked at me for approval. I nodded for him to proceed.

He squeezed my hand as tight as he could, looked at his father and asked, "Uh . . . Pop . . . can uh . . . can I holla at you for a minute?"

Sonny looked at Lorraine in complete surprise, then looked back at his son and said an almost excited, "Sure." He put down the dish towel he was holding and excused himself from Lorraine.

Weston suggested, "Let's step outside on the patio."

He wouldn't let go of my hand. We all went outside, and before we sat down at the table with the umbrella, Sonny looked at me as if to ask why I was still there. Weston saw that and informed him, "I want her to stay for this, Pop . . . I *need* her to stay."

Sonny had no idea what was going on, so all he did was nod, then he pulled out a chair and sat down.

After Weston and I sat, too, Weston took a deep breath and dove right in. He looked his father in the face and said, "Basically, I just need to know why you left us, Pop. I don't really have nothin' else to say . . . I just . . . need you to tell me that, then I'm'a go."

Without hesitation, Sonny began speaking, almost as if he had been waiting forever for this moment and wanted to seize it before his son changed his mind. "The day I left you all, I went and checked myself into a drug rehab center in New York."

I think I stopped breathing for a second. I wasn't expecting that kind of answer. And so bluntly put.

I guess Weston wasn't either, because he scrunched up his face and looked at his father like he had said the most ridiculous thing. "Drug rehab . . . what'choo . . . I don't understand what'choo talkin' 'bout, Pop. What'choo sayin'?"

Sonny continued. "Weston, I hid it very well for a long time, but I had a severe drug problem that I couldn't get over. I had been on drugs for years and after Tamika was born, it spiraled all the way out of control." He stopped to give his son a chance to absorb the mind-blowing information.

Weston shook his head in confusion. "Pop . . . you actually tellin' me you was doin' drugs? I mean, what kinda drugs? I'm not . . . I don't get this . . ."

Sonny went on to say, "It started with just some innocent weed smokin' with some of the boys. You know, just to relax after a hard day's work. Marijuana was all I did for a long time. Then one night, one of the guys came in with some snort, and a few others jumped right on it, like they had been waiting for it to arrive. At first, I looked at all of 'em like they were crazy. They offered me some and told me I didn't know what I was missin'. The first few times they offered, I just shook my head at 'em and went on back to my blunt. Told 'em I didn't wanna be a part of that scene. Then one day, after I had gotten laid off, I was stressed out 'cause I didn't know what I was gonna do. The twins couldn'ta been more than about two or three, plus there was already you and Leslie. Money was tight, and I was worried I wouldn't be able to pull my weight and your mother would leave me."

Weston's mouth was hanging open, and I was trying to do my best to keep mine closed. He was still holding my hand, but he had eased up on the grip.

Then his father said, "So, this one particular day, I was overwhelmed and feelin' sorry for myself. One of the guys offered me some snort. Said it would ease my mind. I thought about it for a second, then, before I thought twice, I told him to show me how it was done. Next thing I knew, I was experiencing my first snort high. After that day, things went downhill for me. I was snorting at least three times a week, and at the time, I was able to do it for free because the guys were being 'generous.' But that was just to get me hooked. Once I was, they started charging me, but by then, I didn't care. I wanted it . . . bad. Even though I finally got another job, that didn't matter. Actually, that was right up my alley, 'cause then I could afford to buy the stuff.

"I started skimming off the top of my paychecks to go buy my stash on a regular basis. That went on for almost a year. Not long after that, Monica was born. I really don't know how I was able to hide all this from your mother, but I managed it. Really, I think she was just so busy with you kids that her attention wasn't focused on me as much."

I think Weston would have said something by then, but he was too flabbergasted, so he just continued to look at his father like he couldn't believe what was coming out of his mouth.

"Eventually, your mother started asking me why I always had the sniffles. She asked me if I had developed an allergy to something, but I just brushed her off and told her it was nothing. After that, I was too hooked to give it up, so I started trying to find other methods to get high. A friend told me about a guy who could hook me up with something even better. And so began my days of shooting up."

Finally, Weston spoke. "Wait a minute . . . my head is spinnin' . . . Pop . . . you . . . you were shootin' up? You had a family and . . . and responsibilities. How could you do that to us? I mean, and how could you do that to yourself?"

"I can't explain what it feels like to be addicted to drugs, son. The only thing I can say is, it had me—

and I was in too deep to just walk away from it. Pretty soon, things started getting bad between your mother and me. I was always high, and even though she didn't know it, she knew something was wrong with me. We started arguing all the time, and I knew something needed to change. I loved your mother and you kids and I didn't wanna lose what I had. By that time, Tamika was about six months old.

"One night, I came home high as a kite and your mother and I got into a terrible fight. I think Leslie was at a party and you were over at Eric's house at that time. Anyway, the fight got so bad that I almost hit your mother. I actually raised my hand to her, but when I saw the fear in her eyes, fortunately, I was able to stop myself. But as soon as I did, I knew it was time for me to go, before I got put out.

"That next day, I left like I was going to work, but I never went. I spent the morning downtown at a pay phone, searching for a rehab center to check myself into. I called at least twenty of 'em, and I finally decided on one in New York. If I was gonna really be serious and try to get myself together, I knew I would need to leave the state, so I made plans to leave the next morning.

"My initial intention was to go home and tell your mother what was going on, but by the time I got there, I changed my mind. I started picturing us talking about it, and me getting cold feet. I wanted to strike while the iron was hot, so as hard as it was for me to do, I got up in the middle of the night, packed a bag, kissed your mother on the cheek while she was sleeping and left her a note on my pillow."

Weston asked, "What did it say?"

He thought back. "It said, *I hate to leave you all this*

*way, but I have to. One day I'll make you understand.
I love you and the kids. Always remember that.*"

Weston opened up just a smidge. "So, what happened after that?"

"I took a cab to the airport at three in the morning and waited there until my flight boarded at eight. Then I left and didn't look back until I got myself together. It was the hardest thing I ever had to do, but I knew if I wanted to be whole again, there was no way around it. I relapsed twice, that's how bad things were. And I wanted to call you guys a thousand times, but I knew if I did, that would open the door for questions I wasn't ready to answer yet. Actually, I did call the house a buncha times, but I would always hang up as soon as one of you picked up the phone. Only one person knew where I was, and that was your uncle Walt. I had to tell someone I could trust to keep it under wraps. I had him keep an eye on you guys and report back to me on a regular basis, so I always knew the family was okay."

There was a superlong pause, and the three of us just sat there. Before Sonny could resume talking, Weston grabbed my hand tight again and said, "'Scuse us, Pop," and started getting up like he just remembered he had something to do. Since he had my hand, I sort of had no choice but to follow him. We got up and headed back into the house, and left Sonny sitting outside alone. He didn't try to stop us. Just pulled out a cigar, lit it, and leaned back in his chair.

When we got back in the house, Lorraine was sitting in the living room in a chair, knitting a sweater and watching television. She looked up at us, but didn't say anything. Weston and I sat down on the couch, and he paused for a minute. He was still gripping my hand.

Weston looked at his mother and asked her with great amounts of curiosity, "Mama . . . you know what all happened wit' Pop?"

She continued knitting, and said a simple, "Yes," and didn't look at him.

Then his brain formed another question, but he hesitated before he asked, as if he were afraid of the answer. "Everybody else know, too?" He looked at her out of the corner of his eye.

Again, all she said was, "Yes."

He wasn't happy about that at all. He finally dropped my hand, raised his voice and demanded to know, "How come everybody around here knows what's goin' on but me?"

But Lorraine was ready for him, and it was as if she already had her answer prepared before he even asked. "Because baby, you didn't wanna hear the truth. It's not like people didn't try to tell you what was goin' on. Whenever someone mentions your father, you just cut 'em off and change the subject. You and I have talked every week since you left home, and every time I tried to talk to you about your father, you told me you didn't wanna hear it. Your brothers and sisters all said you did the same thing to them when they tried to talk to you about him. Leslie told me when she called you and told you that your father had returned, but that we were getting a divorce, you said, 'Good, that's all I need to know; don't say no more on the subject.' Even your father tried to tell you what was going on."

"Mama, that's not true. Pop never said anything to me about this."

His mother put down her knitting, sat upright and looked at her son like she couldn't believe her ears.

"I beg your pardon, young man? Did you just say your father never said anything to you?"

"Yeah." He sounded sure of himself.

Lorraine started in on him. "When you left here to move to California with Eric, your father came out of rehab five months later. He came here and sat us all down together and told us what was going on. You were the only one who wasn't here, and your father wanted to make sure you knew the truth, too. I gave him your address and phone number so he could get in touch with you, and do you know what he told me?" She glared angrily at him.

Weston didn't answer. Just looked away and started tearing up, like he knew what she was gonna say next.

She continued. "He told me he called you numerous times and you never called him back. Said he left message after message and got nothing."

Weston started clenching his jaw, and a vein in his temple started throbbing.

She went on to say, "He also told me he wrote you *eight times* explaining himself, and all of his letters came back unopened and marked return to sender."

I could see Weston tearing up even more so now. His nostrils were making that small, rapid flaring motion that says a million tears are about to be released.

She said, "So don't you sit up here and accuse folks of leavin' you in the dark, when you didn't have the decency and the heart to listen to what any of us had to say, or give your father even half a chance to try to make things right with you."

This was deeper than I could've ever imagined. I still felt sort of uncomfortable sitting right in the middle of all this, but it was too late now. I was all up in the business, and there was no turning back.

Weston let out a small puff of air and gasped it back up, then, I saw a tear drop from each of his eyes.

He tried to defend himself. "He coulda told me about all this when we were all here when you had yo' surgery, if it was that important." He pouted, wiped his eyes and then added, "I didn't hear him tryina fill me in then."

She jumped down his throat again. "Boy, people get tired of chasin' folks that don't wanna listen. Your father made his efforts; more than he shoulda had to, if you ask me. But you made it clear that you didn't wanna have anything to do with him, so he just went ahead and let it go. What did you expect—him to run after you forever?"

The dam broke, and my man started to cry full on. I caressed his back ever so gently, and I think that made him cry even harder. I had never experienced anything so deep with a man in my entire life. The only man I had ever really seen cry was my father, and that was when his brother died. Seeing my baby let his guard down like that and be totally vulnerable was an experience I can't even describe.

Lorraine saw the pain her son was in, so she got up, walked over to him and gently lifted his head up by the chin with her right hand. She looked into his sad eyes and said, compassionately, "Honey, people make mistakes. You expect everybody to be perfect, and they're not. You gotta open your heart a little more. Learn to listen. Learn to try to understand people. 'Specially people you love." Then she wiped her child's eyes, kissed him on the cheek, smiled and winked at me, then gracefully walked away.

The woman was amazing. If I didn't already think my own mother was just as great, I might've been jealous.

The two of us sat for a moment in silence while Weston stared out the living room window into the darkness. Finally, he ran his hands over his wet face, turned to me and said, "I'll be back." He leaned over and kissed my lips, then got up.

I didn't know what to do, so I got up, too. But then he asked me, "You gon' be okay by yourself for a little while?" I knew that was my cue to let him handle this one alone. He started heading back out to the patio where his father was.

"Yeah . . . um . . . I'm gonna . . . go in the den to relax. I brought some magazines I wanna read. You go ahead."

He doubled back and kissed me again. "Thanks, baby. I'm glad you're here. I wouldn't have been able to do this without you. I love you."

"I love you, too."

Weston woke me out of a dream when he got in bed at five in the morning. When he slid his arm around me, I turned over and asked him, "Is everything okay? It's five o'clock, baby."

He whispered, "Yeah. I went over to my pop's crib. He don't live too far from here, 'bout twenty minutes away. We started talkin' and catchin' up. I think we might be okay in time."

"I'm glad. Don't you feel better? At least now you know the truth."

"Yeah." He smoothed my hair. "Go back to sleep, baby. I didn't mean to wake you up."

"That's okay."

"I'm so glad you came with me."

"I am, too."

Weston slept in while Lorraine, Leslie, Monica, Tamika, and I all went to get a spa treatment later that morning. It was our last day in Chicago, and Lorraine said she wanted us girls to do something relaxing before it was time for Weston and me to leave.

By the time we got back, Weston was already up and about, and had packed both our belongings so we wouldn't have to rush to do it later.

At four o'clock, everyone gathered at the house to say goodbye to us, then Lorraine took us to the airport to send us off.

Just before boarding the plane, we said our goodbyes, and I thanked Lorraine for a wonderful time. She demanded that Weston bring me back soon, and he quickly agreed to that.

We both slept for most of the flight home, and by the time we got back on Northern Californian ground, I was wiped out. We both had to work the next day, so Weston took me home. I was glad he didn't wanna spend the night, because I knew if he did, I wouldn't get any sleep.

He helped me get my bags inside, and I thanked him again for taking me to Chicago with him. He assured me that there would be many more trips home for the two of us.

I smiled at the thought, kissed him, and sent him on his way.

11

I believe that every relationship has a defining moment. It's the moment when you know that the person you're with is the one person you don't want to live without. Up until Chicago, I knew I loved Weston. After Chicago is when I knew without a doubt that I wanted to marry him.

I had taken Weston to Lake Tahoe over Labor Day weekend, since he said he had never been. We stayed in a little bed and breakfast inn, saw the sights, relaxed, ate well, and did a lot of lovemaking.

Upon returning home, I felt a cold coming on, and I told Weston I didn't feel good. By the next morning, I had the worst case of the flu imaginable. It just attacked me. My head was throbbing, I was coughing, sneezing, couldn't breathe, had chills, and felt sick as a dog. To top everything off, I started my period, and had cramps for days. I had to cancel all my appointments for that day, and Tiki said she would find a way to fill in for me for a few more.

When Weston called me to find out if I felt any

better, he was mortified at how I sounded, and said he'd be right over. Before I could tell him not to come because I didn't want him to get sick, he had already hung up.

Not thirty minutes later, he was at my door. When I opened it, he blew past me with a duffel bag in hand, mumbling something about looking in the kitchen to see what I needed from the store.

I had never looked more horrific, and I was embarrassed for Weston to see me that way. My hair was matted down, my breath was funky, I had snot-crust under my nose, my lips were white, and my eyes were bloodshot.

I followed him into the kitchen, where he was opening and closing cabinets, looking in the fridge and writing on a pad of paper.

"Weston . . . what are you doing? You shouldn't be here. You'll get sick."

He didn't even look up from writing on the paper, but clearly, he was talking to me. "Let's see . . . you need you some chicken noodle soup . . . oh, better yet, some of that hot 'n' sour stuff . . . that'll knock it out. Well, I'll just get both. Some lemon tea, some fruit, oh, and duh, some orange juice . . . and some crackers. What else you need?" He looked up at me.

Before I could speak, he asked me, "You got any Vicks VapoRub?"

"Um . . . I don't . . . I don't think so. . . . Baby, what are you doing? You need to leave before I get you sick. I can go to the store some other time for all that stuff."

He ignored me.

"You got a cough?"

"Yeah."

"You got any cold medicine or anything like that around here?"

"No, because I hardly ever get sick."

"'Scuse me." He passed me to go into the bathroom.

He started shuffling through my medicine cabinet, and I just stood there, confused, but amazed nonetheless.

When he came out, he asked me, "Where's the tissue?"

"Toilet tissue?"

"No, babe, tissue so you can blow your nose. You got any? I didn't see any in there."

"In my purse, in one of those little travel packs, but—"

"Okay, anything else you need?"

I gave up on trying to get him to leave so he could stay healthy, because it was obvious he had his own agenda.

"I don't think so."

I also forgot I only had a couple of sanitary napkins left. I don't usually let myself get that low, but I was so into our trip and the fun I was having that I completely forgot I was due to start it, and I failed to replenish my stock before we left town. I was most definitely *not* gonna ask him to buy me any, so I didn't say anything.

To my total amazement, he asked me, "Isn't it time for yo' period?"

"Yeah, but how would you know that?"

"'Cause I notice you're always on it around this time of the month. What's the date today . . . the fourth?"

"Yeah."

"Right. I always know not to try to get any around

the first week of the month. So, what do you use, pads or tampons?"

"Okay, I can't believe we're having this conversation. How are you just gonna ask me that like it's no big deal?" I wanted to laugh, but I felt too awful.

"'Cause it's not. What do you use?"

"Pads, but . . ."

"What kind?"

"Always, but . . ."

"You got any?"

"As a matter of fact, I'm down to my last two, but you can't go up in the store buying pads for me."

"Why not? It's nothin' I haven't done before. Remember, I got a mother and three sisters. I prob'ly been to the store for pads more times than you have. Besides, they know I ain't buyin' 'em for *myself,* so what's the big deal?"

I chuckled through my pounding head and snotty nose.

"I guess nothing, then."

"Okay, so I'm'a go to the store and git this stuff on the list. I'll be right back." He moved his duffle bag from the floor to the couch.

"What's in the bag?"

"My stuff. I'm stayin' here and takin' care of you. I'm off today, remember?"

"You can't stay here. We'll both be dead by Thursday."

"No, *you'll* be feelin' *better* by Thursday and I'm'a make sure of it."

"There is no way I'm gonna let you sleep in the same bed with me while I'm sick."

"Who said anything about me sleepin' with you?

I'm sleepin' on the couch. But I'm still stayin' the night. Ay, you got a thermometer?" He felt my head.

I laughed. "Yeah, I think I do."

"What's so funny?"

That made me laugh even harder and made my head throb more.

"I don't know what's so funny, but take your temperature while I'm gone. You feel kinda hot."

I kept laughing, and he looked at me like I was silly, then walked out the door.

He came back about forty-five minutes later and ordered me to get in bed, since I was sitting on the couch watching television. He made me some soup that I threw up not twenty minutes after I ate, and he was right there to help me clean up the mess, since I didn't make it to the toilet bowl in time.

Later, after he made me take some medicine, he rubbed me down with Vicks, changed my bedding for me, did the dishes that were in the sink, straightened up the living room, and stroked my hair until I fell asleep.

When I woke up the next morning, he was sound asleep on the couch. I got up, walked over to the couch, stood over him, and watched him sleep. I knew without a doubt that no matter what, I *had* to marry the man. I had never loved him more in that moment, and it was then that I was sure I had found my soul mate.

12

I couldn't believe how fast time had flown. It was already May, and Tiki was marrying Charles in two days. Weston was supposed to go with me to the wedding, but it fell on the same day as Kevin's graduation from UCLA. Actually, that only happened because Charles sprained his wrist, and they ended up moving the wedding date from the tenth to the twenty-fifth to give it time to heal.

I asked Tiki if it had to be on that day, and she said that was the only other day they could book the church for the wedding. Weston and I were disappointed that he wouldn't be able to be there, but family comes first.

After I sent Weston off to L.A., Tiki and I ran ourselves ragged trying to take care of last-minute details. The flowers, the dress, the food, the decorations—the list went on and on.

Even though Tiki wasn't close to Sabrina, Chantelle, and Genine, they had all met and they got along fine. She had extended invitations to them, but they all had conflicting plans, and told her they wouldn't be able to attend. They helped out with what they could the day before the wedding, and Tiki greatly appreciated it.

Tiki's wedding day was sunny and warm, and my girl was a radiant bride. Charles was handsome and debonair, and looked happier than I had ever seen him in life.

I was looking damn good, if I do say so myself, with my long white Ann Taylor dress on, showing off my figure; and my three-inch-heeled Enzo Angiolinis to match. My makeup was fierce and my hair was sharp.

The wedding was simple, yet romantic, and Tiki and Charles recited their own vows, which were very touching to hear. The church was packed with both friends and family of the bride and groom. At one point, I thought we were gonna run out of seats.

I wasn't a bridesmaid, which was fine, because I was ill-prepared for that task anyway, and I sat in the front so I could see the show up close.

Right after the wedding, everyone drove over to the center that Tiki and Charles rented for the reception. After most everyone had arrived and the bride and groom made their grand entrance, we sat down to a mighty feast and stuffed our faces.

Once the music started, people started mingling and dancing. There were a lot of people from high school there that Charles and I used to hang out with, and it was great to see and talk with them all after so many years. A few of them I still saw every blue moon, but it was nice to catch up with them, too.

Around five-thirty, I had gone over to the punch bowl to get a refill on my drink when from behind me I heard a voice so familiar that it made the hairs on my arms stand on end.

"Sweet Mother of Jesus. Katrice Vincent. Look at you. Still as fine as ever."

My eyes bugged out of my head and I stopped filling my cup with punch. I froze for about three seconds before I turned around, because I already knew who it was.

Royce Phillip Jordan III.

I put my punch down and turned around as slowly as I could, and when I finally faced him, I almost dropped out right at his feet. He was grinning from ear to ear, and was so beautiful I wanted to scream.

I couldn't speak. Literally. My throat locked up on me. I couldn't even swallow. Looking at him at that moment took me right back to high school. I flashed to the day he rejected me, and I had to fight the emotions that were rising from within. I felt like I had a boulder rolling around in my stomach.

Since it was apparent that I couldn't get myself together to speak, he spoke.

"So, how you doin'? Damn, you lookin' *good* girl. Actually, good is a grave understatement."

His voice sounded five times deeper than I remembered it, but it was still the same smooth, soothing voice I used to have fantasies about whispering sweet nothings in my ear; it was just more mature.

Finally, I managed to squeak out, "I'm fine. And you?"

I didn't even blink.

He chuckled. "Damn, girl, you actin' like you scared of a brotha. Can I get a hug or somethin'? I haven't seen you in at least a decade." He opened his arms and stepped closer to me.

Royce and I had never even touched once in the fifteen years we had known each other, so I found his asking for a hug highly unusual. Nevertheless, I tried to loosen up a bit. I gave him a hug, but it was an awfully timid one, and I barely wrapped my arms all the way around him.

His touch was electrifying, and he smelled of an outstanding cologne that I couldn't quite place the name of, but I was too frazzled to ask him what it was. I pulled away before six seconds could pass, because standing there having his arms around me was really messing with my head.

I tried to pull myself together, because now I was curious as to why he was there. Royce and Charles had been good friends in high school, but I had no idea they had been in touch since Royce had moved.

Back in the day, I don't even think Charles knew I liked Royce. I still harbored feelings for him, but once I'd fallen in love with Troy, I made it a point to push those feelings aside. Eventually, I think even Royce assumed I was over him, because my demeanor around him totally changed.

I asked him finally, "So, what brings you here? Didn't you move back East or something?"

"Yep. I live in Maryland. I left here to go work with my dad at his company. He owns a used-car lot, and he had been asking me to come out there and live with him for a long time. I asked him if he would put me on at the lot, and he said yeah. I work in the finance department. His business is big out there. Makes a ton of money. He's always been real business-savvy, which is why I wanted to work with him. I wasn't really doin' much here after I graduated from high school, so I said what the hell. It's been a good move for me. I've grown a lot since I left Oakland.

"Me and Charles stayed in close touch over the

years, so when he told me he was getting married, he asked me if I would make a trip out here. I told him I wouldn't miss it for the world. When he told me he was marrying your shop partner, I assumed you would be here, too, and that gave me even more incentive to come."

I heard that last part about my being there giving him incentive, but since he was never interested in me before, that didn't make any sense to me. I figured I must have misunderstood what he said, so I didn't even ask him to elaborate on that statement.

I looked at him quizzically. "Have you been here the whole time? I mean, were you at the wedding, too? Because I didn't see you."

"Yeah, I was there. I saw you, but I was sitting towards the back. To be honest, I was actually watching you. I wanted to talk to you then, but before I got a chance to say anything to you at the church, you were out the door so quick to get over here that I missed you. I told myself I was gonna make sure I caught you at the reception."

Again, I couldn't figure out where he was coming from. The way he was talking, you would think we had something going back in the day.

He asked me, "You wanna go outside to the courtyard and talk? It's kinda noisy in here."

I was still confused about his whole reaction to me, but I was definitely interested in talking to him, so I grabbed my punch and said, "Sure. Let's go."

When we got outside, we found a private little area and sat down. For about ten minutes, we had small talk. He told me some more about Maryland, I told him all about the shop and meeting Tiki and how she and Charles hooked up, and by that time, the ice was finally broken.

After a long pause, Royce looked at me and asked, "You got a man?"

That caught me off guard.

"Um . . . yes, I do."

"Is he here?"

"No, he's in L.A. at his brother's college graduation. Why?"

"Hmmm . . . already taken. That's too bad."

"Huh?" I said through squinted eyes. "Why is that too bad?"

"Because I would really love to get outta here with you and go somewhere we can be alone. I'm stayin' in Jack London Square. We could go back to my room, if you want."

I almost fell off my seat. It was clear to me now that I wasn't misunderstanding anything he was saying. He was trying to get at me after fifteen years. My head was spinning.

After a moment, I asked him, "How are you all of a sudden interested in me?"

"It's not all of a sudden. I've always been interested."

"No, you haven't. In high school, you gave me absolutely no play. I mean, we talked on occasion, but it wasn't like you tried to get with me."

"I was young and immature back then. I was also insecure, if you wanna know the truth."

I wasn't convinced. "Okay, now young and immature, I'll take. But insecure? You can have that one."

"That's no lie. I was very insecure as a teenager."

"In what way? And what did your supposed insecurity have to do with me?"

"Look, I was sixteen, smart, popular, good

lookin'—and yeah, I knew I could pretty much have any girl I wanted at that time—"

"But, you didn't want me."

"Yes I did. I just never put it out there."

"Do you remember what you said to me that day comin' from the gym?"

"Yeah, I do, as a matter of fact."

"'Cause I remember it like it was an hour ago. And it still hurts."

"I remember what I said. I told you that you weren't my type . . . that you didn't really have what I was lookin' for."

I was surprised he remembered. "Yeah, and I cried every day for three weeks over that. So how can you stand up here now, fifteen years later, and tell me you were interested in me back then?"

I got up and stood about a foot away from him, then, I looked at him angrily and flashed my scarred arm at him.

"You see this scar?" I ran my finger all the way down its raised, textured length. "*You* did this. I got this the day you said that to me. And remember my sprained ankle? That all happened right after you sent me packing and walked away like you didn't have a care in the world. I was so upset that I ran off. I tripped in a pothole and fell right in front of the whole damn school. I never got over that day. Never. You just don't look a person in the face after they've professed their feelings to you, and tell them . . . they don't have what you *want*. You just don't do that to people. You really damaged me, Royce. I was just a girl. Just a *kid*. And you kicked me in the heart."

He got up, too, and came towards me.

"I'm sorry about all that. I didn't mean to hurt you."

I found myself getting angrier by the second. "Sorry? That's all you got?"

"Look, I knew I had it goin' on, no doubt; but I also knew you did, too. You were so fine, and you had yo' head on straight, had yo' little crew, and you carried yo'self like you didn't even *need* a man. On one hand, it was attractive as hell, but on the other hand, wit' all that goin' on, I knew *you* could have any dude *you* wanted, too. I knew if we hooked up, everywhere we went, you'd be turnin' heads and attractin' all kinds of attention. To me, that meant I wouldn't have your full focus. Young ladies like attention, just like guys do. I saw all the play you got in high school, even after you started goin' wit' Troy. I used to wonder how in the hell he dealt wit' that, too. I just . . . I wasn't in a mindset to be able to handle that. If I had you, I knew I wanted to have you all to myself. I didn't even want you *lookin'* at another dude. All eyes on me, that's where I was at, you know? That's just real, baby. Wasn't that I didn't want you, I just couldn't deal wit' nobody *else* wantin' you and tryina take you away from me."

"And what made you think someone would even be able to take me from you? That's pretty presumptuous of you to think I'd be that fickle."

"All I can say is, I guess I was just scared."

"Of what?"

"That I would get sprung. Fall in love with you and you'd hurt me. What can I say? I was a player. A player breaks hearts. And a player always makes sure he's dealin' with a woman who's not likely to break *his* heart. I knew . . . I knew you could be the one woman to break mine."

I couldn't believe my ears. Not for one damn second.

Royce Phillip Jordan III, my lifelong obsession, was
actually standing right in my face, telling me he wanted
me. I wanted to pass out, but then I felt myself getting
offended.

I asked him, "So now, after all this time, you just
wanna hit it right quick? Is that it?"

He looked at me with all the sincerity in the world.
"No. That's not all I want. I want a lot more than that."

He really had my attention then. "But—"

"But I'm leavin' day after tomorrow, and I don't
plan on comin' back no time soon. My life is in
Maryland now. And even if I did come back one day,
I know you'll probably be married with children by
then. A woman like you ain't gon' be on the market
forever. This dude you with right now—I can probably bet he don't have no intention of lettin' you go."

My eyes told him he was right. I knew Weston was
in it to win it.

He continued. "So, since I can't have the long
term, I just want whatever I can have with you . . .
right now . . . for tonight. I can tell by the look on
your face that you love your man. So, it's up to you.
If dancin', drinks and conversation is it, then hey, I
guess I gotta respect that. But, if you say you'll come
with me and be mine for the night, wrong and selfish
as it may be, I'll jump at the opportunity quicker than
you can blink."

And there it all was, right there on the table for me
to drool over. I had fantasized for a decade and a half
about him saying something like this to me, but never
in my wildest imagination did I picture him saying
anything so deep, and I certainly never thought my
fantasy would come true. But now he was here, looking better than I had ever seen him look in life. And

he wanted me. And I had a man. A man that I loved more than I could ever explain to anyone.

All of a sudden, it felt like there was cotton stuffed in my head, and the air got real thin. I wished Weston had come, then, none of this would have ever happened. Then, as soon as I thought about it, his being there didn't sound like such a good idea. I don't think I could've handled the two of them being in the same room together.

The silence was long, and Royce must have seen the horror on my face, because he asked, "Hey . . . are . . . you okay? I didn't mean to upset you. . . ."

"No . . . I'm okay . . . um . . . would you just . . . excuse me for a minute?"

He gave me a worried look. "Yeah, sure. I'll wait out here till you get back."

Without even looking at him, I darted to the bathroom. I tried not to run, so as not to draw too much attention to myself, so I just sort of half-walked, half-trotted.

I passed Charles on the way there and he called out, "Ay, girl, where you been?"

I ignored his question, and instead, pointed toward the bathroom with urgency and said a rushed, "Gotta go! Talk to you in a minute!"

When I got in there, it was full of women. They were talking, laughing, touching up their makeup, combing their hair, and coming out of bathroom stalls. I felt myself about to start crying, but I held it in until I was able to get inside a stall and close the door. I went into the handicapped one, and in my excitement, I accidentally slammed the door. It bounced back open and hit my left arm. As I cursed the door, my purse dropped to the floor and all of my makeup and change fell out. Quarters, dimes, pennies, lipsticks, lip liners, and mascara went crashing down and rolled around inside the stall. I was so flustered and frenzied that I didn't even bother to pick anything up right away. Instead, I took off my jacket, hung it on the door and leaned up against the wall.

I put my hand over my mouth and started breathing heavy. After a minute, I started to cry. I thought about Weston, and how much I loved him. How cheating on him is the last thing I ever imagined I would consider doing. Then I thought about Royce, and how ever since the first day of my freshman year in high school, I had idolized him. How I had told everyone around that I wanted him and that one day, I would make him mine. I thought about how even when I was dating Troy, and every other guy I got involved with, there was always this piece of me that held on to the fantasy of Royce coming to sweep me off my feet one day. My thoughts were all over the place, from Weston to Royce to myself. I thought about all that Weston and I had been through and how much our relationship meant to me. I thought about us getting married and having a family. I also thought about the fact that on occasion, when I was with him, I thought of Royce. Wondering where he was and what he was doing . . . and who he was doing it with.

My head started hurting, and my stomach felt queasy. I looked down at the floor and realized that my belongings were still strewn all over. I wiped my eyes, gathered my senses and started picking up my stuff.

Once I was done putting everything back in my purse, I focused on the subject at hand. There was a man out there waiting for me to make a serious decision. A man I had never fully gotten over. A man who was offering me something I had always wanted from him, and still wanted. It was a dreadful dilemma. If I were to go with Royce and live out my fantasy, would the guilt kill me? Would I be able to look my beautiful man in the face day after day and still feel worthy of him? Or, if I were to pass up Royce's offer, would I regret it forever? Would I spend the rest of my life pining for him and beating myself up for letting this night get by me? So many questions, so much at stake, and so much love involved between Weston and me.

Then, my brain took a different turn. I realized that my wanting to be with Royce had nothing to do with how I felt about Weston. It wasn't like I was dissatisfied with our relationship; in fact, things couldn't have been better between us. This was about me. About a craving that I had for another man that wouldn't go away because I never had the chance to kill the craving. Now that chance was before me, and my gut told me that if I took it, I would be relieved once and for all. Sometimes you just need to do something you've always wanted to do once, then it's out of your system for good. You don't crave it anymore. That was the feeling I was getting from this situation. I honestly felt that if I went with him, that after that night, I would be able to breathe a sigh of relief, tuck the memory away in a special place, and move on once and for all. The more I thought about it, the closer I came to making a final decision.

My last thought was of Weston and me, years into the future. We were married and had a family, but I was still hung up on Royce, because I turned his offer down. I pictured myself constantly thinking back and wishing I had gone with him. Then I pictured myself looking into Weston's eyes and wishing he were Royce. Even for a minute. I paused on that thought for nearly thirty seconds. I closed my eyes and really tried to put myself there, in the future with him, wishing he were Royce. The thought of potentially being in that situation scared me. I never wanted to look at him that way. Ever. And the thought of living the rest of my life with this deplorable craving and taking it to my grave was tearing my soul apart. Fifteen years is a long time to nurse an open wound, and I was tired of it. I wanted to close it up so it could heal, and I could finally be free.

When I opened my eyes, I made my decision. I was going to put this situation to rest once and for all so I could move on in peace with the man I truly loved. I decided to go with Royce.

I left the stall and stopped at the mirror. I was looking haggard, so I took out my mascara, some tissue, and my Fashion Fair lipstick and fixed my face.

One girl who was drying her hands and heading for the door turned to me and asked, "You okay, girl? I heard you crying in there."

"Yeah, just not feeling too good right now. But thanks." I tried to smile a little.

She smiled back and headed out the door.

After I got myself together, I went back out into the hallway and stood for a moment. I thought about the decision I had just made and pondered whether or not it was really what I was gonna do. I checked my watch and looked around. It was going on six o'clock. I thought about Weston, wondered what he was doing. I started missing him, so I pulled out my cell and dialed his number. I got his voicemail. I listened to his greeting, and my eyes started watering. I was gonna leave a message, but then I got a lump in my throat and couldn't think of what to say, so I hung up. Then I headed back to the courtyard to tell Royce I was all his for the evening.

He was sitting, waiting patiently for me, just as he promised.

He asked, "Everything okay?"

It took me a second to answer, but I finally said, "Uh-huh." Then I just stood there and looked at him. I was trying to think of what to say, but nothing would come to me.

He got up and moved slowly toward me, but I took two steps back. I was scared out of my wits. My mouth started feeling like someone had just put dust-balls in it. "Could you . . . um . . . do me a favor and go get me some more punch, please?"

I could tell by the look on his face he knew I was stalling for time. He smiled politely and said, "Sure. Be right back."

After he left, I sat down, rested my elbows on my knees and shoved my face in my hands. I asked myself again if this was really something I felt I could go through with. I felt perspiration running down from my underarms, and my hands went clammy, so I took them off my face. I looked around in the warm, still May night and thought once again about my man. I started wondering if it was all fate. Was it meant for me to go with Royce that night? Weston was supposed to be there with me, but then the wedding date got changed, and now he was down in L.A. None of my girls could come, either; and I know if they had, they would have been my escape. My strength. Was this some sort of sign? I tussled back and forth with all these different thoughts.

One last time, I pulled out my phone and tried to call Weston. I made a deal with myself. If he answered and I got to talk to him, I wouldn't go with Royce. But, if I got his voicemail again, I would take that as a definite sign that it was meant for me to have this time with him, and I would do it.

For some reason, I dialed his number real slow, almost as if I were having a hard time remembering it. I closed my eyes when I finished, and held the phone tightly to my ear. My heart was beating a thousand miles a minute. My call went right to his voicemail. Part of me was relieved, and part of me wished like hell he had picked up the phone.

I noticed that Royce still wasn't back with my punch, and I figured he was giving me a few extra moments alone to get myself together, which was fine with me, because I needed it.

He finally returned with a cup of punch. He didn't say anything to me, just handed me my cup and sat down next to me. I thanked him, took a sip, and set the cup down by my side. Then I looked him in the face and told him, "I'm ready."

As soon as the words came out, I thought I might faint. Royce's face lit up, but I could tell he was trying to tone his excitement down for my sake, since he saw I was having such a difficult time with the situation.

He asked me, "Okay . . . are you sure? 'Cause we really don't have to. Not that I don't want to, but I don't want you to feel like I'm tryina push you into this."

"I appreciate that. And I don't feel like you're pushing me. I'm . . . I'm sure. I wanna be with you tonight. So, like I said, I'm ready."

"Okay." He got up. "You wanna follow me over there?"

"Yeah, I guess so." I was a bundle of nerves.

"All right, how 'bout I meet you in the parking lot in ten minutes? Or is that too soon? I know you need to say something to Tiki and Charles."

I mumbled, "Oh . . . that's right . . ." then I got up and wiped off the back of my dress. "Uhh . . . yeah, gimme about ten minutes. But *you* gotta go now. I don't want anyone to see us leaving too close in time frame. Especially Tiki and Charles."

"I understand. Lemme just go and say goodbye to my boy. I'll just tell him I have an early day tomorrow and need to hit the road."

"Okay."

"I'll be sitting in the car waiting by the time you get out there. I'm in the red Nissan Sentra, over by the entrance to the parking lot. It's a rental. Look for the Enterprise symbol on the back."

"All right. You go inside first."

He did, and I sat down again, feeling like I was about to barf.

A few minutes later, I went back inside and found Tiki. I told her I was beat, and that if I was gonna have any energy to help her and Charles move into their new apartment the next day, I needed to go home and crash for the night. She understood, and I quickly said my goodbyes and congratulations to her and Charles, then headed cautiously out the door.

I pulled my car up near Royce's, and he started the motor and backed out.

All the way to the hotel, I kept dialing Weston's number. I guess I was crying out for help, because I knew if he answered, I would change my mind and go home instead. I kept getting his voicemail, which was frustrating me, because he usually never had his phone off for that long. I didn't leave any messages because I really wanted to talk to him.

We pulled into the hotel parking lot, and I parked on the opposite side of the lot to him. I was paranoid about someone seeing us together, so I was trying to be as inconspicuous as possible.

I guess he felt my vibe, because he walked ahead of me like he didn't know me, which was perfect.

Once inside the hotel lobby, I sort of hung behind him while he stopped at the desk to ask the clerk if there were any messages for him. While the guy went and checked, Royce realized he didn't have his watch on, and looked around for the clock, but couldn't find it.

He turned to me and said, "Katrice, what time is it? I left my watch upstairs."

I had hoped he wouldn't talk to me while we were standing there, and his asking that question messed me up.

I looked at my watch. "Six fifty-two."

There was also a handsome, bald-headed, clean-shaven brother behind the counter, who was helping another couple, but kept looking at me. Not staring, just peeking. I wasn't standing right up at the counter, but I could see that he was definitely trying to make eye contact with me. I was starting to get annoyed, because I felt like he was trying too hard to get my attention, and I had far too many other issues going on without having to fend off some mack daddy.

The clerk came back and told Royce there were no messages. Royce thanked the guy and motioned to me to follow him.

The elevator ride up to the tenth floor was awkward.

Neither of us spoke, but twice on the way up, Royce smiled at me as if he were trying to lighten the mood.

After we got inside the room, Royce took off his jacket, looked at me and said, "Make yourself comfortable. You want anything from room service? I'm gonna order something."

I sat down at the table by the window. "No, thank you. I'm okay."

He sat on the bed and dialed room service, while I got up and went into the bathroom. I didn't have to go, I just needed a moment alone, because I was starting to lose it. I turned on the water at the sink and pretended to be washing my hands; then I pulled my phone out of my purse and called Weston as a last-ditch effort.

I got his voicemail, yet again. At that point, I gave up and turned off *my* phone.

When I came out, Royce had turned on the television and was loosening his tie around his neck.

I went back over and sat down at the table.

"You feel okay?" he asked me.

"Yeah, why?"

"You just got real quiet on me all of a sudden. Are you mad at me?"

"No . . . do I seem like it?"

"I wasn't sure."

"I'm not mad."

That's all I said, and he left it alone.

"You know, there's room for you over here on the bed. You don't hafta sit all the way over there in the window. Don't be scared. I'm not gonna bite you. Just . . . come sit next to me." He stretched out, propped his elbow up and rested his head in his hand.

I got up and moved over to the bed, but I only sat on the edge, and I stared straight ahead at the television.

A minute later, room service knocked at the door, and I jumped outta my skin.

Royce got up, chuckled at me and said, "Relax, girl," and opened the door.

He ordered a fruit tray and some wine. There was also honey, along with whipped cream on ice, which I found strange, but I didn't say anything.

He set the honey and the whipped cream on ice aside, set the fruit tray in the middle of the bed, sat back down, and started eating a piece of cantaloupe. There were also strawberries, grapes, honeydew melon, and watermelon.

"I love fruit like you wouldn't believe," he said, while slurping on a second piece of cantaloupe. "I think I eat more fruit than anything else. Here," he pushed the tray towards me. "You better get'choo some before I eat it all. 'Cause believe me, I will sit my black ass up here and tear this whole platter up. I'll have gas in the morning, but I don't care."

I laughed, and finally let my guard down.

For the next three hours, we talked, laughed, polished off the first fruit tray, ordered another one, and drank wine. I think I was so nervous initially because I assumed that Royce only wanted to get me back to the hotel to have sex. But after we started talking, I saw that wasn't the case. We reminisced about high school, talked about people from back in the day, and talked about what his life was like growing up with just his mom and being an only child. He told me all about what it was like living back East, we laughed at a million things, and then we talked about me and what I had been up to since I last saw him.

By ten-thirty, I was so comfortable that I had taken off my shoes and stretched out on the bed on my side, in the same position as Royce, both of us propped up on pillows and facing each other.

Talking to him was refreshing. I enjoyed his company immensely, and that just made me like him as a person even more. He was still as smart and articulate as I had remembered him to be, and he opened up to me about a lot of things that had happened to him in his childhood, that he said he normally didn't reveal to people.

All of a sudden, he was no longer a god in my eyes. He was just Royce. I was still wildly attracted to him, but something in me changed, and I could feel my obsession with him fading away.

I was in the middle of telling him a funny story about Tiki and me, when he cut me off.

"Damn . . . you are *so* beautiful. I'm sorry, I didn't mean to interrupt you, but I just had to say that."

I was embarrassed. I thanked him and went back to my story, and before I could finish two sentences, he scooted in, touched my face with his index finger, and kissed me. Like a pro, I might add. He French kissed me like I had never been kissed before. His mouth tasted like fruit and wine, and I was sure mine tasted the same. He licked my lips, sucked my tongue and groaned with passion. And I relished every moment of it.

We both started breathing hard, and before I knew it, he had rolled on top of me and started lifting up my dress. To my surprise, I started helping him get under it. He reached under and pulled at my thong. I lifted my butt up off the bed so he could get it off, and after he tossed it on the floor, he reached back under my dress and fingered me so good I thought my eyes were gonna pop out of my head. He ran them up and down the insides of my lips, then, stuck two inside me, moved them around and simultaneously rubbed my magic button until I came long and hard.

When he pulled his fingers out of me, he licked the juices off real slow, as if a savory sauce lay upon them.

He got up off the bed and started taking off his shirt and unbuckling his pants, then he stopped and said, "Take off that dress, gorgeous. I been waitin' for this for a long, long time."

I got up, half-dazed, and started getting undressed. I still couldn't believe I was about to sleep with Royce. I took the straps off my shoulders and let the dress fall to my midsection, then pulled it over my ample behind and dropped it to the floor.

The only thing left was my bra, which I quickly unsnapped and threw off so my melons could break free. I stood in my nakedness in front of Royce, while he looked at me like I was a Nubian queen. By that time, I was no longer embarrassed or afraid. I was ready to get to work.

Royce hadn't finished getting undressed yet; only his shirt was off. He started to unzip his pants and I walked over and stopped him.

"Let me do that," I whispered.

He stopped in his tracks and allowed me to take over.

I unzipped his pants and they fell to the floor. I teased him by reaching inside his boxers, gently caressing his dick, and stroking it with the softness of a feather while I kissed him again.

He closed his eyes and his breathing got choppy. He broke away from my kiss and tilted his head back, licking his lips and moaning, and gyrating in my hand.

Finally, I pulled his boxers to the floor, then I turned him around and pushed him onto the edge of the bed. He fell with his legs wide open, which is exactly the way I wanted them, because then I went to town, introducing him to every oral skill I had learned over the years, and made up some new ones along the way. He wasn't as big as Weston, but he wasn't lacking, either. That was for sure.

About five minutes into my show, he removed the pillow he had shoved up to his face to muffle his sound effects, and he stopped me. "Come here . . . sixty-nine. I wanna taste you again."

This was definitely my kinda party, so I scurried up onto the bed, turned myself around and got into position. We sucked and slurped on each other for I don't know how long, and yes, the man had *mad* skills. With all the moaning, groaning, and grunting coming from the room, I was sure it sounded like an orgy was taking place.

For the second time, I came. I didn't want him to come yet, because we hadn't gotten to the meat and potatoes of the night, so I purposely held back a little on the sucking. I didn't wanna ruin the flow of things by having to wait for him to get a second wind.

Then things got even more intense. I got off his face and turned over onto my back, still reeling from my second orgasm, when I saw Royce reaching for the nightstand. He grabbed the honey and popped it open. Before I could ask him what he was gonna do with it, he straddled me, then he looked at me almost apologetically, and with tenderness in his eyes.

He lifted my right arm, pulled it up to his face, and studied my five-inch scar for a few seconds.

He touched it in a gentle, patting motion and said, "This looks like it really hurt."

My heart was about to pop outta my chest. I couldn't figure out what he was up to, but I decided not to ask. Having him touch my scar had me distracted, and made me remember that day on campus.

I closed my eyes, recalling my fall, remembering how much it hurt and whispered like a seven-year-old, "It did. It hurt bad."

He turned the bottle over, held my arm up, squeezed honey directly onto my scar, put the bottle down on the bed and said, "Lemme make it up to you."

He gingerly rubbed the thick, sticky honey in like lotion, licked his fingers, then, in slow motion, began licking and sucking the honey off my scar. With extreme concentration, he softly ran his tongue down every inch of my abrasion, making sure to connect with each small lump the keloid left me with.

I started crying uncontrollably.

He stopped licking my arm and whispered, "Shhhh . . . don't cry . . . I'm sorry . . . I'm sorry . . . I didn't mean to hurt you, Katrice, I *swear* I didn't. I was an asshole . . . you were too good for me . . . I wasn't ready for a girl like you back then."

That made me cry even harder.

"*Please* don't cry . . ." he pleaded, as he licked the honey off his lips. Then he started kissing my arm as if he were appeasing an injured child. I guess to some extent he was, because in my mind, at that moment, I was fifteen again.

He licked the last of the honey off my arm, then leaned down and kissed my lips ever so softly. I let the sweet taste fall into my mouth, and we kissed for a minute. When he stopped kissing me, he cradled my face in his hands and lovingly wiped the tears from my cheeks with the tips of his thumbs. I let out a long sigh, releasing all of my mental tension into the air.

"You okay?" he asked.

"Yeah. I'm all right."

"Okay."

Next, he put the honey back on the nightstand and reached for the whipped cream. It was time to change gears. He put some on both my nipples, inside my belly button, and a small dab on each of my toes.

He got busy, licking the whipped cream off my breasts, driving me crazy, and making me scream. Once he was through there, he scooted down and sucked it out of my navel, sticking his tongue in and wiggling it around inside the hole to make sure he got it all out.

He then moved down to my feet, and sucked the whipped cream off each and every one of my toes, giving them each special attention. I thanked God I had gotten a pedicure that morning. I had never had my toes sucked before, and the feeling was incredible. It gave me chills down my spine.

Finally, he reached in the nightstand drawer and pulled out a condom. The whole time he was unwrapping it and rolling it on, he was staring me in the eyes, looking serious.

I didn't say a word.

I spread my legs for him and he guided himself into me. Having him inside me felt out of this world. He took it slow and easy, feeling me out, taking me in. He closed his eyes while he stroked me, taking long, deep breaths and mumbling about how wet I was, and that he thought he might scream.

After he got a good sense of me, he quickened his pace and started letting loose. I wrapped myself as tight as I could around him, gently biting his shoulders and kissing his neck.

He worked a lot quieter than Weston, but he didn't lack passion, and he certainly knew what he was doing. He was by far one of the most smooth, most rhythmical "strokers" I had experienced.

First, he stayed on top for a while, giving it to me hard, then he flipped me over, and we doggie-styled it for a while. I held tightly onto the headboard while he pounded me from the back, gripping my ass firmly, spreading my cheeks apart, stroking powerfully, sliding one hand around my midsection to hold me while pressing the other one gently into my back. He slapped my ass, pulled my hair, and called my name over and over like a broken record.

He threw in a few new, harder-to-describe positions that Weston and I hadn't tried yet, but that I made sure to remember. I followed his lead, went with the flow, felt the pleasure, asked for a little pain, dug my nails into his back, broke the skin, wiped the sweat from his brow, kissed his salty lips, and made the ugliest pleasure-and-pain faces ever.

Soon, I flipped *him* over and got on top, rode him like a champ in a rodeo, kept strong eye contact, told him how good he felt, leaned forward, pressed my hands into his chest and bounced like a rabbit: slow, then fast; hard, then soft; side-to-side, grinding slowly—then, I put a mean hurting on him until finally he started to yelp in a strange, off-key, high-pitched tone that startled me, considering how deep his voice was.

I knew what that meant, so I stepped up the pace and worked my hips like a pro. He grabbed my breasts, squeezed them, fondled them, told me he was about to explode, and then one last, good time, I slammed down on him with attitude and rocked back and forth, while he shrieked for all the world to hear.

I was spent. He was half dead. I collapsed on top of him and stayed there. We breathed together; we breathed separate. We kissed; we clasped hands. We laughed softly; we whispered sweet nothings. We complimented one another; we looked deep into each other's eyes. We fell asleep.

I woke with a start and found that Royce was still partially inside me, since I hadn't yet gotten off him.

I looked over at the clock and saw that it was after one in the morning. I jumped up, scaring Royce, and hurried to find my clothes. I was panic-stricken for some reason. I couldn't figure out why, but all I knew was I could not spend the night with him. Waves of guilt started hitting me from every direction.

"Hey . . . what's wrong?" he asked me while rubbing his eyes, trying to get focused on me.

"I gotta go. I can't stay here."

"Why not?"

"I just can't."

He sat up. "When's your man coming home?"

Hearing him refer to "my man" reminded me of the seriousness of what I had just done. I continued gathering my clothes and putting them on while I talked, but I didn't look at him.

"Tomorrow night. But, that's not the point. I can't

stay here with you. I need to go home. I just cheated on the man I love, and I'm freaking out about that right now. I've never cheated on a boyfriend, ever. This is bad, Royce. Very bad."

He got up with the condom still dangling from his limp penis, and tried to comfort me by giving me a hug. But now, all of a sudden, I didn't want him touching me at all. I moved away from him and he looked hurt.

"Damn . . . so it's like that? I can't even touch you now?"

I was finally dressed, and I was fumbling in my purse for my car keys. I stopped and looked at Royce.

I sighed. "I'm sorry, don't take it personal, but I don't think you understand the position I'm in right now. I have to find a way to deal with what I just did here. Figure out how I'm gonna look Weston in the face when he comes home. I'm sorry, Royce, but I hafta go."

He nodded. "I understand. But can you tell me something?"

"What?"

"Do you regret coming here with me tonight?"

I paused for a long time before I answered that question.

"Yes and no. But what bothers me is that the answer is mostly no."

I turned to leave and he stopped me.

"So . . . I guess this is it then . . . I'm not gonna see you again, am I?"

I shook my head. Then I walked to the door, and he stopped me again.

"Katrice. I wish . . . I wish I had treated you the way you deserved to be treated back then. I mean, we

coulda probably . . ." And then he trailed off, knowing it wasn't even worth finishing the statement.

I just said, "Yeah. I wish you had, too." I paused
before I said, "Bye, Royce."

And when I said "Bye, Royce," I really meant it.

I took one last look at him, standing there in all his
beautiful, black glory, opened the door and walked out.

All the way home, I was in a trance. When I walked
in my front door, I went to look and see if there were
any messages on my home phone. There were none.
Weston hadn't called all day. Not even to leave me
one of his *I love you* messages. I turned my cell phone
on and waited for the new message indicator to pop
up, but it never did. I was disturbed by the fact that
I hadn't been able to speak to Weston all day, but
mostly, I was exhausted.

I peeled off my clothes and let them fall right in
the middle of the floor, which is not like me, especially
with my more expensive items, but I didn't care.

My body was starting to ache from all the different positions Royce had had me in, and I could smell
him all over me. For some odd reason, I felt guilty
about getting in my bed with his scent still lingering
on my skin, so as tired as I was, I went and took a
quick shower to wash off all the evidence of my
crime.

Around two, I fell into bed and was asleep before
I even had time to think about what I was gonna say
to Weston when I finally did talk to him. I was glad
he wasn't due back for another day and a half, because I knew I would need at least that long to get my
head together.

13

I was dreaming that I was standing on the rooftop of a building in the middle of the night. The wind was whipping at about thirty miles an hour, and my hair was standing on top of my head. I was in a nasty-looking white nightgown with a bunch of rotten apples all over it. All of the apples had worms coming out of them, and the worms were moving. Holding hands and dancing around me in a circle, were about ten little Mini-Me's, dressed in the same nightgown I was wearing. They were smiling and skipping around, singing the theme song from *The Smurfs*.

I was dancing as they sang, but then, all of a sudden, one of my "selves" stopped in her tracks and started growling like a rabid dog, flashing sharp fangs. I stopped dancing and looked around at my other pint-sized "selves." One by one, they all stopped dancing and started growling. I panicked and tried to run, but they had me trapped in the middle of the circle.

After a minute, the Mini-Me's closed in on me and began trying to bite me. I screamed and started kicking at them, but they just kept coming at me. One of my "selves" bit my leg and broke the skin. My shin started to bleed, and as the blood flowed, worms like the ones in the apples on my nightgown started crawling out of my leg. First, it was just a few; then they started coming out by the dozens. I screamed and slapped at my bloody, wormy leg, but they kept squirming out. The Mini-Me's stopped growling and started laughing at me. I screamed for them to get away from me, but the more I screamed, the harder and louder they laughed.

As they continued to close in on me, I started backing up. I took about four steps back, and the next thing I knew, the "selves" had disappeared, and I was now standing backwards on the ledge of the building. I turned around slowly to look behind me and I lost my balance and fell off the roof.

As I fell at breakneck speed to the ground, I closed my eyes tight, and I could feel my heart racing as I prepared to hit the ground. Just as my body was about to splatter all over the streets of wherever I was, someone caught me. When I opened my eyes to see who it was, I nearly choked on my tongue. It was a man, but not just any man. He was one half Weston and one half Royce. I mean, literally—one half of his body belonged to Weston, and the other half to Royce—from head to toe. I was looking into a half dark chocolate, half brown-sugar-colored face of two different men, joined together as one. The Weston side had one of his beautiful eyes, and the Royce side had one big, dark-brown eye. The Royce side was smiling and the Weston side was crying.

The whole scene scared the hell out of me, and I screamed at the top of my lungs. Then, something even freakier happened. Both sides of the face started talking. First, the Royce side said, "You're mine now. You'll never escape me. Tell your man goodbye." Then, the Weston side said, through his tears, "How could you do this to me, baby? I thought you loved me."

Just as I was about to answer Weston, his side let me go and I fell to the ground. I landed on my back with a thud, and my head hit the sidewalk hard. I could feel the pain in my dream, and when I reached back to try to touch my head, the Weston side stepped on my hand. I yelped in pain; then the dual man bent down and the Royce side started gently stroking my face with the back of his hand. The Weston side got mad and slapped the Royce side's hand away from me.

Then, the worst thing happened. The Weston side looked me in the eyes, reached out, wrapped his large hand around my throat, and began strangling me. I tried to kick, but for some reason, my legs wouldn't move. I looked to the Royce side for help, but his half of the face and body were suddenly frozen. I gasped for air, but Weston kept choking me, harder and harder. I felt myself begin to cry, as my windpipe rapidly shut down on me.

Finally, as I felt myself giving in to the Grim Reaper, Weston started shouting my name repeatedly. After he had said it about ten times, he started ordering me to open up. I remember thinking in my dream, *What does he mean by "open up"?* Just then, Weston squeezed my throat one last time, and then my eyes popped open.

When I woke up, I found myself on the floor, on my back, next to my bed, crying. My head was touching the leg of my nightstand, and I could feel a huge bump forming. What scared me the most was that my own hand was wrapped firmly around my throat in a chokehold. I quickly took my hand from my throat, realizing I had actually been strangling myself in my sleep. Then, a loud knock on my door startled me. Someone was outside pounding furiously like the police and yelling my name. I sat up, drenched in sweat, listened for a second, and realized it was Weston.

I scrambled to get off the floor. I used the side of my bed to pull myself up, and when I looked at the clock, it glowed a bright red 3:07 A.M. Weston was still knocking and shouting, and I couldn't figure out what the hell he was even doing at my door when he wasn't due back from L.A. yet. My first thought was that something bad happened while he was away.

I rushed to the door and turned on the hall light. When I opened it, I didn't even get a chance to say anything. Weston pushed past me in a heat of anger with a near-full forty-ounce in his hand, and started shouting at me.

"What the *fuck* took you so long to open the goddamn door?! Is that muthafucka up in here wit'choo?!"

I was totally confused, plus, I was still reeling from the dream I had just had. My head and throat were throbbing, and I was feeling dizzy.

"What . . . are you talking about? What's wrong with you? Are you drunk?"

"Don't worry 'bout whether I'm drunk or not! You worry 'bout tellin' *me* where the hell you went after the reception!"

"I . . . I don't understand . . . what?"

He barked in an angry, exaggerated tone, "I *said*, in case yo' *deaf ass* missed it, where were you after Tiki and Charles's reception?! And I'm just *waitin'* for you to stand up here and tell me a bold-faced lie, too!"

I needed a moment to get myself together, because it was obvious to me that he knew something, but I wasn't exactly sure what, so I didn't answer him. At that point, I didn't even care that he had burst into my apartment in the middle of the night cussing me out. I had much bigger things to worry about. Like what he was doing back, and how he found out I had been doing something I shouldn't have that night.

He got up in my face, his eyes red and watery, blazing-hot breath loaded with alcohol, and hollered, "Don't stand up here and act like you don't hear me! Answer me, goddammit! WHERE . . . THE FUCK . . . WERE YOU?!"

I was scared he was gonna clock me in the eye or something, so I tried to move away from him, but he blocked my way and wouldn't let me get past him.

His tone turned sinister. "Where you goin', baby? Huh? What—you need some help rememberin'? I mean, wassup? You need time to git'cho *memory* together up in here?"

I was so scared I almost shit on myself. "No . . ."

He moved in close enough to kiss me. "Then I'm'a ask you *one more time,* and yo' best bet is to *answer* me this time before I *really* get mad—WHAT . . . DID YOU DO . . . AFTER THE MUTHA . . . FUCKIN' . . . RECEPTION?!"

I gasped, and in my nervousness, I bit my tongue so hard I could taste the blood. The pain made my eyes water, but when I looked into my man's angry eyes, tears started to cascade down my face. I didn't know how he found out, but clearly, I was busted.

I still couldn't bring myself to tell the whole truth, so I told him, "I . . . um . . . left with a friend, and—"

Before I could finish what was already turning into somewhat of a lie, Weston drew his body back, and just when I thought he was about to beat me to a bloody pulp, he threw his bottle of beer against the wall behind me with all the strength he had. The bottle shattered into pieces, and beer sprayed all over the wall, the hallway, and on me. Dozens of chunks of glass, large and small, flew in five different directions and ricocheted everywhere. I flinched and closed my eyes to keep from getting glass in them. I felt several pieces graze my face, and one of them bounced off my top lip.

With all the commotion coming from my small apartment in the dead of the night, I was sure at least one of my neighbors were already calling the police, reporting some sort of domestic disturbance.

I was too scared to scream or try to move again, so I just kept my eyes closed as tight as I could, tensed up my shoulders, and waited for my life to come to an end.

Instead, Weston stunned me by yelling, "You didn't leave wit' no *goddam friend!* You left wit' *Royce* and had yo' ass all up in the hotel wit' him!"

"Oh my God . . ." I sobbed, "how did you find . . . ?"

He backed me into the beer-soaked wall and started hollering at me like an Army drill sergeant. "Did you give up the pussy?! Don'choo fuckin' lie to me, Katrice! If you did, you tell me *right now!* Did you fuck him?! You give my pussy away?!"

Tears that felt like fire continued to fall down my cheeks as I prepared myself to reveal the truth to the man I loved.

I forced out a weak and horrified, "Y-yes."

He balled up his fists, and I watched as his face turned as red as it possibly could underneath his beautiful brown skin. He turned away from me, threw his hands up to his face and covered his eyes, and let out a long, gut-wrenching, bloodcurdling yell that sounded like he was being stabbed to death. Then he whipped back around, looked at me with an Incredible Hulk-like madness in his eyes, and went completely berzerk.

"I can't *believe* you! Why would you *do* some shit like that to me?! I came back early to be with you tonight! I spent money to change my flight, and then I left my *family* to come back here and surprise you so we could be together at the wedding, and this is what I get?! Yo' *trick ass* can't even keep yo' *mutha fuckin'* draws up?! What the *fuck* is wrong wit'choo?!"

I fell into a hysterical cry, the kind where your breathing is choppy and you're snorting and coughing.

"Weston, I'm s-s-sor-ryyyy! I know it was wrong, but it didn't have anything to d-do with y-you!"

"Aw, you fulla *shit,* you know that?! You done lost yo' muthafuckin' mind! How could you *do* this? *Knowin'* I'm in love wit'choo! You don't love me?! Huh?! You don't love me?! Is that the problem?!"

"YESSS! I DO! You're the *only* person I wanna be with!"

"Oh, I *know* you didn't just tell *that* lie! You can't *possibly* love me! I turn my back for TWO DAYS . . . TWO GODDAMN DAYS, and you just gon' run off to a hotel wit' this dirty muthafucka when you KNOW you got a man?!"

"I'm *sorry!* I *am!* I love you *so much!* You *have* to believe me . . . this was *not* about you!"

"Yeah, you got that right! You about as *sorry* as they come!"

I wiped tears from my eyes and snot from my nose and tried to calm myself. "Weston . . . I love you . . . I do . . . lemme explain what happened—"

"WHY do you keep lettin' that lie come out'cho *mouth?!* You selfish! Only person you love is YOU! You don't give a shit about me! And I can't *believe* I let myself fall so *deep* for you! You ain't nothin' but a spoiled, ungrateful, tramp-ass BITCH!"

I was so spastic I thought I might have a stroke. "No . . . Wes . . . I'm . . . oh my God . . . oh my *GOD* . . . pllleeeeeeaaasse . . . just lemme tell you the whole story first!"

My head was pounding. And I couldn't believe that Weston had just called me a bitch. It was like a stab in the heart.

"Nah, you know what? Fuck yo' tired-ass story! And *FUCK YOU!*"

And on that note, before I could even begin to speak again, he shoved past me, practically knocking me over, flung the door open with so much force that it crashed against the doorstop and bounced, then he disappeared into the night. As I looked out the door, I wanted to call after him, but I knew at that point, there was nothing I could do to get him to listen to me.

I looked out into the darkness as I cried the heaviest tears of regret ever. I could see people from the next building over, peeking out their windows. There were no police cars in sight and no sirens in the distance, so I guess that night, folks decided to stay out of our Kool-Aid and let whatever was gonna go down go down. I knew one thing for sure: Everyone in my neighborhood heard all of my business. How could they not? As quiet and still as it was at three in the morning, and as loud as the two of us were yelling, I'm sure we woke all the neighbors *and* their dead-as-doornails relatives. I really couldn't have cared less. The love of my life had just walked out on me, and I had no idea what to do next.

I closed the door and collapsed in the hallway on top of the scattered glass and puddle of beer. I didn't even care about being careful not to cut myself on the glass. I felt like taking a chunk and cutting my throat. I balled myself up into an upright fetal position, leaned myself up against the wall, and sat there and cried until my eyes were almost puffed shut.

While I cried, I kept wondering how in the hell Weston found out about everything. And he said he came back early to be with me at the wedding, but he *wasn't there,* so I just kept thinking, *Where the hell was he?* It just didn't make any sense to me. Then I drifted into thoughts about Royce and our night together. I thought about how undeniably satisfying it was. I thought about how I had wanted to be with him for so many years, and how relieved I felt now that I had been able to get that longing out of my system. But there was also this large part of me that wished he had never even shown up at the reception. I had a good thing, and his coming back into my life for that one night tore everything apart. I had crushed the man I knew I wanted to spend the rest of my life with, and all I could do was prepare to let him and all his awesome love go.

I'm not sure what time Weston left, but when I got up off the floor and dragged myself back to the bed-room and looked at the clock, it said 4:19 A.M. I was thoroughly exhausted, and I wanted so badly to call my girls for some much-needed support, but I wasn't trying to get cussed out for a second time that night, so I crawled back into bed, every cell in my body wracked with pain, and fell out. I didn't even bother to clean up the lousy-smelling mess in the hallway, or clean *myself* up prior to getting back in bed. Before the word "sleep" could even cross my mind, I was out like a light.

My alarm went off at seven-thirty, blasting in my ear. When I reached over to turn it off, I was so delirious that I ended up pushing the clock off the nightstand. That shut that madness down. I stared at the ceiling for a few minutes and had to try to remember what day it was, and why my clock was beeping at me at such an early hour. Then I remembered. I promised Tiki I would finish helping her move the rest of her stuff into her and Charles's new place. At that moment, the last thing I wanted to do was get out of bed and go out into the world to face the public, much less friends. I really didn't even wanna talk to Chantelle, Genine, and Sabrina anymore. I just wanted to stay in bed until the year 2000, and by then, hopefully, I would have an answer as to how I was gonna get my life back together.

I rolled over to contemplate how I was gonna get through the day, and the damn phone rang. At first, I was pissed off, but then, when I realized it could be Weston, I nearly threw myself out of the bed in attempt to hurry up and get to the table where the phone was. I didn't even bother to look at my caller ID; I just grabbed the phone at the beginning of the third ring, out of breath, and hoped to hear my man's voice on the other end.

It was Tiki. I wanted to start crying again, but I was too tired, and I didn't think I could come up with any more tears.

"Katrice? Are you okay?"

"Oh . . . um . . . you know what, girl? I'm actually not."

"What's wrong?"

"God . . . um . . . I got . . . I got really sick in the middle of the night, and I just got back to sleep around five o'clock this morning. I don't think I'ma be able to help you today. I'm sorry . . . I just . . . I just need to get some sleep and get myself together and then I think I'll be okay."

"What happened?"

"I just . . . my stomach started cramping up around two and then I got the runs really bad. Maybe it was something I ate at the party. I just need to stay home today."

"Okay, well, don't worry about it; just do what'choo need to do, girl. Charles can probably get Robert to help. You got any appointments today?"

"Um . . . n-no . . . I didn't schedule anybody 'cause I knew I'd probably be with you guys all day."

"Okay. Now, you know we leave for the cruise early tomorrow morning, and I won't be seeing anyone till about three days after we get back."

"Yeah, I know. I'll call you later tonight when I'm feeling a little better, 'kay?"

"All right, girl. Take care. Love you. And thanks for being there yesterday. It wouldn't'ta been the same without you. Sorry Weston missed everything."

"Yeah . . . me, too . . . you have no idea. . . ."

"Okay, girl, lemme let'choo go; you sound beat up. Talk to you later."

"Okay . . . bye."

"Bye."

When I hung up the phone, all of a sudden I went into autopilot mode and started packing an overnight bag. I called my mother and told her I was on my way over, that I had a problem and I needed help. She got scared and asked me if I was sick. I told her not to worry, I was just upset, and that I would be there shortly.

Then I called the girls' cell phones, which I knew would be off that early in the morning, and left them all messages telling them I would be at my parents' for a day or so, and I would call them when I got back home. I told them we had a little family issue to deal with and not to worry, that I would fill them in later.

I threw on some jeans, a T-shirt, and some sandals, then raced out of the house, leaving the hallway smelling like beer. I decided I would deal with that when I got back. Right now, I needed my mommy and daddy.

When I got there, my parents were sitting in the living room, waiting anxiously for me. I couldn't even get in the door before my father started grilling me about what happened, why was I rushing over there at eight in the morning, and was someone hurt.

I quieted him down, put my bag on the floor, sat on the couch and told them my story. I was so thankful that I could talk to them, especially since they knew my history with Royce.

When I was done, they both looked at me like I had just said something in Greek and they didn't know how to respond.

After a long pause, Daddy said slowly, "Sooooo . . . are you satisfied now?"

I was surprised at his response, because I was expecting him to judge and criticize me. I think he knew I had enough problems already, and that would only make me feel worse.

I answered, "You know what, Daddy? I am, in a big way. But then again, I'm not. There's all this stuff with Weston now. I cheated on him . . . and he found out somehow . . . and now he's angry . . . and rightfully so. But, what am I gonna do? I really screwed up this time, I know that, but he didn't even give me a chance to explain why I did what I did."

Mama finally spoke on the subject. "Leave him alone, Katrice. Lord knows you're lucky he didn't strike you last night. I would have to kill him if he did, but my point is, now is not a good time to be trying to talk to him. Give it a week or so, then see what happens. He might have come around by then."

My mouth fell open. "A weeeeek? I can't wait a week, Mama. I'll go crazy."

"Your mother's right. Let the dust settle for a minute. You just concentrate on getting yourself together. Weston'll come around eventually. He loves you."

"I don't know if I can do this, you guys. I'm already a basket case as it is."

Mama said, "You'll be fine."

Then I asked, "So can I stay here for a coupla days? I don't wanna be in my house right now."

Daddy frowned at me. "Now that's a silly question, Chickadee. Of course you can stay here. This is still your home, even though you don't live here anymore."

"I know, I just . . . I don't wanna be in you guys' way."

"Oh, don't be ridiculous, Katrice," Mama said. "You not gon' be in nobody's way around here."

"Are you sure?"

They both just looked at me.

I called Joan-Renee that night and spewed the entire saga to her over buckets of tears and anguish, and she was totally floored. We had kind of gotten away from our weekly talks since she moved to Texas shortly after high school, and then even more so after she got married, but this particular conversation was *very* necessary, and we stayed on the phone for nearly four hours. She said she'd known he was gonna come to his senses about me one day, but was mad as hell that he chose that night to do it. Although she understood my dilemma and the difficulty of my decision, she also didn't fail to put me in my place about it. She gave me the loving scolding that Mama and Daddy didn't, and refused to attend the pity party I was throwing. And I needed that. I love her so much.

Two days later, I returned home and called the girls. Tiki and Charles were still on their honeymoon, so I would have to fill her in when she got back.

I asked them to come over and help me clean up a huge mess. They thought it a strange request, but I told them I really needed them to help me. Within the hour, they were at my door.

When they walked in, the smell of the old beer sopped into the rug made them frown up.

Genine asked, "*God,* 'Trice . . . what's that smell? And what's with the glass all over the floor? What the hell happened here?"

I told them all to have a seat, and went into my

blow-by-blow description of what happened the night of the wedding.

For the first time since I had known them, none of them had anything to say except, "Damn."

After they all stared at me for quite a few seconds, Sabrina asked, "So . . . I mean, what'choo gon' do, girl? This is *serious*."

I shook my head. "I have no idea. Absolutely none. Right now, I need to get my house back in order. So, can you guys please help me clean up the hallway? I can't do this by myself. I just don't have the energy."

Chantelle smiled. "You know we got'cho' back, girl. Whatever you need."

It took us several hours to scrub the walls, shampoo the carpet, and find all the glass fragments, but by evening's end, we got it done. I could still smell the slight stench of beer, but at least the mess was gone.

When Tiki returned, I told her the story, and she felt terrible. She told me if she had known having Royce there was gonna cause problems for me she would have told Charles not to invite him. I told her it wasn't her fault, and that I would be okay.

I wanted to believe that everything would turn out fine between Weston and me, but deep down, I knew I was in for the worst ride of my life. I was just glad I had my girls to hold onto for support.

14

The first three months after our breakup were utterly ghastly. I cried every day and I could hardly think straight. I fell into a deep, dark depression that I had no intention of pulling myself out of. If the girls called, I would get on the phone and snivel. If my parents or P.J. called, I would fake like everything was just fine, then as soon as I hung up, I would fall right back into the semi-suicidal state of mind I was previously in.

I had called Weston, but needless to say, I was never able to actually speak to him. He made sure of that. Part of the reason I wanted so badly to talk to him, aside from the fact that I missed him more than you could imagine, was that there were two things that were driving me totally crazy. One was that I never got a chance to explain myself to him, and the other was trying to figure out how he even found out about that night to begin with. I tried to answer that question a hundred different times, and could never come up with anything that made any sense.

So yeah, I had become obsessed with the whole

situation. It took everything I had in me to keep from becoming a stalker. It's funny how you can live in the same city with someone, even minutes away, and when you're on speaking terms, you manage to see that person all the time. But when something happens between you, all of a sudden, that person is like a ghost. You couldn't even run into them if you camped outside their damn house. Barring knocking on his door and popping up at his job, because that would be suicide in and of itself, I went to all the places we used to go together around Oakland, and not once did I see him. Not around the lake, not in the grocery stores, not in the eateries, at the gas station, at the ATM, nowhere. It was as if he had dropped off the face of the earth—only I knew he hadn't. Other people told me they had seen him. Clients, acquaintances, even P.J. ran into him one day when he had come to Oakland to see Mama and Daddy. But could I run into him? No. And of course, he found someone else to cut his hair for him, because the last time he set foot in the shop was the day before he left for L.A. for Kevin's graduation.

For nearly three months, things went on this way. Then, one day, everything came to a head and I got a huge, painful rude awakening.

As usual, I was half-crazy, missing the man I loved, and once again, I tried to call him. I had come in from work around eight-thirty one Friday night, and I turned on the television to HBO. One of Weston's favorite movies, *A Low Down Dirty Shame,* had just come on, and I couldn't help but watch it. I curled up on the couch with a huge bowl of ice cream. I pretended Weston was lying right there with me, munching on tortilla chips and drinking an ice-cold beer.

Those were two of his must-haves when watching movies at home. I always kept the brews in the very back of my fridge for him so they would stay extra chilled.

Halfway through the movie, I couldn't take it anymore, and I jumped up and grabbed the phone. I didn't even have to dial his number, just simply pushed redial, since he was the only person I ever called, and then I waited for an answer. I got an answer all right, and it went *exactly* like this:

On the third ring, someone answered Weston's phone, but it wasn't Weston. It was some other guy. In the background, I could hear a bunch of people laughing and shouting, and there was a lot of commotion going on. Plates and silverware clanging, music playing, the microwave beeping, the garbage disposal rumbling, and I even heard a few girls talking and giggling.

The guy said, "Yeeeuh, Porter residence, wassup?"

I was confused. "Ummm . . . hi—yeah, is . . . Weston there?"

"Who's callin'?"

I was offended. I wondered who this common thug thought he was, asking me "*Who's calling?*" But, nonetheless, I told him, "This is Katrice."

"Ah'ight . . . hol' on. . . ."

He set the phone down on the counter, and unfortunately, I heard everything that transpired after that.

"Ay, man, some girl named Katrice on the phone askin' fuh you."

Weston said, loud and clear and with ice in his voice, "I don't know nobody named Katrice."

My heart sank.

Dude said, "You don't?"

"Nope. Hang up the phone."

"Ay, you sure? 'Cause she asked for you like she knew you."

I could hear the tension and growing irritation in Weston's voice when he repeated in almost a robotic tone, "I don't know nobody named Katrice. Hang up."

"Ah'ight, but . . . so what'choo want me to tell her?"

Weston lost it and yelled, "NOTHIN', MAN, *FUCK DAT BITCH!* HANG UP THE MUTHAFUCKIN' PHONE! I SAID I DON'T KNOW THE HO!"

I heard dude pick up the receiver and say to Weston, "Okay, man, damn . . . why you . . . ?"

And then my ear met with the humiliating sound of the abrupt and intentional end of a phone call.

For at least two full minutes, I just stood there with the phone still mashed tightly against my left ear, in shock from what I had heard.

Eventually, when it was clear that I was the only one still on the line and I really had been dissed to the highest degree, I threw the cordless receiver across the room and it bounced off the wall. Then I hurled myself onto the living room floor and bawled like an abused child for half an hour. I knew Weston was mad at me, but I never expected that kind of treatment from him. I had seen him in his most evil, hostile moments, but most of the time they didn't involve me. Now, things had taken a nasty turn, and in that instant, I never regretted making a phone call as much as I did then.

After I wallowed around in self-pity, I picked up the phone, put the battery that had flown out of it when it hit the wall, back in, and then called Chantelle. I was still crying when I called her, and no sooner than I finished telling her what had happened, she cut me off and said, "Lemme call you right back," and then *she* hung up on me, too.

I was completely bewildered. I called her right back, but my call went straight to her voicemail, which meant she was on the phone. I thought maybe she was trying to call me back, so I stood there for another couple of minutes, waiting for my phone to ring, but it never did. I tried to call Genine, but she didn't answer. Then I just got pissed off and started stomping through the house talking to myself like one of those people from *One Flew over the Cuckoo's Nest*. I cursed Weston, Chantelle, myself, Royce, the guy on the phone at Weston's house, the giggling girls in the background, everybody.

About forty-five minutes later, after I had calmed myself some and resumed my position on the couch, watching Nick at Nite, my doorbell rang. I didn't even feel like trying to figure out who it could be, because I already knew it wasn't gonna be Weston, so it really didn't matter who was on my stoop. I was tired, my eyes were puffy and red, and I was on the verge of calling one of those suicide hotlines, so all I knew was, whoever it was, they were gonna have to make it quick.

When I opened the door, there, staring me down, were Genine, Sabrina, and Chantelle. All of them had that famous intervention look on their faces, and I knew what was coming next. I also knew I wasn't in the mood. Looking at the three of them standing there angered me to the core.

"What happened to you calling me back?" I asked Chantelle, while I stood defiantly in the doorway, *not* inviting them in.

She pushed past me, and the other two trailed in right behind her.

Chantelle said, "This shit has gotten *way* outta hand. I'm sick of you always crying."

"Great, thanks a lot. Love the friendly support. Can you guys get out now?"

They all ignored me.

Genine jumped in with her two cents. "Chantelle told us what happened. Girl, you have *got* to stop calling him. I know you love him and I know you're sorry about what you did, but you gotta stop setting yourself up for this kinda pain. That man does *not* wanna talk to you. You need to accept that. It's time for you to move on and let him go."

Sabrina asked Genine, "Wait a minute . . . how many times has she called him?"

Genine shrugged and looked at me. Then Sabrina looked at me, too, and asked, looking annoyed, "Katrice. How many times have you called him?"

I was embarrassed to say, because I knew my damn self that it was pitiful, so this time I shrugged *my* shoulders and looked away. But you can't fool those who know you best.

Sabrina snapped viciously, "Don't shrug your shoulders at me, goddammit! I asked you a question. How many times have you called him? And I know you know, so answer me!"

"FINE! Ninety-six times, okay?! I've called him ninety-six times and no, I'm not proud of it, but that's what I did!"

Outdone, she screeched, "NINETY-SIX TIMES?! You've called that bastard ninety-six times over the past three months and all you've managed to get is disrespected, ignored, and hung up on?! That don't make no sense!"

"He's mad at me! I cheated on him!"

"Yeah, I know that—we ALL know that, but if you ask me, he's actin' like an asshole! Regardless of what you did, he should have the decency to *tell* you *personally* not to call him anymore! But, nooooo, he wanna play head games! He's doing this *strictly* to hurt you! To make you suffer! What he did tonight was rude and mean! He ain't stupid! He knew you could hear him! But instead of havin' the balls to just get on the phone and be a man about it and deal with you, he pulls this shit! Callin' you a *ho* and talkin' 'bout '*Fuck dat bitch,*' no, *he's* the bitch!"

"Why are you yelling at me?!"

"Because you're my girl and I *love you!* And YOU are dying! Spiritually, YOU . . . ARE . . . DYING! This—the way you're living—is not healthy! YOU are not healthy!"

Chantelle jumped in, waving her hands from side to side. "Okay—hey—you guys need to tone it down. Let's try to keep our business our business, all right?"

My bottom lip started quivering, and I got ready to cry, yet again, and now I was ashamed, given the comment that Chantelle made when she walked in.

I tried to hold the tears back. "There's nothing wrong with the way I'm living. I'm doing fine."

Sabrina took it down a couple of octaves, but was still fuming. "Oh, *bullshit!* Look at you! It's obvious you're not eating—you've lost at least twenty pounds—and when's the last time you did your hair?"

I let out a frustrated sigh. "I don't know . . . right before the wedding."

"Now see, that's what I mean. The Katrice I know

wouldn't even *think* of lettin' thirty *days* pass without doin' somethin' to her hair. Come here."

She grabbed me by the arm, dragged me to the bathroom, and stood me in front of the mirror.

"And *what* is *this?*" She made an angry hand gesture towards the tacky little ball in the back of my head.

"A bun. So?"

"YOU DON'T WEAR BUNS, KATRICE! You hate buns!"

She snatched my bun holder off my head and started separating chunks of my hair, which had grown almost two inches since the wedding—and of course, I hadn't bothered to even trim my ends to keep it healthy.

"Look at this! Look at these roots! This is ridiculous!"

And she was right. I looked horrible. My face was flushed, I had dark circles under my eyes from the lack of sleep I had been experiencing, my clothes were ill-fitting from the weight I had lost, and basically, I just didn't care about anything anymore. Truth be told, the only reason I went to work was so I could pay my bills. I had even lost that passionate feeling I had for doing hair, and I had never had that happen before. All I did every day was go to the shop, come home, and either crawl into bed or slump on the couch and watch Lifetime, MTV, or VH1 until I fell asleep. On occasion I'd watch a movie channel. I only got up to pee and maybe eat a bowl of Top Ramen or cold cereal, simply to keep myself from dying of malnutrition—although the nutritional value of Top Ramen is *clearly* questionable.

I hadn't flossed my teeth since the morning of the wedding, and some days I didn't even brush them;

my skin had broken out; and since I hadn't bothered to change my bedding even once since the night Weston tore through my house in a tirade, everything was crusty, soiled to the max and smelled like stale feet and unwashed ass.

As I stood looking at myself while my friend scolded me, I realized she was right. It was time. Time for me to get back to loving and respecting myself. Time for me to pick up the pieces of my life and put it back together. I loved Weston, and I missed him more than I cared to think about, but the truth was staring me right in the face. He was through with me, and there wasn't a damn thing I could do about it. I finally had to admit that it was time for me to bury my dead relationship and work on getting back to being the sexy, sassy, saucy woman I used to be. It wasn't gonna be easy, but I knew I had to try.

Ashamed, I turned away from the mirror and looked at Sabrina. "Okay. You're right," I surrendered.

Genine and Chantelle were now standing in the bathroom doorway, looking worried.

Finally, Sabrina started looking at me like she loved me instead of like she wanted to kick my ass. She smiled and said, "I know I'm right. Now get yourself together. Pick out some clothes, do your hair, and take a shower. We're goin' out."

"Where to?"

"Jimmie's. It's Flashback Friday. Old-school music all night."

"I don't know if I'm ready for all that—goin' to the club and—"

"Okay, you know what? I'm'a need you to be quiet and just . . . do what I said. We're going. You need to do this. Now," she looked at her watch, "it's getting late, so you need to put a rush on it. You got an hour and a half to get ready."

I wasn't thrilled with the idea of going out, but to shut her up, I gave in. "Fine. You guys can come back and get me. I'll be ready."

Genine poked her head in the bathroom. "Uh-uh. We're waitin' right here."

"But you're not even dressed."

"Our clothes are in the car. You forget that nobody knows you better than us. If we leave, you'll be back in that germ-infested bed quicker than we all can spit. So thank you, ma'am, but we'll do just fine to stay and get dressed *here,* so we can all leave together."

Chantelle added, "For real, 'cause right now, you know you can't be trusted."

I sucked my teeth and frowned. "Damn, y'all. I can't stand either one of you right now."

Sabrina said, "Whatever. Get your stank ass in the shower, please. The clock's ticking."

I wanted to put up a fight, but deep down, I knew they were right. If they had left, I would have gone straight to bed and called one of them to say I wasn't going. As much as I hated to admit it, I did need to get out and be around people other than my clients.

After they came back from getting their clothes out of the car, the girls made themselves comfortable in the living room while I perused my closet for something halfway decent. My eyes caught sight of something way in the back, and I pushed my way through all the other clothes to get to it. It was a brown leather pants outfit that I had gotten a couple of years prior, not long before I met Weston. After we got together, I put on a little weight and had to hang that 'fit up for a while, but now that I had shrunk back down a size or two, I knew it would be perfect.

I pulled it out, draped it across my bed, and then went back into the bathroom to begin to transform myself into a once-again-hot item. Since I hadn't done anything to my hair since the wedding, and my new growth was out of control, I popped open a brand-new kit and relaxed it right quick. When it was time to wash the cream out, I turned on the shower and hopped in.

I'll be honest; it did feel good to take an actual shower again. I didn't tell anyone this, but for over a month, because I was so depressed, I had been sleeping until the very last minute I could in the mornings. When I would finally force myself out of bed, I would go in the bathroom and take a ghetto bath— you know, fill the bathroom sink, put some soap and water on a washcloth and wipe yourself down, then rinse off using the water in the sink. It's not the most effective way to clean oneself up, but it gets the job done in a pinch. I also used up several containers of baby wipes keeping my private parts clean. After running some water and gel through my hair, I would tie it back in the bun that Sabrina was so offended by. It was the best I could do considering the state of mind I was in at the time.

The steaming-hot water felt wonderful. I still had the soap from the Elysium set that Weston bought me for my birthday right after we met, so I used that. It costs too much to be using every day, so I made sure I saved it for special occasions. I also still had half a bottle of lotion and some perfume, so I had plenty of product left to layer with.

It's true what they say about taking a long, hot

shower when you're depressed, making you feel like new person. By the time I got out, I felt totally rejuvenated. My hair felt good, my body was fresh, and the smell of the perfumed soap lingering in the bathroom lifted my spirits.

After I dried off, lotioned up and dabbed on some perfume, as fast as I could, I whipped my hair into shape. Once I put my clothes on and looked at myself in the mirror, I smiled at what I saw. Aside from the dark circles under my eyes and the mild acne that would take a couple of weeks to clear completely up, I actually felt attractive again. Those two obstacles could easily be taken care of with some makeup, so I wasn't too concerned about them.

I hadn't seen myself dressed up since the wedding, and the outfit was just right. I admired myself for a few minutes, and I started to feel good again. The girls had gotten dressed and had turned on the radio, and while I put the finishing touches on my face, we all danced and sang to some of the jams that came on.

Finally, shortly after midnight, I was ready to hit the streets with my sisters. On the way out the door, I stopped and told them, "I really love you guys. I don't know what I'd do without you."

They all said, "We love you, too, 'Trice."

The four of us stepped out into the balmy night, looking like models, and I was finally ready to begin my new life.

15

I can't remember when I've had more fun at a club. Jimmie's was off the hook that night, and I danced harder and better than I realized I knew how.

When I walked in, I felt like a celebrity. Men were all up on me like bees to honey. It felt good being back in the game, and I felt hopeful for a bright and happy future with someone new.

I stacked up on the phone numbers, and didn't give mine to anyone, of course, 'cause that's how I stay in control of things until I'm ready to move forward.

I decided to keep two guys' numbers and toss the rest. It turns out that I should have tossed them all, because those two that I chose to keep turned out to be duds, and my total dating time with both of them amounted to all of a month.

The first guy, Sydney, was a handsome, well-spoken brother from Detroit. He was a freelance photographer. I called him a couple of days after meeting him at the club, and our rapport was good. We talked for a long time about all kinds of interesting things. We went on

236   *Charlene E. Green*

three dates. On that third date, I realized I had to shut
him down when he told me about how he punched his
ex-girlfriend in the mouth when they got into an argument and she told him to kiss her ass. Trouble was, he
really thought he was entitled to that, and couldn't understand why she left him.

That night, when he dropped me off, I thanked
him for the date, went in the house and erased his
number from my phone. He called me for about a
week after that, but when he realized he had been cut,
he went on about his business.

The second guy, Wendel, but pronounced *Wen-dell*,
was a tall, succulent-looking man from New Jersey.
He was a professional mover and worked for May-
flower. I soon found out why he chose that field.

One day, while we were having lunch in Berkeley,
I used the word "collaborate" in a sentence, and he
looked at me funny. When I asked him what was
wrong, he asked me what collaborate meant. I was
shocked that he was even serious, but nevertheless,
explained the meaning of the word. Five minutes
later, when I used the word "nuisance" in a sentence,
and he asked me what *that* meant, I politely asked
him to get the check, and as soon as he took me
home, I checked out of that relationship before it
went any further.

About a week after I had done away with Sydney
and Wendel, the girls and I were at House Burgers,
the family-owned restaurant that Charles opened
back in 1995 with his brother, Robert, and older
sister, Rishidda.

We were discussing Genine's new job at the phone
company when a smooth brother with short, wavy

hair and a cute little mole on his nose, dressed in a business suit, stopped at our table.

He spoke to the others, then looked at me and said, "You are by far *the* most beautiful thing I have seen all year. My name is Evan Turner. What's yours?"

The girls smirked, and I smiled at Evan.

"Well, thank you, Evan Turner. I appreciate the compliment. I'm Katrice."

He stuck his hand out for me to shake, and when I extended my hand, he kissed the back of it, winking at me at the same time.

"I hope I'm not interrupting you young ladies here, but I just had to come and talk to you, Katrice. I feel like I need to get to know you."

Before I got a chance to respond, he whipped out a business card, wrote something on the back real quick, then looked at me.

"I'd like to give you my number, if you don't mind, and I hope you'll call me sometime soon." He handed me the card and looked at me like I was the one, the two, *and* the three.

"Thank you. I just might do that."

He looked at the girls and told them, "You ladies have a wonderful day." Then he looked at me. "All right now, Pretty, gimme a call." And he strutted out the door with his bag of food.

Sabrina shouted, "Girl, holla at *that . . . tonight!* Hell, right now. Call him from yo' cell . . . tell him you wanna hook up after we leave here!"

We all laughed.

I said, "He *was* a cutie, and he did have him some manners, huh?"

Chantelle asked me, "What's on the business card?"

I looked at the front. "Some real estate company."

"I bet he wrote his home number on the back. Look and see," Genine said.

I turned the card over, and sure enough, he had done just that.

"Yep. I got the home, cell, and job. All three numbers present and accounted for."

She said, "Well, then, I say call him. You got the magic three on the first day . . . you battin' a thousand. It's hard to get a home number these days."

"True . . . so true. I'm'a check him out." I put the card in my purse.

Sabrina got up to go get a refill on her drink, and when she came and sat back down, she asked me, "What's the deal with that head cook, Rishidda? That's the older sister, right?"

"Yeah, why? What happened?"

"Nothing really, she just seems so dry and rude. She never smiles, and I don't think I've ever heard her say anything to anyone."

"You remember, I told you about how she witnessed her fiancé, Cash, the big-time drug dealer, get killed in a drive-by a few years ago."

"I don't remember that. What happened, now?"

"Yes you do. That was the story that was all over the news. She was meeting him to pick up some money. She had their three kids in the car, and when she got out to get ready to walk over to him, a black Caddy with tinted windows drove by, slowed up, and someone in the car shot him in the head four times. She was standing right there, watching the whole thing. Then they sped off, and since there were no license plates on the car, she couldn't even give the police a license-plate number."

"You know what? I'm trippin'. I remember that.

That's right, because they said she started screaming and then the kids started screaming and all hell broke loose in the middle of the street. Okay, I gotcha. I didn't realize that was her."

"Yeah."

Chantelle said, "Well, I probably wouldn't talk to anybody, either. I'd be too messed up in the head to even come to work."

Genine jumped in. "I gotta jet, y'all. I got a lot to do before tomorrow. First day at a new job; gotta be on my A-game."

I said, "I need to get up outta here, too. I got a perm to do at four." I looked at Sabrina and asked her, "You workin' tomorrow?"

"Nope. I'm off."

I asked her, "How much longer you plan on workin' at that damn convalescent home?"

"Shut up. I like my job, Miss Prissy. It's peaceful to me."

"If you say so. Come on, y'all. Let's be out."

16

I called Evan the next night, and we talked for two hours. I liked him immediately and couldn't wait to go out with him. He was from the Bay Area and had been in real estate for six years.

He called me every day, and we went out at least five times in three weeks. He was a gentleman, had class, was educated, and handsome to boot. I started to feel like this was gonna be a relationship I could sink my teeth into.

I didn't sleep with him right away, because I wanted to make sure it was something I was really ready to do. I knew I wasn't over Weston, and I didn't wanna move too fast, even though I was looking for love again.

One evening, Evan took me out to an early dinner in Pleasanton, then we went back to his townhouse, which was in Hayward. I decided that morning that I was ready to do the do with Evan, so I made sure that when he picked me up for our date, I put the small pack of condoms that I had bought that morning, in my purse.

I had been to his house a few times by then, so when we walked in, I made myself at home on the couch and turned on the television. Evan put his wallet and cell phone down, took off his jacket, and went upstairs to hang it up.

No sooner had he left the room than his cell started ringing. For some strange reason, my women's intuition told me to look at the screen and see who was calling, which is something I normally wouldn't do.

I picked the phone up off the coffee table, looked at it, and saw the word "home" flashing across the screen and a phone number with a Richmond prefix blinking underneath it. I stared at the screen, hoping this wasn't what I thought it was, and started to panic.

I heard Evan coming down the stairs, so I looked really hard at the number, logged it into my brain, and put the phone back on the table. I wanted to go somewhere to write it down before I forgot it, so when Evan came back into the living room, I excused myself to go to the bathroom. I didn't bother to tell him his phone had rung.

I took my purse in with me, shut the door, and shuffled through it to find a pen. I found one, snatched it out, and in the process, accidentally pulled my pack of gum out, which fell on the floor next to the toilet. I wrote the number on an old receipt I had found, put the number and the pen back in my purse, then, reached down to pick up my gum.

Unfortunately, more than my gum was on the floor by the toilet.

When I picked it up, I thought I saw a familiar-looking item sticking out from behind the bowl. I stuck my head a little further back, and I couldn't believe my eyes.

It was a used condom.

I was furious.

I flushed the toilet so Evan wouldn't get suspicious, ran the sink water, and came out of the bathroom, ready to fight.

Instead, I said to him, "Evan, um . . . could you please take me home? I really don't feel good. I feel like I'm gonna throw up. I think it was the crab salad I ate."

"Oh, I'm sorry. I didn't know you were feeling sick, Pretty. You sure you don't wanna crash here tonight . . . go home in the morning? There's plenty of room here."

"No, no . . . I really should go home."

"Okay, then, lemme just get my jacket."

As soon as Evan dropped me off, I ran in the house, pulled out the number and rushed over to the phone.

I blocked my number, then dialed the one I got from Evan's phone. On the fourth ring, a soft-spoken woman answered. I almost hung up, but I had to know if what my intuition told me was right, so I went ahead and did my thing. I pretended to be a representative from the *Costa Times* newspaper. I got that little trick from Genine back in the day, when she found herself in the same situation I was in at that moment. She said it worked like a charm, so I decided to give it a try.

"Yes, good evening, is this the Turner residence?"

"Yes it is. May I ask who's calling?"

"Yes ma'am, this is Faith with the *Costa Times*. We were wondering if you or your husband . . . er . . . would that be . . . Evan?"

"Yes, that's right."

"Yes, okay. Would you be interested in a subscription today?"

"We already have a subscription with you guys."

"Oh. I'm sorry. Looks like we need to update our records, then. Sorry to have bothered you. You have a nice evening, ma'am."

"Thank you. You do the same."

The dirty bastard *was* married. I wondered what the hell the deal was, like if they were separated or something. Clearly, he spent a decent amount of time at the townhouse, because I had been there several times. No matter. Married was married. All I knew was, there would be no Evan and Katrice.

After I paced my floors for twenty minutes, thinking of ways to get my revenge on Evan, I realized that he wasn't even worth wasting my time on. I hadn't slept with him, we hadn't developed a solid mental bond yet, and although I was starting to really feel him, we really didn't have anything worth me going ballistic over. I was damn hot that he was a lying bastard, and that I *almost* gave him my goods that night, but other than that, it was early enough in the game for me to just stop returning his calls and move the hell on.

I will say that deep down, I was really hurt, because for a minute, I thought I had found a replacement for Weston. Evan seemed to have so many of the qualities that drew me to Weston, and I was just starting to feel comfortable about letting someone new in. Now I was back to square one, and *that* is what bothered me the most.

The next day, I woke up close to eleven in the morning with a terrible headache and a heavy heart. The Evan thing really disturbed me during my sleep. I had one bad dream about him after the other, and when I woke up, I realized I was more upset than I had antic-

ipated I would be. It wasn't so much that Evan had lied
to me; that was part of it, but mostly, I was really looking forward to starting a new relationship, and finally
getting over Weston, and now that wasn't going to
happen. I started thinking about us and the way we
were in the good ol' days. I fought back loads of tears,
because by then, *I* was tired of crying.

I was hungry, and I didn't feel like cooking anything. I decided to drive over to House Burgers to pick
up one of Charles's famous Big Bang Beefer cheese-
burgers, some seasoned curly fries, and a chocolate
shake with extra whipped cream falling off the top.

I went alone. I didn't want any company for some
reason. Normally, I would have called one or all of the
girls to join me, but that day, I felt like I needed time
to myself. Originally, I had planned on eating there,
but something happened to change my plans. It also
changed my life.

When I walked in, the place was unusually empty
for a Saturday afternoon. House Burgers did a booming business, so a slow day was a rare one. There
were all of seven people inside, and several of them
were on their way out.

I walked up to the counter and peered into the
kitchen. I saw Rishidda and we waved to each other.
I wasn't offended by the fact that she never smiled at
me, even though I was a regular and was friends with
her brother. In fact, everyone who knew about the in-
cident back in the day understood that with Rishidda,
there would be very little communication, if any at
all. I wasn't in a smiling mood, either, so we pretty
much acknowledged each other with stone faces.

One of the cashiers came out and took my order. I
went and sat down at a table in the corner to wait for

my food. About three minutes after I sat down, all of a sudden, Rishidda was standing at my side, looking down at me.

I was stunned, because I had never seen her anywhere except in the kitchen. I wasn't sure what was going on, but for some reason, the way she was looking at me was scaring me.

"Rishidda . . . hey . . . what's . . . what's up?"

She sat down at my table and continued to stare at me, which was starting to freak me out.

"I know a lot about pain," she started. "Deep pain. The kind that eats at your intestines every second of the day and makes you start looking old and worn down before your time. I been feelin' that kinda pain for three years."

She stopped and looked me deep in my eyes. My heart was thumping so hard I was sure she could hear it. I couldn't figure out where she was going with all this, and why she was telling me, of all people.

She went on to say, "I been in therapy for two and a half years. Before I started going, I was oblivious to other people and their pain. Now . . . I can read it on their faces in one glance. Sometimes, they exude pain from deep within their souls and they don't even know it. You been comin' here for a long time. You used to be happy. Now you're not. These days, when you walk in here, your pain is off the charts. Sometimes, I see you smiling with your girlfriends, but you're just pretending."

I was speechless, because she was right. I *had* been faking it since my breakup with Weston. Yeah, after the girls made me go out to the club that night, I did start feeling better, and I had my good days; but underneath it all, a large part of me was still numb. I was merely living day to day, going with the flow. I didn't respond, but gave her a look that said she had my full attention.

She continued, "When you came in today, I looked at you, and I knew that you needed help. You look like I used to look right after Cash was killed. I don't talk to too many people. Hardly anyone, really. But you . . . you need someone right now who understands the kind of pain you're in, and I do, even though I have no idea what your pain is about yet. So, if you wanna talk about it, I wanna listen. Maybe I can help."

My eyes started to water, I was so touched. I didn't know Rishidda at all, only through Charles and the restaurant. We were never friends, never had a conversation, never exchanged more than some hellos and how-are-yous. But at that moment, I felt like she was the best friend I ever had. Something in me wanted to share everything with her. I felt like I was gonna explode. I nodded, and the tears began to fall.

She looked at me with all the compassion in the world, reached over and touched my hand and said, "Come on. Let's go out back and sit on the steps. It's quiet out there."

She told the other cook to hold off making my order, took off her apron, told him she'd be back soon, and led me out to the back steps. We sat, and for the next hour, I spilled my guts to her about everything. I went back to high school and told her all about Royce, how I had always felt about him, what I went through when he rejected me, all of it. Then I told her all about Weston and our relationship. Next, I told her about Royce showing up at the wedding and our night together, and everything that happened after that up until that very moment.

She listened intently. She was totally focused on me and every word that came out of my mouth. I gave more details to her about my situation than I gave the girls. I let out every frustrated, hurt, angry, guilty feeling I had in me. And it felt damn good. I hadn't realized how tense I still was, and some of the things that came out were a surprise to me. I felt like a hose that hadn't been turned on in years. When it finally is turned on, the first thing that comes out is the built-up dirt inside; then after a moment, the clean water comes out.

After I released everything, we sat in silence for a few minutes. I dried my eyes, breathed a sigh of relief and looked out into the distance. At that point, I didn't even care if Rishidda had anything deep to say. It just felt good to finally get everything off my chest.

Finally, she looked over at me and said, "Katrice, you need to deal with your feelings. That's your problem. I can already tell by the way you just purged that you been tryina feel better without acknowledging how bad you feel. You can't do that. You'll never heal that way. Today was a good start for you, because I'll bet you haven't talked about this situation like this since it happened."

"I haven't."

"I can tell. But, you need to take it a step further."

"Meaning what?"

"In simple terms, somehow, through your own spiritual work, you need to find a way to make peace with what you did and why you did it, accept the outcome, and then let it go. I mean for good. I'm saying that, but I don't mean to sound like it's easy, 'cause it's not. The letting go is the hardest thing. You gotta find a way to be able to hold onto the good memories of you and your ex and be able to smile about them, and be okay with the fact that you're not together anymore."

"I don't know if I can do that. Be okay with our breakup, I mean. I want him back. It's not okay that we can't be together."

"But that's my point. When you do your work, you'll get to a place where yeah, you'll probably still love him, and you'll miss him, and if you *could* get back together, that would be great, but you'll fall into a mode of, 'Well, if we don't, I'll be all right.' That's what I mean by being okay with it. It's not like, 'Oh, I'm just so happy I lost the man I love.' It's more of an acceptance that it's over and time to move on."

"How are you dealing with Cash's death? How can you possibly be at a point where you wanna move on with your life?"

"I'm dealing with it, day by day. But I don't have a choice but to move on, 'cause Cash is never coming back. I know people think I'm rude and unfeeling 'cause I don't talk, but I have my reasons. I'm still working through a lot of pain. Cash's death isn't something I wanna talk about all the time. When people approach me, it seems like all they wanna talk to me about is Cash this and Cash that; how am I feeling, do I need to talk. No, I need to be left alone so I can heal.

"So, eventually, I got so annoyed with all the questions that I just stopped talking. People called me cold and mean, but hey, this is *my* pain, not theirs. I don't owe them *anything*. You're the first person I've talked to at length in over a year and a half. I don't even talk to my family that much, because they're the main ones harassing me about how I feel. I just go home, spend time with my kids, and when they have questions or feelings, we talk about them. But all in all, with my therapy, I'm doing okay. I'm not happy yet, but I can make it through the day without crying, and for me, that's a big thing."

"So, why did you choose me to talk to today?"

"I told you . . . I could see your pain plain as day, and I felt for you. It was just something I needed to do."

"So, what do I do now? I just feel lost."

"Well, I'll tell you what worked for me. Journaling. My therapist recommended it to me in the first month of my seeing her, and it's been the best medicine for me. We say a lot of things, but we think even more. We think about things we're not even aware are on our minds during the day. I guarantee you, if you start writing your feelings down every day in a journal, you'll be able to clear up so much stuff that you'll be amazed. But you gotta write something every day. Even if it's just a line, or even two words. That line or coupla words will lead into a whole journal entry that will blow your mind, mark my words. Even on days when you don't think you have any feelings to write, do it anyway. You'll be surprised at what comes out of you. I'm telling you, journaling is the quickest way I know to heal your mental wounds. When you leave here today, go to a really good stationery store and buy yourself a nice journal. Not some cheap, tacky one, either. Find one that really catches your eye, and spend some money on it. You'll understand why I say that when you buy it. Oh, and buy a few special pens to write in it with. Don't use them for anything else but your journal. Trust me, you won't regret it. You let me know how it goes, okay?"

"Thank you, Rishidda. I think you just saved my life."

I smiled, reached over and hugged her tight. After

a few more minutes of encouragement from Rishidda, we exchanged phone numbers, and she made me promise to call her before a week passed. We went back inside, I got my food, and then I headed straight for a stationery store to get my journal.

I had a diary once when I was about nine, but I didn't really use it, so writing in a journal was definitely something that would be new to me. I scanned the aisles until I found one that "caught my eye," as Rishidda had said. It was purple, burgundy, and dark blue, and the pattern kind of reminded me of little puffs of clouds. It was a hardback book, and the pages were thick, sturdy, and lined in gold. When I turned it over and saw that it cost almost thirty dollars, I almost put it down, I was so shocked. But then, I remembered what Rishidda had told me about splurging on one that cost a little bit of money, so I went ahead and bought it. I found three way-too-expensive multicolored pens and added them to the pot. In the end, I felt good about my purchases.

I took my food home, which had gotten cold, and while I warmed it up in the toaster oven, I set up a spot on my little balcony to prepare to write. I had no idea what I was gonna put in that journal, but I was damn sure gonna make a go of it.

Three hours and twenty-five pages later, I had written my very first journal entry, and let me tell you, I was shocked at the content of those pages. I figured my entry would consist of a repeat of everything I told Rishidda, but I was sorely mistaken. I won't go into detail, but suffice it to say, I had learned a lot of new things about myself by the time I was finished. Not to mention, I felt refreshed and so much lighter mentally. And Rishidda was right: I fell in love with my journal, and was glad I spent every penny of the thirty dollars on it.

Over the next two months, I not only wrote every day for at least an hour, but I also incorporated something else new into my daily life: complete and total silence. I noticed that when I was at home, I needed some type of distraction, be it the television or radio or a CD constantly going. I realized I was using the distractions to keep me from thinking, because if I was thinking, I was hurting, and the pain was too much for me to bear. So, in preparation for my hour of writing, I spent at least an hour either sitting or lounging quietly, with nothing but my thoughts. No phone calls, no television, no music. Just me. I had no idea how messed up in the head I was, and not just about the Weston situation. Other things started coming to light that I never even thought of.

By December, I was finally feeling like I had gotten a grip on the reality of my life, and just like Rishidda promised, I did reach a point where I felt like I could survive and be okay without Weston in my life. I definitely still loved him, but I was ready to let him go, if that's the way it had to be. I had made my choice that night in May, and it cost me a great guy. But the one thing that remained constant within my heart was that I was not sorry I spent that time with Royce. Don't read malice into that statement. I was sorry I hurt Weston, and that everything turned out so badly between us, but I honestly felt that night with Royce was necessary for me to be able to get on with my life. It just so happened that now, my life would be without Weston.

17

Five days before Christmas, I was at the shop in the evening cleaning and getting ready to leave. All my customers had already gone, and I couldn't wait to get home.

I had been feeling a little sad since it was the holidays, and even though I had advanced in a major way with the whole Weston situation, I still missed him, especially since Christmas and New Year's were near. The year was about to come to a close, and I was glad. It had been, hands down, the worst year of my entire life.

Around eight-thirty, while I was folding some bibs and putting away products, I heard a knock on the shop door. I turned around to see who it was, and my jaw dropped.

I shoved the bibs into the cubbyhole where I kept them, tossed the bottle of leave-in conditioner in my hand onto the counter, and ran to the door.

I unlocked and opened it, then stood there, staring at him in amazement.

Weston said, "I know you're closed, but can I come in for a few minutes?"

"Of course." I stepped out of the doorway.

My eyes followed him as he walked in. It was the first time I had seen him since the wedding. He had put on a little weight, his hair wasn't groomed all that well, and he needed to shave. He didn't look totally beat down, but he definitely wasn't his usual top-of-the-line self.

He walked over, pushed up a dryer head and sat down in the seat.

I sat down at the dryer next to him and waited for him to say something.

At first, he just sat there, looking across the room, spaced out. Finally, he looked over at me and said, "So, how you been?"

"Good. Okay. Terrible. All of the above. What about you?"

"I been better."

Then, neither of us said anything for about thirty seconds.

Just as I was about to make some more small talk to try to break the ice, Weston blurted out, "Tell me what happened. Don't leave nothin' out."

He thought about that statement for a second, then changed his mind.

"Except the sex. I don't wanna hear about the sex."

I took a deep breath and recalled the entire evening of May twenty-fifth, action for action, word for word, thought for thought. Everything but the sex.

After I told him the story, he stared at me for a moment. There was still so much curiosity and confusion in his eyes. I could read his mind, so before he even had a chance to ask his next question, I started explaining further.

"I don't know if you've ever had anything just stay with you and gnaw at you for a really long time, but it's nerve-racking. It's like, an obsession or something. You don't know what it is or why it is. All you know is you need to do something about it, and if the opportunity ever presents itself, you're gonna jump at the chance to see what it's all about. So, when my opportunity came around, yeah, I knew it was wrong, and yeah, I felt guilty about it. I also knew if you ever found out, we'd probably be having this very conversation sooner or later. And believe it or not, I didn't jump right on it. It took me awhile to make my decision because of you. Because I love you and I didn't wanna lose you."

"Oh, so just 'cause you didn't do it right away, that's supposed to make it okay?"

"No, it's not okay. It was never okay. That's not what I'm saying."

"Then why didn't you stop yourself?"

"Because—I had to kill it. I had to kill the craving. It had been killing *me* for so many years that I thought I was gonna lose my mind. I just had to get it outta my system once and for all. Weston, you have *no idea* how I struggled with that decision. I'll never be able to put into words how hard it was for me to do what I did. But the honest truth is . . . I did it so I could get on with my life . . . with *you*. I didn't want a bunch of Royce what-ifs haunting me for the rest of my existence."

"And you think it's out your system now?"

"Definitely."

"How can you be sure?"

"I just know how I felt after it was all over, and all I can say is that I knew that was the end of it."

"So, what if you didn't get it out your system? What then?"

"I can't answer that. It's out of my system, so I can't speak on any other feeling except what I feel."

"But, just for argument's sake, what do you *think* you would do if you didn't kill the craving all the way?"

"Weston, I really can't answer that. I'm not in the situation."

He huffed, then, realizing that conversation was a moot point, he let it go. But I could tell it was still bugging him.

"You know what hurts the most? That this dude can just step to you after fifteen years—*fifteen years*—and just straight break you down in one night. Every time I think about it, I just . . ."

I went to touch him, but he pulled away from me and continued talking.

"I gave you more of myself than I've ever given any other woman on this earth. How could you just . . . go with him? After all these years? After everything we been to each other? We had a serious bond. How could you just throw all that away for one night with a man who obviously don't have no respect for you or *care* nothin' about'choo? He knew you were weak for him. He *knew* it. He took advantage of that weakness to get what he wanted, and you let him. It's not like he came to try to build a life with you or anything. I mean, I woulda had more respect for the man if he had come at you like, 'Look, I wanna be with you and I'm'a do whatever I need to do to take you from yo' man, 'cause I believe you're the one for me.' I mean, hey, you can't fault a brotha for goin' after what he wants, but that ain't even what he's about. You don't just blow into town, sex some other man's woman for one night, and then leave. That's the coward's way. Hell, if a man is gon' go through all that to ruin a relationship, at the very *least* he should be tryina have somethin' long-term wit' the woman. But he ain't tryina do that wit'choo. *I was,* and you tossed all my love and commitment aside and stepped on it, all so you could fulfill a damn fantasy. I mean, you just told me the man said he was always interested in you, right? You ain't seen him in what . . . ten years? He ain't called, wrote, or tried to see you . . . that don't sound like a man who's truly interested in a woman to me. I may not *be* a dog, but I do know the ways of 'em, and I'm'a tell you right now, you got bit by one of the big ones."

He took a breather, and I stayed silent. It had taken him seven months to finally confront me, and I wanted to make sure I heard every word of how he felt.

He continued. "Bottom line, you put a man who wasn't serious about you over me. I showed you every day, in every *way* how serious I was about you, and that wasn't enough. I just couldn't deal wit' that. I just can't believe you let that cat use you and talk you into disrespectin' me like that. I thought you were smarter than that, Katrice."

I felt small, smaller than the Mini-Me's in my dream seven months prior. Weston was making me feel like I got played like a super-sucker, and my ego was bruised.

I don't know why, but I tried to defend Royce by reminding Weston, "But remember, he *did* say he wanted the long-term with me, it's just that he had already made a life for himself back East."

After I said it, I realized maybe it wasn't the best

thing to say. Weston might take it as a slap in the face. I was afraid of what might come out of his mouth next.

Instead of getting mad, he just laughed as if I sounded ridiculous. "And you *fell* for that? Of *course* he would say somethin' like that. He wanted something from you. A man is gon' say what a man has to say to get what he wants in the heat of the moment, Katrice. *Come on.* I know you know that."

I was feeling more and more stupid by the minute.

He went on. "Lemme tell you somethin'. If he *really* wanted the long-term, he woulda either been tryina pack *you* up to move out there with *him,* or he woulda been makin' plans to pack his *damn* self up to move back out here to throw down wit' me so he could have you. Leslie's husband did it. Packed up and moved out to Chi-Town from Boston to be with her. My boy Guy just did it. He helped his girl find a job and an apartment out in D.C. and helped pay for her to move out there to be wit' him. Plain and simple, if he was about you, he woulda had no problem fightin' for you. Period. I'm just . . . I'm *hurt.* You let another man get between us. And on top of that, he never even came *close* to havin' the feelings for you that I do."

When I thought about it, Weston was right. It had been seven months since that night, and not once had Royce tried to contact me. Granted, I purposely didn't exchange numbers with him, but he knew who to call to find me if he really wanted to. He was a coward in high school, and apparently nothing had changed.

While on one hand, I was still glad I got Royce out of my system, on the other hand, I had caused a lot of unnecessary pain and suffering for both Weston and myself, and for *that*, I was truly regretful.

We sat in silence for a few minutes. He stared out the window and I sat with my head hung low. I wanted to tell him I was sorry, but at that point, after everything he had just said, I knew it wouldn't have meant much. Besides, I felt ashamed. Words had pretty much escaped me.

It had started to rain pretty hard. I felt awful. I had waited so long to hear Weston's feelings, and now that I had, I was upset all over again. I wanted to cry, but I was all cried out, so I let the raindrops be my tears while I waited for Weston to say something . . . anything to let me know that somehow, we were gonna be okay. I hadn't stopped loving or wanting him, and something told me he felt the same way, or he never would have shown up that night.

I asked him, "What made you come here tonight? After all this time?"

"Lotta things. But mostly, my mother."

I already knew I wasn't gonna get an elaboration on what a "lotta things" were, but I was curious to know what his mother had to do with it.

"Why your mother?"

"We talked for a long time one night about a month and a half ago, and she reminded me that what I was doin' to you was the same thing I did to my pops for all those years. She told me I needed to work on the part of me that shuts down on people when they hurt me. Said it's not healthy for me to harbor all that negativity. I've always been like that, though. People betray me, I cut 'em off. She told me it was time for me to leave that habit in the past and evolve into a more mature person."

He paused in deep thought.

"My mother knows how to reach me when nobody else does."

"Well, I'm glad she did."

In a split second, something major dawned on me. I realized that Weston had some very important information that *I* needed. Before he could speak again, I told him, "I need to know something. How did you find out about that night?"

He continued looking out the window as he filled in the blanks for me.

"Like I told you, I came back early so I could surprise you by showin' up at the wedding. I got there around seven. I woulda been there a lot sooner, but my flight was delayed almost two hours. By the time I got on the plane, I knew I was gon' be late, but I still wanted to make an appearance. When I got there, everything was over and people were already cleanin' up and leavin'. I asked one of the girls there if she had seen you, and she told me she saw you outside talkin' to Royce about an hour before I got there. I started trippin' when she said that, 'cause I remembered the story you told me on our first date, so I went and found Tiki and asked her where you were. She said you told her you were tired and you were gon' go home so you could get some rest so you'd have enough energy to help her move the next day.

"I went straight to your house, but you weren't there. I didn't wanna think the worst, but somethin' kept tellin' me you were with him. I sat outside your house in my car for three hours and I called your cell every ten minutes. I just sat there gettin' madder and madder by the second.

"Around ten-thirty, I got ready to leave and my

phone rang and it was Eric. He asked me what happened between me and you. I said, 'Nothin', why?' And then he asked me if I was sure we didn't have a fight or break up and just didn't wanna tell him, and I told him no. Then he said, 'Well, then why was she checkin' in the hotel tonight wit' some dude named Royce?'"

I jumped in. "Wait a minute . . . how does Eric know what I did and where I was that night? He wasn't there."

Finally, Weston turned away from the window and looked at me. "Eric *was* there. You just weren't payin' attention. Matter of fact, he said you looked him dead in the face a coupla times while y'all were at the counter checkin' in."

"*What? Wait* . . . I still don't get it. Where was Eric to see me checking in with Royce?"

He started getting mad, like he was having flash-backs of that night. He raised his voice at me. "Behind the damn counter, Katrice."

I got scared. "Behind the counter?"

"Yeah. He shaved off all his facial hair and cut off his dreads right after he got that job. But you were so preoccupied, you didn't even know who you were lookin' at."

I felt like the biggest asshole alive. "Oh my God . . . I feel *so* stupid." I rested my right palm on my forehead and looked down at the floor. "That's why he kept look-ing at me."

Weston got sarcastic on me. "That would be why, yeah."

So, the mystery was finally solved. Eric was the snitch, and I stood right there, looking him in the face, thinking he was just another sleazy brother trying to peep me out. How arrogant of me. Granted, I had only seen Eric a few times since the day I first met him, and really, I wasn't looking that hard at him, so it's no wonder I didn't recognize him without the mustache, beard, and dreads. But Weston was right: If I hadn't been so damn preoccupied with what I *wasn't* supposed to be doing, I may have been able to figure out it was him.

"Oh my God . . . I'm *so* sorry. That must've been so embarrassing for you."

"Actually, I was glad he called, 'cause I already had a feelin' y'all were together somewhere, and he just confirmed it for me."

"So, what did you do? How did you know I'd be home when you came over?"

"I told Eric what was up and what I was thinkin' before he called me. He told me to meet him down at Club Dimension, and that's where we stayed till about two-somethin'. We had a few drinks, talked, and I got seriously buzzed.

"When I left him, I stopped and got me a forty, then headed to your house. I knew you'd be there 'cause I know you too well. You mighta fucked him, but I knew you wouldn't be able to bring yo'self to spend the whole night with him. You ain't got that kinda boldness in you."

"Weston, I don't know what else to say. I'm just . . . so sorry about that whole night."

"Are you? Sorry about the night, or just sorry you got caught?"

"Weston . . ."

"Don't answer that . . . I already know the answer." He looked so hurt.

I was afraid to try to touch him again, so I left that

alone. I was anxious about our next move, so after a few seconds, I asked him, "So, what now? I mean, what are we doing? What about us? *Is* . . . there an us?"

He wasn't ready to talk about "us" yet. I could tell, because he got up and started putting his jacket on. I was sorely disappointed, but I don't know why I expected anything different. It was our first conversation since that night. I guess it would have been too much to hope for to have him tell me he loved me, kiss me like he did when we first started out, tell me there was no way he was ever gonna let me go again, and then take me home for a night of passionate make-up-for-lost-time lovemaking.

Instead, he headed for the door. "I gotta go."

"Weston, wait—"

He turned and looked at me, and I could see his eyes beginning to fill with tears.

"I . . . I love you." I swallowed the lump in my throat. "I only love *you*. That's not gonna change, no matter what. Even if you leave here and never speak to me again. You're the only man I wanna be with, whether you believe that or not."

He sniffed, blinked hard two times, then slowly walked out the door with no response.

Of course, I wanted him to take me back, but I realized I meant what I said to him. No matter what, I would always love him. Even if there never was an "us" again, I felt spiritually cleansed and ready to deal with whatever the outcome might have been. We had finally had it out, so to speak. Now, the ball was entirely in his court.

18

Sixteen days had passed since Weston and I talked. I had hopes of us at least speaking again, but I had accepted the fact that we may not be anything more than friends in the future, if that. I also had hopes that the year 2000 would be better than the last one.

Around ten-thirty-one Saturday morning, my phone rang. When I looked at the caller ID, I saw Weston's name and nearly fainted. I didn't wanna seem too anxious to talk to him, so I let the phone ring three times before I answered.

He wanted to meet me at the lake, in our favorite spot, a little area near Fairyland away from the main trail, where we used to sit and talk. He said he had something he wanted to tell me, but wouldn't say what it was. I didn't push the issue by asking. I just told him I'd be there.

I was nervous. Since Weston didn't tell me what the news was on the phone, I had all kinds of things running through my head. We had said one o'clock, and lo and behold, he actually showed up at one on the nose.

He walked up to me and paused. The moment was awkward, because I don't think either of us knew what to do with the other person. Of course, I wanted to jump into his arms and kiss him, but I didn't dare do that, because I didn't wanna risk him pushing me away from him. I still didn't know where his head was at. So, instead, I just stood there, waiting for him to make some sort of move.

To my disappointment, he didn't even touch me. He simply said, "How you doin'?" and kept his distance.

"I'm good. You?"

"All right."

He jumped right in. "Look. I don't wanna do this anymore. I wanna work things out. I love you. I need you in my life. I haven't been right since we broke up. I been workin' hard on gittin' past . . . what'choo did. I hate that you did it, but I think I can forgive you . . . now that, you know, we talked and everything. I just . . . wanna know if you feel the same way. I mean, if you wanna work it out, too."

I could have turned a cartwheel right there. I couldn't believe he had just said it. He wanted me back, and he was asking me if I felt the same way.

"I don't even know why you're asking me that, Weston. I been waitin' for you to say this to me since the night of the wedding. Of course I wanna work it out. That's all I've ever wanted."

He had an urgent look on his face. "Are you sure? I mean, really sure?"

"What do you mean, am I sure? Yeah, I'm sure. Why? 'Cause if you're worried about me cheating on you again, that's not gonna happen. I guarantee it."

"No, that's not it. I just need to be certain . . . 'cause . . . I need to tell you somethin', first."

"O . . . kaaayy . . ." I already didn't like the sound of things.

He blew out a long puff of air, looked away for a few seconds, then looked at me and didn't say anything. I couldn't take the suspense anymore.

"Weston . . . what's wrong? Say something. You're making me crazy, here."

He started wiping his palms on his pants, and I was so scared I nearly lost my breakfast. He only wiped his palms on his pants when something major was on his mind or about to happen.

Finally, he spoke. "I'm sorta . . . uhh . . ." he struggled for a few seconds, then blurted it out. "I'm sorta expectin' a baby next month."

My face got hot, my whole being deflated, and I stood stiff as a statue, with my eyes fixed on his. I stopped breathing, as I waited for him to start laughing and tell me he was just kidding. But he didn't.

After I stared him down and got nothing, I forced myself to speak. *"WHAT . . . DID YOU . . . JUST . . . SAY?"*

He didn't answer me. He just stood there, looking ashamed.

"WESTON . . . did you just say . . . you're expecting a *BABY? NEXT MONTH?"*

He nodded, then started looking scared.

"Weston James Porter . . . you *BETTER BE JOKING, AND YOU BETTER LAUGH IN THE NEXT FIVE SECONDS!"*

But he didn't laugh. He didn't even blink.

I went off.

"ARE YOU FUCKING KIDDING ME?!" I charged at him like a bull on crack, then I slap-shoved him as hard as I could in the middle of his chest. The force from the blow knocked him off balance, and he nearly fell over. I wasn't even scared he would hit me back, because I knew he wouldn't.

"WHAT THE FUCK DO YOU MEAN YOU'RE EXPECTING A GODDAMN BABY, WESTON?! YOU BETTER START TALKIN', 'CAUSE I'M ABOUT TO *KILL* YOUR ASS OUT HERE!" I had never screamed that loud at anyone before. People were staring at us, but I gave *less* than a damn. I was in the rage of my life.

"Wait a minute . . . stop hollerin'." He took three steps backward, then put his hands up, surrender style.

"I will holler all I feel like it! Who's havin' your baby? If it's due next month, that means you were with her sometime in May! What . . . did you cheat on *me*?! 'Cause if that's the case, we can git 'em up right here for all the torture you put me through!"

"Whoa, whoa . . . hold on . . . I didn't cheat on you. That's your arena, remember?"

I almost punched him in the goddamn face. "You're a *real bastard*, you know that?"

"Hey, I'm just statin' the facts, baby. If you'd let me talk, I could *tell* you what happened."

"Fine. Talk."

"This girl I used to work with . . . Yolanda . . . she had a party about a week after we broke up, and she came by the job to invite a bunch of us. I didn't really wanna go, but I needed to get out the house 'cause all I could think about was you. So, I went over there and kicked it; me and a few guys started talkin' and it got late. Pretty soon, everybody was leavin'. I started talkin' to Yolanda right before I was about to leave and she asked me about you. I told her we broke up. Next thing I know, after everybody's gone,

I'm spillin' my guts and we're sittin' on the couch, havin' a drink. She listened to me. And I was hurt and lonely. I appreciated the company, and we had been cool anyway from when we used to work together, so talkin' to her was easy.

"Anyway, she hugged me and said everything was gon' be okay, and when she released me, I just kissed her. I don't know what came over me. I had never really been attracted to her, even though she's an attractive young lady, but we just never felt each other like that. I was just in need of some physical attention. She didn't stop me from kissin' her, and she was kinda buzzed anyway, so one thing led to another and we ended up hookin' up, right there on the couch. It wasn't even nothin' romantic, it was just sex. And before you ask, no, we didn't use anything. I know it was stupid, but at the time, I just didn't care. I wasn't really trippin' off any kind of aftermath or consequences. I just wanted to feel better. I didn't even stay the night with her. She knew I wasn't into her, so she wasn't even offended. She understood what was up.

"About three weeks later, she called me and told me she was pregnant. She started cryin' and sayin' how she thought about havin' an abortion, but if she did, it would be her second one, and she didn't wanna keep doin' that to her body."

I huffed, "And you didn't stop to think that it might not be yours, I guess. If she's lettin' *you* hit it raw, no tellin' *who* else she's been with."

"It's mine. I ain't crazy. We had a paternity test done. She was mad at first that I told her I wanted one, but she got over it quick."

That shut me up. I should have known he wasn't gonna just take her word for it.

"Anyway, after we got the results of the test, we talked about it for a long time, and I told her I would be there to do what I had to do as a father. She wasn't askin' me to be her man, plus, she already knew that wasn't gon' happen anyway. We get along and we're friends, but that's it. She's good people, but I don't wanna be with her."

"So, wait . . . lemme get this straight. You got me out here to tell me you *do* wanna get back together, right?"

"Right."

"But you're havin' a baby with another woman, which you've obviously known about since June, yes?"

"Yes."

"And now I'm supposed to just jump for joy over the fact that after it took you *seven months* to finally talk to me, you've decided you want me back? Then you tell me you're expecting a *child* and that's just supposed to automatically *work* for me?"

"I don't know why not. You wanted yo' little tryst with Royce to be okay with me, so what's the difference? It's not like I love Yolanda."

"Oh my God, that's not the point! We're talking about the difference between me spending a few hours with a man, versus *you* bringing a whole new *life* into the world and being bonded with the mother forever! There's no comparison! I can't even *believe* this! And then you didn't even bother to tell me sooner. What's *that* about?"

"Tell you for what? We weren't even together, and to be honest, I wasn't sure I was even gon' try to get back with you. So, why would I just call you up and tell you somethin' like that?"

I didn't have an answer.

"Look, I made a mistake. We *both* made mistakes.

Big ones." He moved toward me. "But I know we can work past 'em if we really want to."

"Weston. *My* mistake left the state. I don't ever hafta see *my* mistake again. *Your mistake* is gonna be up in our faces for as long as we're together. It's just not the same thing and I think you know it! I can't *believe* you . . . gettin' with that girl like that."

"Wait, hold up. You ain't in no position to be judgin' what I did *after* we broke up, considerin' what *you* did while were were *together.* If it wasn't for *you*, none of this would even be jumpin' off!"

"Uh-uh . . . don't blame *me* 'cause *you* acted irresponsibly! At least I did use protection with Royce!"

"You gave your *body* to another man while you were supposed to be committed to *me!* Just 'cause you used protection don't make it no better!"

"We already went through this two weeks ago, and I told you why I did what I did and I said I was sorry! Now either you forgive me or you don't, but do *not* keep throwing it in my face, 'cause I can't *live* like this! I WON'T LIVE LIKE THIS!"

"I'm here with you, aren't I?"

"And what does that mean?"

"It means . . . I wanna be with you, whether I have a baby with another woman or not. I don't love her. I love *you*. I miss you. We belong together. So just . . . work with me, here. I know this is a bad situation, but I can't fix it. The baby's due at the end of next month. And I *have* to take care of my child, Katrice. I just can't turn my back on my own baby."

"I'm not asking you to. It's just . . . this was supposed to be *us*. *I'm* supposed to be having your baby. This is *awful*."

"Do you wanna be with me or not?"

"You know I do."

"Okay. Then be with me. That's it. Let's just be together."

"But, what are we gonna do?"

"I don't know . . . just . . . we gon' . . . do whatever we have to. But we gon' be together."

He wrapped those arms that I missed so much around me, and I collapsed into his thick chest. We stayed like that for a long time. No words, no tears, just us, hugging for the first time in months.

I told Weston that I needed to go home and think, and that I would call him later. He said that was fine, and that he had some errands to run.

By dusk, I had already told everybody the good and the bad news about Weston and me. No one could believe the turn of events, but they were all glad we were getting back together.

One thing was for sure: The year 2000 sure was getting off to a rocky start. All I knew was, the tunnel was very, very dark, and I needed to see the light at the end of that bitch *real fast*.

I also knew that even though I finally had my man back, things would never, ever be the same.

19

Dealing with Weston's baby issue was hard. It seemed like he never had enough time to spend with me, and every time I turned around, Yolanda needed something from him. I tried not to say too much about it, because our relationship was still in the fragile state, but one day in particular, I just couldn't take it anymore.

Weston and I had just gotten back to his house from going to a matinée. We had planned on hooking up with P.J. and Lateshia to go to an Eric Jerome Dickey book signing at Mark's Bookstore later that day.

Around half an hour before we were supposed to meet P.J. and Lateshia, Weston's cell phone rang. It was Yolanda, calling to ask Weston if he could come over to her house to help her put the baby's crib together. She had ordered it online, and it had just been delivered. Originally, her brother was supposed to help her, but he had to work.

Weston said, "Sorry, babe. I'm'a hafta catch E.J.D.

another time. I gotta go do this. You go ahead without me."

I sucked my teeth and started mumbling underneath my breath.

"I'm *so* sicka this shit."

"What'choo say?"

"I said, I'm sicka this shit."

"And what shit is that?"

"I'm sicka her. I'm sicka you always runnin' off and leavin' me for her. I'm sicka this whole situation."

"What the hell is yo' problem?"

All out of the blue, I burst out, "What about our kids?"

"What kids?"

"Our kids . . . if we have any."

"So, what about 'em?"

"What would you do if you needed to be in two places at once?"

"What'choo talkin' about?"

"What would you do if there was something going on with her baby and there was something going on with our baby, and you needed to be in two places at the same time?"

"What kinda question is that?"

"The kind of question I need you to answer. What if it was between her baby and our baby? What would you do?"

"Why you keep sayin' 'her baby' like I'm not involved? That's my baby, too, and you need to start acknowledgin' that. It's not *her* baby, it's *our* baby."

"Well, you know what I mean."

"Yeah, that's yo' psyche talkin'. You don't want it to be my baby, that's why you keep sayin' 'her baby,' 'cause you wish it wasn't mine."

"Well, of course I wish it wasn't yours. But there's nothin' we can do about that now, is there?"

"So then why you trippin'?" .

"I wanna know which baby is gonna come first. Are you gonna love her—*y'all's* baby more 'cause it came before ours?"

"You doin' *way too much*."

"No I'm not, I'm just asking."

"Of course I'm not gon' love one of my kids more than the other."

"How do you know?"

"'Cause no matter how many kids I end up with, I'm'a love 'em all the same 'cause they mine."

"Okay, but you still haven't answered the original question."

"*What original question?* I'm still not knowin' what'choo trippin' on."

"About our kids and the one you got with her. What would you do?"

"Hell, I don't know. I can't even answer that."

"Why not?"

"Because it's not *happening* right now."

"So, you sayin' you don't know which baby you'd be there for?"

"I just said I can't answer that."

"Well, I don't see why not."

"For the same reason you couldn't answer me when I asked you not two damn months ago what you woulda done if you couldn't get Royce out yo' system. And what did you tell me? You couldn't answer the question 'cause you weren't in the situation!"

"Why are you bringin' up that thing with Royce? I don't wanna talk about him!"

"We *not* talkin' about him! We talkin' about the

fact that you askin' me the same type of question right now that I asked you that night, and you wanted me to accept yo' answer then, and I'm tellin' you to accept the same one from me now!"

"Well, can you at least *think* about what you'd do?"

"No! Why would I think about somethin' that ain't even happenin'?"

"Because it's an issue that needs to be taken into consideration!"

"No it ain't!"

"Why not?"

"BECAUSE WE DON'T HAVE KIDS, KATRICE! *Damn*, I *hate* that about you!"

"So now you're *hating* things about me all of a sudden? Wow."

"You always wanna get all hypothetical about shit and be tryina cross bridges that ain't even built! You need to just deal wit' stuff when it happens insteada creatin' extra worries! You makin' things harder than they need to be!"

"No! *You* just don't wanna think about it 'cause you don't wanna have kids with me!"

"Oh, *MY* God! What the *hell* are you talkin' about? I mean, do you even *know*?"

"I didn't hear you deny it!"

"You know how retarded you sound right now?"

"I'm not retarded!"

"I didn't say *you* were retarded; I said you *sound* retarded!"

"Fine, if you don't wanna answer my question then don't!"

"This whole conversation is fuckin' preposterous!"

"Great, then let's end it! I'm gone!"

"Gone where?"

"I dunno . . . just gone!"

And I slammed out of Weston's house in a fit of rage.

I really didn't know where I was going, so I just got in the car and started driving. I called P.J. and told him Weston and I wouldn't be going to the book signing, and to go on without us.

Before I knew it, I was headed to my parents' house. For some reason, I needed my daddy.

When I got to the house, I went in through the back entrance where the patio is. I could smell Daddy's cigar smoke floating over the fence. When I opened the gate, Daddy looked up at me and smiled. He was drinking some iced tea and reading his newspaper. I walked over, kissed him, and sat down in the chair next to him.

"Hey, Daddy."

"Hey there, Chickadee."

"Where's Mama?"

"In the kitchen."

"So, how you doin'?"

"Just fine." He studied me. "And how are you today?"

Daddy always knew when something was bothering me. All of a sudden, I felt overwhelmed. I felt all my pent-up emotions rising to the surface, about to erupt. My throat got tight, and a few seconds later, the tears climbed to the corners of my eyes.

My voice cracked. "I don't . . . know."

Daddy raised his eyebrows and looked at me over the top of his glasses. "You don't know? Look like you cryin' to me, so you must know somethin'."

"Well . . . I just . . . can't deal with this whole baby thing. It's just getting to be too much already and Weston and I haven't even been back together a full month. I'm sicka this. Sicka *her*. She's always calling and interrupting our private time together 'cause she needs something, and he's always running off to do stuff for her. It's like we can't even get a moment's peace. I just want it to be me and him . . . like it used to be. Every time we get ready to do something or go somewhere, his phone rings and it's *her* . . . beggin'. I just wish she'd find her own man and leave mine alone. The closer the due date gets, the more she calls."

"Treecie, that's *his* baby, not some other man's. What'choo expect her to do?"

"I don't know . . . just . . . fend for herself or something. Why does she always hafta call him? Damn. He got a life, too."

"Lemme tell you something, Katrice."

Daddy only says my name when he's about to break me off.

"You young people need to start taking care of the good things you got in your lives, 'cause you can easily lose those things if you don't. And ain't no guarantee that if you get somethin' back, it's gon' be in the same good shape it was in when you lost it.

"Now you made a choice that night when you went with that boy. You chose to risk your relationship with Weston and all the good things you had goin' for yourselves as a couple. You chose to risk breakin' somethin' that wasn't broken in the first place, and I'm'a tell you right now, you lucky you got it back. Now if you wanna keep it, you gon' hafta learn to deal with things the way they are *now* and let go of the way they *used* to be. Those days ended when you did what you did. I'm not tryina make you feel guilty; I'm just tryina get you to understand that these are the consequences that came with your actions, and you can't go back. What's done is done, and what is now, is.

"So, it's up to you. Either you want what'choo got or you don't. If you do, then my suggestion is you need to stop hatin' and start supportin'. I'm warnin' you, don't get in the way of that man takin' care of his responsibilities and bein' a good father to that child. These black men today got a hard enough time committin' to they kids. You got a man who wants to do the right thing. Let him. Respect him for it. And don't cause no trouble."

I didn't say a word. I just sat there with my head hanging down. I knew he was right. I was being selfish and childish, and I owed Weston an apology ASAP.

After a moment, I looked up. "I know . . . you're right. Thanks, Daddy." I got up and kissed his forehead. "I gotta go. I'll call you later, okay? I love you. Can you tell Mama I said I'll see her later on? If I go inside, she'll wanna talk, and I got somethin' I need to do right now."

"Sure thing, baby. No problem. Go on."

After I left Daddy, I needed a little extra time to get my head together before I faced Weston, so I walked the lake once really fast. When I was finished, I called Weston's cell. He answered on the first ring.

"Where you at, babe?"

"Lake."

"What'choo doin'?"

"Just finished walkin' it."

He paused. "We need to talk, you know that, right?"

"Yeah. Come over to my house when you're done, okay?"

"Okay. We almost through. Gimme about another half-hour."

"All right."

Weston showed up about an hour later. I apologized and told him I would try to be more understanding. He assured me that along the way things would get easier, but I didn't really believe him. I just went along with what he said to avoid another argument.

We got comfortable at my place and spent a quiet night in, just talking. He even turned off his cell, which made me feel a lot better. No interruptions; just us, the way we used to be.

20

One night, Weston and I had just gotten back from having dinner in Jack London Square. We settled in at my apartment to watch a couple of movies we had rented earlier that day.

A couple of weeks had gone by since the baby blow-up when I stormed out, and finally, I was feeling like Weston and I were our old selves again. We had gotten back to interacting the way we used to in the beginning, with only a minimal amount of tension between us. Now that I had cheated on him and another woman was carrying his child, both of us had our "moments."

Sometimes, I would catch Weston just staring at me with a blank look on his face. When I would ask him what was wrong, he would always say nothing, but I knew he was still fighting to accept my indiscretion.

I, on the other hand, didn't so much stare at him, but sometimes when we would make love, I had horrifying visions of him groping and sweating all over the mother of his unborn child as they did their dirty couch deed. I hadn't met her yet, and really, I didn't want to, but I knew the day would soon come when it would be necessary.

About nine-thirty, just as we were getting ready to pop in a Bruce Lee movie so Weston could get his kung fu dose, my home phone rang. The caller came up "private," and I usually don't answer those calls, but something told me to pick up this time. I was shocked at who was on the other line.

"Hi . . . is Weston there? This is Yolanda."

I spun around and mean-mugged him, then said in my most professional tone, "Just one moment, please."

I extended the receiver to him, and he got up to get it while looking at me like he couldn't figure out what my problem was. I stood there with my arms folded, mad as hell.

After they talked for less than twenty seconds, Weston went and sat back down like everything was everything, which made me madder than I already was.

"So, what was that call about, if you don't mind me asking?" I asked sharply.

"She was just remindin' me about her doctor's appointment tomorrow. I told her I'd take her since her car's in the shop. Why, is there a problem?"

"Uh, *sort of*. How did she get my number?"

"What'choo mean how did she get it? I gave it to her."

"For what?"

"So she can reach me if I'm here."

"*You* got a cell phone."

"What's the problem?"

"I'm just wonderin' why she needs to have my phone number. Why does she hafta call you *here*? Why can't she call you on your cell?"

"Katrice, the baby's due in less than two weeks.

Wherever I am, I need her to be able to reach me. Anything could happen."

"Well, if something happens, then wouldn't you think the best place for her to reach you would be your cell? What if we decided to leave?"

"Jesus! Why you trippin'?! It's no big deal, shit! Grow up and stop actin' like a damn brat!"

"Excuse me?"

"You heard me; now git off the subject! Sit down and watch the movie! We supposed to be havin' quality time and you messin' it up!"

"*Me?!* I'm not the one jumpin' up takin' phone calls!"

"Katrice! SIT DOWN! And quit it!"

Before I could say another word, all I heard rolling through my head was my father telling me not to cause any trouble, and there I was, causing trouble again.

Immediately, I apologized. "You're right. I'm sorry. I'm . . . I'm not gonna cause any more trouble, okay? I'm sorry. I swear, this won't happen again."

"We can't keep havin' these fights or this isn't gon' work, Katrice. I know this is hard for you, but I'm strugglin', too. You gotta stop bein' so insecure. I'm here with *you. Period.* Yes, I'm havin' a baby with someone else. I know it's a big thing, but we gotta deal with this if we gon' make it as a couple. I can't keep havin' you wig out on me every time I hafta associate with Yolanda. You gon' hafta get used to that.

"And yeah, she might hafta call me . . . *here.* Sometimes I might hafta cut out early. Sometimes we might not be able to do stuff, dependin' on what I need to do for the baby. If you think you can handle that, then cool. But if not, let me know now, 'cause I already got enough on my mind without you makin' things worse."

"No . . . no . . . I can handle it. I'll be okay. I promise."

"Okay, then. Now rewind the movie, 'cause I'm missin' Bruce's moves."

I did what I was told, and that was the last time I made waves about Yolanda and the baby.

21

Nine days later, at four forty-five A.M., while Weston and I were dead to the world in my bed, his cell phone started ringing. Instantly, I knew what the deal was. The baby was coming. This was it. My man was about to become a father.

Weston jumped up and snatched the phone, bumping his knee on my nightstand. He cursed, then answered. After fifteen seconds of hurried conversation, he hung up and looked at me.

"Come on, babe, we gotta go. Yolanda's in labor. Her mother's takin' her to the hospital right now."

"Um . . . what do you mean, '*we*'? You want me to go *with* you?"

He looked crushed. "Of course I want you to come with me. I need you there."

I didn't know what to say, and it wasn't like there was a whole lot of time for me to think on it. A baby was on the way.

"Wow . . . um . . . oh . . . okay . . . I just wasn't expecting you to . . . well anyway. Lemme . . .

uhh . . . you go ahead. I'll meet you there in an hour. Kaiser in Richmond, right?"

He looked abandoned. "You're not gonna ride with me?"

"Baby, I just . . . I need some time to get prepared for this. Just a little time."

Barely above a whisper, he said, "I'm scared. I don't . . . I don't know how to do this. I don't know what to do."

"Well, sweetie, I don't either, but . . . you'll be fine. Go on. I'll meet you there in an hour. I promise."

"Please make sure you come. I can't do this without you."

"I will. I promise. Now hurry up."

Distressed, he threw on his clothes, grabbed his phone and wallet, and started making a phone call. On his way out the door, I heard him telling his mother that he was on his way to the hospital, and that the baby was coming.

I got up, grabbed my journal and wrote a quick entry. Ever since Rishidda suggested I start journaling, it had become a daily ritual for me. It had gotten to the point where if I didn't write in it at least once a day, my day didn't feel complete.

After I spilled my guts in my journal, I threw on some halfway-decent-looking clothes, tied my hair back in a scarf, brushed my teeth and headed out the door for the hospital.

I still wasn't ready for what was about to take place, but like my father told me, there was no going back to the old days.

I drove in silence and thought about everything that Weston and I had done and been through since we met. I realized how special our love really was, and even though he was about to be a father to another woman's child, even though I had cheated on him, we were still managing to make things work. I felt lucky. Now that the baby was coming, I knew there would still be more difficult times, but I made a vow to try my damnedest to be mature about things.

When I got to the hospital, I was told that Weston had already gone in with Yolanda and her mother. It was an uncomfortable feeling, knowing that my man was in there watching his firstborn enter the world. I tried not to think about it, and picked up a *Parenting* magazine and skimmed through it. Something told me I had better brush up on my skills. Inevitably, I would come in contact with Baby Porter, and I would definitely need to know a little somethin' about caring for a child.

Surprisingly, the magazine was quite interesting, so I looked through a few more. Soon, I found myself dozing off. I tried to stay awake, but I just couldn't, so I went ahead and fell asleep.

I felt someone tapping my shoulder and calling my name. I opened my eyes and Weston was standing there, looking proud.

"Hey, is everything okay? What time is it?"

"Quarter to nine." He smiled. "It's a girl. I have a daughter. Seven pounds, six ounces. I saw her." His eyes lit up. "She looks just like me."

I tried to smile like I was happy for him, but inside I was a wreck. He was so proud and so excited. That hurt. I wanted to be the one in the room holding our newborn.

I sucked it up and said, "I'm glad everything went well. How's Yolanda?"

"She's fine. She did a good job in there. She's gon' be a good mother, I can tell."

The more information he gave me, the more I wanted to run out the door screaming; but I knew I couldn't do that, so I just kept the fake-ass smile on my face.

"What's her name?"

"Lydia Marie Porter. Isn't that pretty, babe? It has a nice ring to it, don't'choo think?"

"Yeah. I like it." My tone couldn't have been any drier.

"Oh, um . . . Yolanda wants to talk to you."

"Talk to me like what? You mean, right now? Like, go in the room?"

"Yeah. Just for a minute. She has something she wants to say to you. Plus, you guys need to meet."

I sat up straight. This, I most definitely was not ready for. Coming face-to-face with Yolanda was something I knew I would have to do eventually, but I didn't wanna do it right after she had just given birth to my man's baby. I started feeling overwhelmed.

"Weston . . . I don't think I'm ready for that . . . to meet her right now. Can I talk to her later or something?"

"I know you're uncomfortable, and I'm sorry about that. But can you please just go in there and meet her, hear what she has to say? Please? Do this for me, okay?"

"Do you know what she wants to talk to me about?"

"Yeah, I do. But you need to go in there and hear it from her."

Of course, I wasn't gonna say no to him, so

reluctantly, I went in to meet the mother of Weston's child.

First, I just peeked my head in the door. Yolanda looked up, smiled, and motioned for me to come in. She was by herself, and she wasn't holding the baby, thank goodness, because I don't think I could've handled that.

Yolanda was a pretty, light-skinned woman with short hair, and she had the face of a child. Weston had told me she was thirty-two, but to me, she looked all of twenty.

After we introduced ourselves to each other, I congratulated her, which took every ounce of maturity I had, but I didn't wanna seem petty and jealous.

"How are you feeling?" I asked her.

"I'm okay. Just tired."

There was a long pause.

She said, "I've heard a lot about you. As a matter of fact, Weston talks about you all the time."

I wasn't sure what to say to that, so I stayed quiet.

"He loves you more than I think you know."

"I'm lucky to have him," was all I could come up with to say.

"I just wanted you to know that . . . I'm not in love with Weston. I never have been. And he doesn't love me. But we do care about each other as friends. Now that we have Lydia, things are probably gonna be strange for a little while. This whole situation is gonna take some getting used to for all of us. I just hope you and I can be friends one day, because I'm not trying to get in the way of what you and Weston have. The only thing I expect from him is that he love and be there for our daughter. That's it."

I was glad Weston made me go in and talk to her,

because what she said was exactly what I needed to hear, and it took a huge load off my mind.

"Thank you, Yolanda . . . for saying that. I'm sure we will be friends one day."

She smiled at me, and I knew from that point on, things would be okay.

22

Six months had whizzed by and things between Weston, Yolanda and me were good. We were adjusting well to the changes, and I felt confident about my relationship with Weston once again.

I had even started doing Yolanda's hair, and we were actually becoming good friends. To be honest, the more I talked to her, the more I realized she was one of the nicest women I had ever met.

It also didn't hurt that she had met someone she really liked, and he seemed to be into her, too. He didn't mind that she had a six-month-old, and she said she felt good about the relationship.

I had, of course, spent time with the baby, who, I have to say, was an absolute doll. Weston wasn't kidding when he said she looked just like him. She had the same golden eyes, dimples, skin color, and soft, curly hair. Not to mention, she was the most mild-mannered baby I had ever dealt with. She hardly ever cried, and didn't have a problem letting other people hold her.

Weston was a great father. He fawned and doted on Lydia every chance he got, and he was so good with her. He knew what every movement, sound, and facial expression of hers meant, which I found fascinating.

I had come to terms with the fact that I would never have his firstborn, and soon, began to really enjoy watching them together.

The one thing I had not done was babysit Lydia by myself. I had done it with Weston a few times, but he did all the work, since he knew what she needed. I just basically played with her.

One Saturday while I was cleaning the kitchen, Weston called me, sounding urgent.

"Babe . . . I need you to watch Lydia for a few hours. I gotta go to work . . . somethin' came up."

"Watch her by myself?"

"Yeah, just for a few hours. You'll be fine. But come over here, because I don't have time to pack her up and bring her over to your house. Plus, she's asleep. I don't wanna wake her up. She's kinda fussy today, and I had a hard time gettin' her to calm down."

"Okay . . . I'll . . . I'll be there in a few minutes."

"Thanks."

When I got to Weston's, he rushed to the door, ran down a list of dos and don'ts, kissed me, thanked me, and then bolted.

Lydia was still asleep, so I went into the living room and started watching television. About twenty minutes later, I heard her crying.

I went in the room and just looked at her for a minute, not sure what to do. Then, I remembered Weston's do's and don'ts, so I picked her up and rocked her. That didn't help, so I walked around the house with her for a few minutes. When that didn't work, I checked her diaper, but she was dry as a bone. She wasn't hungry, because Weston said she drank a whole bottle right before I got there.

So, now I was stuck. Lydia continued to cry while I walked her around the house, trying to think of all the reasons babies cry. All of a sudden, something dawned on me that I don't think even Weston thought about, because he didn't mention it.

I put Lydia on the bed and shuffled through her baby bag. I pulled out a teething ring, rinsed it off right quick, then I jiggled it in Lydia's mouth. She resisted it at first, but after a minute, she started gnawing on it furiously, and her cry fell into a whimper. I picked her up and walked her, keeping the ring in her mouth, and she finally quieted down. Pretty soon, she started getting heavy-eyed.

I was tired, too, so I lay across Weston's bed and positioned Lydia next to me on her back. I stuck my index finger into her little hand and she started grabbing it. Not long after that, we both went to sleep.

Something woke me up all of a sudden. It wasn't a sound or a dream; it was a presence. When I opened my eyes, I looked at Lydia, who was still sleeping, and my finger was still in her hand.

When I looked up, Weston was standing in the doorway of the bedroom with a strange look on his face. He was staring at the two of us like he was contemplating something too deep for words.

"Hey. How long have you been standing there? You scared me. Are you okay? You look . . . confused or something."

"I'm fine. I've only been standin' here for about a minute or so."

"Oh."

He continued to stare at us with that strange look on his face.

"You sure you're okay? You keep staring at me . . . at us."

"Uh-huh." His expression still didn't change. "You have any problems with her?"

I rose up and took my finger out of Lydia's hand.

"No, but that reminds me . . . I know what's wrong with her."

"What's that?"

"She's teething."

"Is that right? How'd you figure that out?" He kept studying us.

"Process of elimination. Plus, she's at that age. I gave her a teething ring, and that did the trick. We were cool after that."

"Really?"

"Yup."

"Okay, well, thanks. That's good to know. Glad you were here." He sounded monotone, and his eyes pierced through me in a way that chilled me to the bone.

I got off the bed.

"What's wrong with you? Are you mad at me or something? Because the look on your face is trippin' me out."

All of a sudden, his demeanor switched, and the look on his face changed.

"Naw . . . I'm not mad at you. Not at all. I'm just . . . thinkin' about somethin' right now, that's all."

"What are you thinking about?"

"Nothin'. I'll tell you later. Come here."

I walked over to him and he kissed me, ran his palm down my face, and walked away.

"I just remembered, I got one other thing to do. I need to make a run right quick. Can you hang out here for a little while longer?"

"Yeah, but . . . where you goin'?"

He was already halfway out the door when he said, "I'll be back soon."

I couldn't figure out what his deal was, so I went back in the living room to finish watching television.

Two and a half hours later, he came back. I didn't ask him where he'd been; I figured he would tell me later. Besides, it seemed like he had something on his mind that he didn't wanna talk about, so I just left him alone.

I had some things to take care of at home, so I told Weston I needed to get ready to go.

He said, "Ay, let's go to Café Soul tomorrow morning, okay? We haven't been in a minute."

"Okay. What time?"

"I'll pick you up at ten."

"'Kay. I'll see you in the morning. Love you."

"Love you, too, babe."

23

When we got to Café Soul, Weston insisted on waiting for the table towards the back of the restaurant. I asked him why, but he just said he preferred that table. I didn't argue with him.

About fifteen minutes later, we were finally seated. We were regulars there, so everyone knew us by name. I spoke to the waiters and waitresses, and they spoke to me, but I could have sworn they were all looking at me funny. I couldn't put my finger on it, but something was strange about the aura in the restaurant that morning.

Weston picked up his menu and started looking through it. When I got ready to look at mine, one of the waitresses came over and said, "Oh . . . wait a minute, Katrice . . . that's the wrong menu. You need the new one."

"I didn't know you guys changed the menu." Then I asked Weston, who was still looking in his, "Baby, is yours new?"

"Hang on a second."

"Lemme see yours."

"Wait a minute, babe. I'm lookin' at somethin'."

I was about to get annoyed, but then the waitress came back with another menu.

"Here you go."

"Thanks."

I took the menu and looked at the front, which didn't look any different than the one she had just taken from me. I opened it up, and it still didn't look any different. Five seconds later, I gasped and started hyperventilating.

"Weston, Weston, Weston . . . what is this?"

He was calm. "What's wrong?"

I pushed my seat back and looked inside the menu again, to make sure I really saw what I thought I saw.

"Weston . . . what's this . . . in the menu?"

"Lemme see. . . ." He took the menu from me and looked inside, then said, "Ohhhhh . . . that's where that went. I been lookin' for this all doggone morning."

I looked around the restaurant and everyone was staring at us. I felt my eyes start to water.

Weston reached into the menu and pulled out the fourteen-karat white-gold diamond solitaire ring from under the little piece of tape, got up, grinned at me, then, knelt down on one knee and took my left hand in his.

The tears came before I could stop them.

"Katrice, right here at this very table, on our first date, is where I started fallin' in love with you. We been through a lot, and I know for sure that I will *never* love another woman like I love you. So now, I'm bringin' it back to where it all began to ask you, Katrice Nicole Vincent, to be my wife. Will you marry me?"

I managed to whisper "Yes" through my sobs.

Weston glided the ring onto my finger, and everyone started clapping and cheering. The diamond in the ring was at least a half-carat.

Weston got up off the floor, and I got out of my seat and hugged him.

We stayed and ate breakfast, on the house, of course, and I could hardly wait to get home to tell my parents and the girls.

That night, the girls, my parents, Tiki and Charles, and P.J. and Lateshia went out to dinner with Weston and me at Crusty's Station, our favorite seafood place in San Francisco, to celebrate our engagement.

Later, Weston and I spent the evening cuddling and planning our new life together.

24

On July 24, 2001, I finally became Katrice Vincent-Porter. Weston and I had a beautiful, romantic wedding held at the Chicago Botanic Garden, with all of our friends and family in attendance. Even Joan-Renee flew in for the occasion with her husband, Neal, and their son. The biggest surprise of all was the person who tapped me on my shoulder about ten minutes before I got ready to walk down the aisle with Daddy. It was Troy Parker. I completely lost my mind, I was so happy to see him. Joan-Renee tracked him down after I told her Weston and I were getting married. She figured having him there would make my day, and she was right.

Of course, Lorraine made both my and Weston's wedding attire. We were both stunning, and my dress was exquisite. She made me a pearl-colored silk strapless gown with a long train and beautiful veil. Weston was decked out in a beige suit and looked more handsome than I had ever seen him.

Sonny was there, looking at Weston with pride in

his eyes, and Lorraine cried every fifteen minutes. She was so happy for us, and she said she knew this day would come, even after all we had been through.

Like Tiki and Charles, we, too, recited our own vows. Surprisingly, I made it through mine without crying, but Weston didn't. Halfway through his speech, he choked up, and a couple of tears fell. Then, of course, I cried. But then, I do that very well anyway.

Chantelle's wedding gift to us was a gorgeous, incredibly lifelike portrait she had worked on for two months. It was of Weston and me at a party we'd all gone to a while back. Weston was on one side of the room talking to someone, and I was standing close by talking to someone else, but we were looking at each other instead of the people we were supposed to be talking to. Chantelle said she snapped that shot of us by accident. She was trying to shoot Sabrina, but ended up getting us instead because Sabrina kept moving. When she got it developed, she said she knew she had struck gold and started working on the portrait. She called it *Soul Mates . . . Across a Crowded Room.*

The very rich owner of the art supply store where she went to get it framed, and which she frequented to buy her drawing materials, was so taken by it that he asked if it was for sale. When she told him no and the reason why, she nearly fell to the floor when he then offered her ten thousand dollars to draw him a replica to give to his daughter, Maya, who was an art major. He also referred her to some "artist buddies" of his, who hooked her up with dozens of freelance jobs drawing portraits for parties, weddings, and other events.

Weston and I bought a small home in Oakland

right after we got married, and things couldn't have been better.

Lydia and I loved each other to death, and Yolanda and I were tight. She married Thomas, the guy she'd started seeing shortly after Lydia was born, and the five of us hung out frequently.

Epilogue

On September 16, 2002, Weston and I became the proud parents of a gorgeous pair of fraternal twins, a boy and a girl named William Weston and Eleanor Katrice—we called them Willie and Ellie for short. My parents were thrilled to have their grandchildren named after them, and it was Weston's idea to give them our first names as their middle ones.

As for me, I finally saw the light at the end of the tunnel, and it was far brighter than I could have ever imagined.

UNBREAKABLE
BOND

Sometimes when you love someone
No matter what they say or do
There's just no letting them go

Your souls have become one
And to split them apart
Assures a spiritual death for both

If you try to move on
Without your one and only
Your heart incessantly ails

The cure that you need
Is the one you let go
All others are pieces of gauze

No replacement will do
For there is no room
The one you crave still lives in the space

If your love breaks your heart
And you two fall apart
They walk away with the piece in their hand

Now you are halfhearted
Everywhere you go
And in every single thing that you do

There is no other match
For the chunk that is gone
But the one that your soul mate has seized

You want wholeness again
And need the rest of your heart
But now it's part of a package deal

You can't get it back
Without taking as well
The lover that you sent away

So you dig deep within
Find the forgiveness you need
Then bestow it on the one with the key

All gauze is discarded
Your cure has arrived
And your once-destroyed soul is now healed

About the Author

Charlene E. Green is a Northern California native who has been writing since very early childhood. In 2003, she relocated from Oakland to Los Angeles to pursue her career in writing, as well as in film and television. After completing her first novel, *One Man's Treasure*, she connected with publisher, author, and philanthropist Dr. Rosie Milligan, and began an internship working as a copy editor and proofreader. She further interned for literary agent and best-selling author Dr. Maxine Thompson as a copy editor and story editor. She has just completed her second novel, *And They'll Come Home*, the sequel to *One Man's Treasure*, and is working on her first book of poetry, titled *From Me to You . . . Through Mine Eyes*, as well as several other creative projects.